Hamilton's...
DEEP CATCH

Published in the UK in 2025 by DR Enterprises

Copyright © Douglas Roberts 2025

Douglas Roberts has asserted their right under the Copyright, Designs and Patents Act, 1988, to be identified as the author of this work.

All rights reserved. No part of this book may be reproduced, stored in a retrieved system or transmitted, in any form or by any means, electronic, mechanical, scanning, photocopying, recording or otherwise, without the prior permission of the author and publisher.

This book is a work of fiction, and except in the case of historical or geographical fact, any resemblance to names, place and characters, living or dead, is purely coincidental.

Paperback ISBN 978-1-7392935-0-5
eBook ISBN 978-1-7392935-1-2

Cover design and typeset by SpiffingCovers

Hamilton's...
DEEP CATCH

DR Enterprises

DOUGLAS ROBERTS
BOOK THREE IN THE *CATCH* SERIES

ALSO AVAILABLE IN THIS SERIES

THE CHASE SERIES

To all of those who consider it worthwhile knowing me.

'Greed has no boundaries' - Aristotle, circa 384BC

Chapter 1

As he plummeted the hundred feet or so downwards, he had just enough time to wonder if things could get any worse, but during those final few seconds he never had time to reach any kind of defintitive conclusion. He'd previously thought about the prospect once when they had disembarked from the helicopter, and a second time just a few minutes ago; and on both occasions he'd decided that he would very probably die during the drop. He'd only ever heard of the expression *'terminal velocity'* and didn't think he'd have time to reach whatever ridiculous speed it referred to before hitting the rough seas below. No matter how hard he tried to rationalise his predicament, staying alive was his primary concern.

Despite his lack of awareness of time, he had managed to take in that the strengthening winds were approaching gale force and driving the rain so hard that that it swirled round the huge metal stanchions in unpredictable directions. Eye goggles would have protected his delicate irises from the stinging droplets had he been wearing them, but they would have either fogged-up from the inside or been spattered with rain from the outside, rendering them next to useless. Even then, the only light able to penetrate the obsidian darkness came from distant flood lamps, and their piercing rays would have only managed to blurring any image. There was also the simple matter of placing one foot in front of the other which depended upon the wind direction, especially when it came to grated steps on which to bark one's shins. All made slippery by the rain.

Any human being would have struggled in this hostile environment and yearned for the blessed warmth and dryness of a cabin towel, but his job title of computer analysist didn't mention anything about being blown all over a deep sea oil rig's platform. He had focussed on the man crouching in front of him, knowing that one of them, probably him, would end up as fish bait that very night. No sooner had he brushed his arm across his face and wiped away the spray than he had to do it again, but now he watched the silhouette of the man in front of him change shape from crouched to upright. Just as he was wondering why his opponent was ceding his advantageous position, he felt the sharpness of the knife being drawn across his throat.

There are very few people in the world who have managed to live through this deadly process, but those who have will tell you that it is actually painless. One's numbed mind struggles to comprehend what is actually happening, and instead, instantly focuses on the most important issue of survival. When given the option of managing pain or working out a way to supply oxygen to the most important organ of the body, there's no contest; it totally ignores the pain. Realisation that life-giving air will be denied in very short order overrides all other considerations and while one's senses continue to work, the brain all but shuts-out the incoming messages that it has relied upon its entire life.

While overcoming the shock of having his throat cut, he strangely found time to realise that he had been tipped over the safety guard rail and was now hurtling towards a very nasty end, It would be worse when he entered the sea.

He couldn't breathe. Nobody could have drawn breath. Not with their throat cut. Especially underwater.

Not that he registered it, but his impact at the wrong angle dislocated his shoulder and ripped his gullet wide open, allowing an inrush of bitterly cold salt water. He died.

Miles Glen peered through the gloom and watched the sad saga unfold from the relative safety of his perch nearly thirty feet above. He cursed, and silently vowed revenge on his colleague's untimely passing. Vengeance was not normally a part of his character, but he would gladly set that inhibition to aside on this occasion. He fervently hoped the opportunity would coincide with the priority task he had been given.

There were two of them, and the murderous pair were dressed in black, as he was, but he felt he had the edge on them since he wore a hooded wet suit. He watched one of them shout at the other, trying to be heard over the whistling wind. What was said was a mystery, but the outcome was obvious as they both looked about them as if looking for something; or someone. That someone was him.

He was confident that they couldn't see him as he

hugged the round support much as a bear would hug a tree trunk, but nevertheless, despite his dark skin, he briefly shut his eyelids so that the whites of his eyes didn't betray him. When he opened them again, he caught the outline of them splitting up and heading in opposite directions. They were definitely on the lookout for him with similar murderous intent, and much as he would have liked to have stayed where he was, he knew that sooner or later the cold would penetrate his wetsuit and render him useless. In any case, he had a job to do and it wasn't going to get done by hiding in the shadows.

He decided to stay virtually invisible a while longer, three-quarters of the way up one of the helicopter supports on a very small ledge, to see if either of the pair was going to make an appearance near him or if they were waiting for him to make the first move. From his perspective it was ideal. He could far better manage them one at a time rather than both together. Right until the moment his colleague had had his throat slit, he hadn't known that there were two of them, and neither had his colleague. Somehow they knew that he was one of a pair, and he would try to fathom that issue out later. Right now, as they hunted him down, he would become the hunter. Now aware of their modus operandi, he'd keep one eye over his shoulder.

He remained stock-still round his metal tree trunk, and that was now paying dividends as he watched one of them furtively ascend the steel staircase below him. Any sort of noise he would make would remain unheard, as the wind lashed the heavy rain against the structure and drowned out all but the loudest sound. Just about the only thing that was making sense was the ability to see; and that was not much more than fifty feet. He could hardly believe his luck when the killer made a U-turn at the top of the steps to follow the walkway past him.

He drew his own knife and repositioned his feet in order to pounce on the man as he passed beneath. He was about to do so when a sixth sense caused him to hesitate. Just as well, because at the far extremity of his vision he saw the second killer flit from behind one upright to another nearby. Same scenario. One killer acting as bait while the other came from behind. To Miles' mind there was only one way to deal with this pair and that was to take out the man in the background first - providing he could keep tabs on him.

The pair crisscrossed their way towards the accommodation wing, and Miles reckoned that they would then scour the western arm of the rig, the one in front hoping to flush him out while the other stayed in the shadows ready to deliver the final fatal blow with his knife.

He blessed the stormy weather knowing that it would help disguise his movements, as only rain-free line-of-sight would betray him. He allowed another few seconds after the second killer had taken up temporary residence behind a square pillar before dropping down flat onto his stomach on to the metal grating a few feet below.

Feline-like, he made his way towards the western edge of the platform and looked up with relief to see similar ledge to the one he had been standing on a few minutes ago. He heaved himself onto it using a handy bunch of pipes as purchase. He struggled to make it due to the rain-soaked metal, and managed to bruise his knee trying to reach its safety, but once there, and having had a brief look about, he saw that it was ideally placed for where they would pass underneath. Assuming that they would..

He smiled to himself as the wind gusted more ferociously than ever, hurling larger and larger rain drops almost horizontally, and drew comfort from the fact that their vision would be seriously impeded by facing into it. So far, he hadn't seen them looking above themselves, but then again, he hadn't been able to watch them for nearly long enough to assume that they wouldn't be checking each and every ledge. He couldn't see them right now as deep shadow shrouded the part of the platform in darkness where they ought to be, which meant that they couldn't see him either.

He took the opportunity to ease himself around the circular ledge just a little further and instantly froze. The bait man was twenty feet away and coming towards him from a different direction, and his initial thought was that he had been out-guessed, but as he passed underneath him for the second time that night, he breathed out in relief. He had time to wonder why he had held his breath because nobody without a stethoscope was going to hear any breathing that night.

A loose halliard somewhere up top was making a rhythmic racket, and on top of that, the shriek from the wind had been joined by a low-resonance noise that vibrated throughout. Making any kind of noise tonight was not going to be an issue. He briefly considered his dead colleague before returning to the task at hand, and sure enough, he just about managed to spot the second killer as he took up station next to a girder which had an odd shaped bulbous box attached to it. All he had to do now was wait until number two came anywhere close and he would be able to send him to his own watery grave.

Miles had two knives. One was broad stainless steel, archetypal-shaped with one edge being partially serrated and much favoured by the American elite special services. The other was much thinner and more like a stiletto; made from titanium and almost exclusively used by the British. Instead of drawing the serrated one as he had done before, he chose the slim one as it would be better for penetration through clothing..

He looked down and with chagrin noticed that number two had not taken the obvious path and was now by a staircase; The very next instant, he moved in Miles' direction.

His dagger entered number two's neck obliquely as Miles thrust it sideways on his way to the metal grating. It was just as quickly withdrawn with a slight twist allowing copious amounts of warm blood to flow from the jugular. Not that it mattered, but it was soundless except for the vague thump of Miles landing heavily on the deck.

Within three seconds he had achieved the first part of his task. If number one spotted him he would hopefully assume that it was his partner and not his enemy, and Miles thought it likely that there would shortly come a time when their paths had to converge. He put away his dagger and took out his serrated knife, thinking that what was about to happen might come down to a face-to-face engagement. He didn't want to be out-knifed.

He saw that they had just about come to the end of their search leg, and would logically be making an approximate ninety degree turn, so he cut across the corner, all the while trying to remember how number two moved. At the same time, he was trying to think of a way to attract number one's attention to get him to come closer and very quickly concluded he'd have to be seen; perhaps even beckon him over. Either that, or ambush him as he was going to do in the first place.

He looked around, and ran at a crouch to a medium-sized vertical steel pipe so that he was ahead of number one. As he waited a nasty thought entered his mind. Were there three of them? He looked about but could see nobody, but that didn't mean that nobody was there. He also remembered to look up.

Number one was now only feet away and with a shift of his body from behind the pipe, he briefly showed his torso, then vanished again. He hoped number one would come over, but after a few seconds it was apparent that he wasn't going to. Patience was one of Miles' virtues, but he counted only to three, took the few necessary steps and thrust his knife into number two's side under his rib cage, twisted it and yanked it sideways on the way out to ensure maximum damage. Number one was naturally stunned but it still took him several seconds before he collapsed. Miles looked on

First one, then the other body was tipped overboard to join the growing fish bait in the middle of the Irish

Sea, and Miles didn't concern himself with cleaning up any of the evidence as the storm was doing that by itself.

He now had two options: Either stay on board and continue with his alias as an oil rig worker and be questioned, along with the others, by the police when they arrived, or to hide-out and smuggle himself onto the shore-bound boat, whenever that might be. He chose the latter because remaining as a worker could well take a few days too many, and there was always the chance that the police might pick up on his false documents. First, he desperately needed to warm-up, so headed for the crew accommodation quarters and took a much-needed shower.

Chapter 2

Ignoring and being ignored by the only other person in the communal changing room as he dried-off, he considered what had actually triggered the most recent violence. He mentally kicked himself again for not having greater forethought. Of course there was going to be some sort of alert as his colleague had accessed the rig's main computer, but it hadn't occurred to either of them at the time. Hindsight is usually reserved for losers and he cringed at the thought of himself not being alert enough to recognise the tiny flashing icon near the top left of the computer screen in time. To be fair, he had been looking mostly the other way, looking for anyone returning to the console room, but even when he had glanced briefly at the screen it still didn't register. This time, it was his colleague who had lost, but it could quite easily have been him had their roles been reversed. A voice from the door the other side of the lockers shouted loudly "Hey. Anyone seen Carnegie or Danny… Hello, anyone in here?"

He looked towards where the other man had been and saw he was in the shower, so shouted back "Not in the last few minutes." As the door closed on its spring and the man walked away, he heard a fading "Shit."

So those were the names of the killers and he immediately doubted their veracity. He had maybe ten minutes to hide himself away before a roll call and a search, but he knew exactly where to hide. They would question the whereabouts of his colleague but only he knew the approximate whereabouts of all three of them. Additionally, his name would also be on the missing persons list but that would just add to the numerous questions that would arise. Why had four perfectly healthy men just disappeared?

He paused his drying and spent all of two seconds wondering what his colleague's name was, but then carried on in a hurry as it was irrelevant now. There might have been a time when he would have wasted more precious seconds but not now; especially after what he had just witnessed. They had only met less than nine hours ago on the way over in the transit helicopter. No names and no formalities, but each knew who the other was, and they both knew what had to be done; and quickly. What mattered now was that he had to return to the mainland and report back to his superior; complete with the waterproof memory stick that he now slipped into a skin-tight pouch strapped to his inside leg.

He didn't want to be caught leaving the changing room in a thick wetsuit and instead stowed it in his sailors' bag. Even being caught with a bag would have been suspicious enough on an oil rig where discipline was extremely strict, but at least it was less likely to raise eyebrows. A man dressed in a wetsuit in the middle of the night during a force ten storm on an oil rig, at the extremity of The Irish Sea in February, would have certainly been queried.

He made it to the leeward outside door without being

seen and closed it as quietly as the wind would allow. He was soaked within a couple of seconds, but he only needed to endure the most unpleasant of conditions for another couple of minutes as he made his way to the cabin of one of the crane derricks. The one he had personally put out of action almost as soon as he had arrived, and hence his confidence in it not being called upon for use until it had been attended to by a qualified engineer.

Once inside he changed out of his wet clothes, used the dry towel on himself before squeezing himself into the outrageously tight wetsuit. Anyone who has ever tried to get into a wetsuit by themselves will understand the effort required to do so, especially if it is six millimetres thick. The neoprene clings and stretches all at the same time and the thicker the suit, the more awkward it is to fit into. It is a lot easier if one is standing up with plenty of space around, but doing so in a confined cabin with arm rests, pedals and levers protruding just where one wants to manoeuvre oneself drains energy in such a way that one is exhausted by the end of the process.

At last, Miles could relax as he managed to pull-up the zip at the back with the help of the cord that dangled down, and he collapsed in the surprisingly comfortable seat. All he had to do now was wait until the authorities arrived and with any luck, due to the number of missing personnel, there'd be more than one boat of policemen, immigration inspectors, health and safety officials, medical staff and so on. He would also have to wait until the storm abated enough.

* * * * *

It took nearly a day before the wind lessened for no apparent reason, and while the rain continued to fall heavily from the leaden skies, at least it was no longer approaching the horizontal. It was a squawking gull perched on the cab's roof that woke Miles from his most uncomfortable and sporadic slumber, not the approach of the less noisy helicopter that now hovered relatively easily before touching down one of the designated platforms at the far end of the rig.

From his elevated vantage point, he watched several people disembark but couldn't see who they were due to their head coverings, and he guessed that they would be officials. He twisted round to look in the other direction and was glad to see that his gamble would be paying off, in that he could see a reasonable-sized boat approaching. He needn't rush as it would take at least quarter of an hour to reach the rig's dock a couple of hundred feet below him and he hoped it wouldn't leave straight away. Dusk was imminent and would be the perfect time for him to slip aboard undetected. What he wanted most now was a drink of water as he had been perspiring heavily in the enveloping suit, but knew that if he did so that it would go straight through him and he really didn't want to go round smelling like a public toilet for the next couple of days. He didn't fancy trying to keep his legs crossed either.

Seagulls don't usually attract attention but this one above his head hadn't stopped making a racket. It was as though it was saying 'Oi. There's someone hiding in here. Come and have a look.' He was crouched down below the glazing with just the top of his head visible but in the improving weather he now saw someone looking in his direction, probably drawn by the din emanating from the noisy bird. He waited a few minutes but it was time to move in any case, so he eased himself out of the door with his satchel bound over his shoulder and climbed down to below the top platform level. He was far less detectable here and could choose his route down to the motor cruiser below with ease.

Obscuring himself next to one of the large supporting beams, he chose his moment to leap silently on board while the boat's mate attended to one of the mooring ropes at the other end of the vessel. As he made his way down to the bowels of the boat where he planned to hide out, his path took him within a whisker of being seen by the skipper who was just emerging from one of the cabins. He heard his receding footsteps and then a cry to his mate that they needed to get underway soon as there was another storm front coming in. A few comments about being given a chance to dry out mixed with a few colourful swearwords, completed the scenario.

Soon after the boat got underway, he began to have serious doubts if he could stay hidden where he was. As far forward as he could go, he was sandwiched behind the heads which tended to leak whenever they hit a bad trough, but worse than that were the fumes from the diesel's exhaust which crept back down to his location. Coupled with the horrible twisting motion and the unexpected slap-bangs from waves smashing into the bows next to him, all-in-all he endured an extremely uncomfortable and sickening ride back to Fishguard on the Welsh coast.

He waited until all sounds of berthing had receded then counted to three hundred, about five minutes, before daring to move. As he stretched out, he nearly threw up, but resisted the urge to get his own back on the errant head. Opening the cabin door and gingerly showing his face above the deck, he quite rightly assessed that nobody was left on board and gulped down the salty fresh air until he felt normal again. It had stopped raining and the wind had temporarily dropped, so he blessedly eased himself out of the wetsuit and went in search of some water. He didn't want to leave any trace of him ever having been on board and carefully replaced everything he touched before dressing into the driest clothes from his satchel.

He actually enjoyed the relatively short walk from the quayside into the village of Goodwick, next to its better-known big brother of Fishguard. He stopped at The Rose and Crown for a couple of pints of Brains bitter and a fish pie, and felt a bit more human. His next stop was the transport parking area where he found a lorry driver willing to take him to London, providing he didn't mind stopping off for half-an-hour in Swindon en route so he could see 'his sister'.

Chapter 3

Miles waved a casual goodbye to the driver in his mirrors as the articulated lorry trundled away from the commercial parking area in Oxford services. He wasted no time hunting down another lift that would take him where he wanted to go. Northwood, not far from the urban town of Pinner in north west London, was a very useful liaison hub housed mainly in underground bunkers, and was where the three branches of the military co-ordinated and sought co-operation with each other. The Royal Navy, The Royal Air Force and The British Army had their own headquarters, but shared this common location so as to speed-up communications.

Miles had been dropped-off by a white van-man near Uxbridge on the A40, and had walked a mile or so before getting on the tube at Ealing and then used a variety of buses and trains before approaching the guarded entrance of Britain's equivalent of America's Pentagon. He was safe in the knowledge that nobody would have been able to trace his movements during the past eight hours. The sentry accepted his pass and another checked it again as he waited at one of the hangar doors. There was third and final check by one who wrinkled his nose by a lift entrance, and then he was inside one of Britain's sanctums.

He knew his way around and had to walk almost

to the very end of a long carpeted corridor before he entered the toilets. Once there, he washed himself down as best he could as he really didn't want to go in front of his superior dishing out bad odours as well as bad news. The only good news was that he still had the memory stick, but he had no idea as to what his colleague had managed to download on to it.

He knew without looking at his watch that she was likely to leave the building soon, but he still took measured paces back down the corridor towards her door. He paused and took a deep breath before letting himself in. The smart gent behind the desk looked up, and while not showing any surprise, from the way he fidgeted his feet, Miles knew he had caught him unawares.

"Miles…didn't expect you back for another week or so yet." When it was clear to him that Miles wasn't going to tell him anything, he continued after a sideways check to see if she was on the phone. "I'll let her know you're back."

"Tell her I have to see her straight away."

The master-servant relationship between them had rapidly re-established itself. As he walked into her office, Miles didn't bother to even notice the reaction of the functionary who guarded access to Commodore Janet Waters OBE.

As far as The Admiralty was concerned, her rank was that of Commodore in order to relay their hopes, wishes, and sometimes demands to a similarly ranked officer in the Royal Air Force or The Army. Nobody in Northwood would refer to Janet Waters by her rank unless it was official since she had made it abundantly clear that the use of 'Commodore' was only to be used as a last resort. Her ethos was that if it couldn't be negotiated, then it ought to have been ordered and not requested.

She'd joined the navy straight from college and immediately showed up her contemporaries, and soon after the Falklands War had even managed to come to the attention of Prince Phillip when he had visited Dartmouth College in his capacity of admiral of the fleet. As the highest ranked liaison officer outside of Whitehall, she was usually the first person approached when there was some sort of sticky problem, since her knife-sharp mind would very quickly pinpoint whatever the problem was and analyse the best way out of it. She had no family other than her sister with whom she lived with in Buckinghamshire, and if anyone even thought of mentioning retirement at the age of fifty-three, they'd likely or not end up with a broken nose. She wasn't particularly tall but could clearly handle herself.

She swivelled her low leather armchair as Miles entered and she beckoned him to sit on one of the opposite sofas. "As you're back sooner than anticipated, it's either very bad or very good news."

Miles handed over the small memory stick as he sat down. "I hope you find want you want on there, but that's all the good news there is."

She placed it on the table next to her without taking her eyes off him. "Tell me more." She instructed.

He'd spent his recent transit time wondering how he was going to present the news to her but it didn't quite go the way he'd planned. He started with his colleague's demise. "Our friend from Natural Resources gave me that just before he was murdered and thrown into the sea, and those who did it are now also at the bottom of the sea." He paused. "They were professionals, not your usual thugs, which tells me they'd been paid to protect something or someone, and I suspect it's what's on that stick that they were trying to guard." Miles wasn't foolish enough to ask what that was..

Her face didn't betray her thoughts, but after a while she asked "And you left no trace of your involvement?"

"None. But that's not to say that one body or another isn't going to turn up on a beach on the English Riviera in a few days' time. Half-eaten by the local crabs of course, which ought to hinder identification a little. But there's nothing to link them to me."

"Good. Because if there was....." She didn't need to finish the sentence. She changed tack. "If you recall, I charged you with two things on this assignment. You failed on the first which was to look after our Natural Resources friend, so did you gather any information on your second task? That memory stick may be the one thing to come out of this episode clean, so tell me you found out something worthwhile."

He didn't consider coming up with the excuse that he had been aboard the rig for about eight hours only, as it would have been ignored. It would also have belittled him in his superior's eyes, but he told her what he had learned. "This was straight from one of the foremen's lips... 'This oil is shit' and from another seasoned worker, a similar comment together with something about their own shit being more valuable. From the tone of the few men I'd had time to come across and talk with, they were quite happy with their employment, and I think they were expecting a healthy bonus in the near future."

"Do you think their union rep. had any influence?"

"I came across him just once and all he did was tell me not to catch a cold on my first day. Other than that, nothing."

She mulled over his words for a moment. "Go home and get some rest. Only a few hours ought to be sufficient."

"Yes. Ma'am."

She waited until he had closed the door before inserting the stick into her computer and while it loaded, she acknowledged to herself that Miles Glen was indeed a gift from heaven, but she would never tell him so to his face. This was the third time he had come in extremely useful and each time he had achieved what had been asked of him; and with total discretion.

She leaned forward to inspect the screen in front of her as it ceased its search and stabilised. "Right then… let's see what you're up to, then." She mumbled.

Forty-five minutes later she was on the phone to Commander Gibbons of Special Branch.

Chapter 4

"What am I going to do with you? You're hopeless." Justin managed to say what he meant in between peals of laughter as he watched his fiancée tangle the fishing line into a knotted spiders web. "You haven't even got a rod and I'm not sure we can trust you with another hook 'cos you'd probably catch your own foot." He was ribbing her as much as he could, mainly because she was sitting down more than an arm's length away and couldn't reach him. "Oh... ha haa... and now it looks like you've managed to catch a healthy bit of duck weed. Quick haul it in before it escapes. Haaaa..."

Despite the fact that it was still officially winter, there wasn't a cloud in the sky and what little wind there was bought relatively warm weather across the country from The Atlantic. The shallow stream off the River Mole not too far from Guildford afforded Justin the perfect backdrop for teaching her the rudiments of fishing; but only with a line, not a rod.

"Pull it in, pull it in, come on."

It was just as well she was wearing gloves otherwise her fingers would never have been able to gather in the thin nylon line, but when she eventually did there was an even larger pile of line collecting around her feet. Plus a few feet of bright green duck weed.

"See, I told you. Duck weed."

"At least it's more than you've got." She looked down at his line that disappeared into the gently flowing crystal-clear water. "And what's more, my bait is still on its hook."

"Well, cast it back in. But this time try to throw it upstream a little."

Sitting in a couple of rustic chairs on the edge of the rickety wooden jetty in the sunshine was exactly what they both needed after an intensive couple of weeks. This was the first opportunity they had had to spend time together, and they spent it catching-up with almost irrelevant chatter. Patricia, more so than Justin, looked forward to discussing their wedding plans over dinner that evening and wanted to avoid mention of it until then.

Justin wasn't expecting to catch anything, but he'd promised her that he'd show her how satisfying fishermen found it. If she didn't try it for herself, she surely couldn't criticise others, so she had given in when Justin produced a pair of wooden blocks with fishing line wrapped round them. On their way down, he'd picked up a small tub of worms for bait in the fishing shop and when he explained that one warms them up in one's mouth, he'd had to shut hers with his hand. It was fortunate that the warming-up process wasn't obligatory.

"I've got one... I've got... Justin look... the line's jerking."

Justin was about to dismiss her claim but looked over just in case, and was surprised to see her line reacting. There really was a fish on the end.

"Well, don't just sit there, pull the line towards you so and hook it properly. Play with it gently. Here, let me help you." He got up but had to stand behind her. "Oh no you don't. I caught this one and it's mine." Now she was standing and started to pull the line in. "Look, there's a fish on the end of it."

As the end of the line neared the surface it became clear that a small brown fish was definitely hooked and to Justin's surprise, she deftly lifted it out of the water and landed it on the deck. "Ha ha, I've caught a fish." She jumped for joy but soon calmed down. "Now what do I do with it?"

Justin was happy for her and decided to rib her for as long as possible. "Well, that depends upon what you're planning to do with it, but I think you have two choices. No, three choices." He kept her waiting.

"Go on then, what are they?" She was crouching down looking at the tiny flapping creature as it gasped.

"If you're planning to eat it, then it needs to be put in a plastic bag with some of that river water so that it stays fresh right up to the time you place it in the pan."

"It's hardly going to make a mouthful."

"Another option is to gut it here and now so that it's ready for later on."

"Urgh." She grimaced. She waited for the third option and had to prompt Justin. "Go on."

"Or you can just take it off the hook and throw it back."

"I like that option." She retorted quickly as she eyed the poor creature. "But it's all slimy, and how do I....."

Justin put her and the fish out of their misery by unhooking it for her and holding it in his cupped hands. "Now it's up to you to throw it back."

With trepidation, she went to pick the fish up with forefinger and thumb but before she got the chance to, Justin grabbed her other hand and put it in it.

She instinctively shrieked and shied away, dropping the little feller as she tried to get rid of it as though it would bite her hand off, and watched it bounce just once before disappearing over the edge and back into the stream.

"Now you can call yourself a fisherman." He jibed.

"I think I'd rather visit the supermarket fish counter." She replied as she wiped her hands on a tissue she had found in her coat pocket. "At least they look edible there."

Justin wound the excess nylon line back onto the wooden reel as they walked along the grassy bank back to the car. "Right then, answer me this: How many fish can you get in a pair of tights?"

She gave him a knowing sideways look without commenting.

"Two soles, two eels, a couple of crabs and one wet plaice." He grinned.

"Trust you to know that one."

Chapter 5

She let out a sigh of satisfaction as she sat back on the leather sofa opposite the telly. "You know, I'm really glad we decided to stay in tonight, and that steak and kidney pie was just right. I haven't had once since…it might have been my college days. And now for a couple of relaxing days off." She put her unstockinged feet up.

Justin finished his, looked up and pointed at her with his fork. "Looks like you've still got a bit of kidney stuck to your bottom lip."

She instinctively put her hand up to her mouth to feel for it.

"Other side."

She inspected the merest of brown smudges on her fingertip; then licked it clean. "Shall we see what's on TV or start sorting out our wedding?" She'd have been cross if he'd said TV.

"Wedding." As he tidied his tray onto the floor, "Because if we put off discussing it again, we'll end up getting married next year instead of this. Besides which, there's no cricket on TV tonight." He jested.

"We'd better pick a date that doesn't clash with a Test match, then." She parried. "What about the August bank holiday weekend?"

Justin opened his mouth to answer but was beaten to it by Patricia's mobile ringing. She dropped her head in chagrin before getting up to retrieve it from the sideboard and listened for all of twenty seconds. "Nine o' clock. Yes." Then hung-up and lobbed her phone onto the hard surface of the sideboard without caring if it bounced or broke. "You can guess who that was, can't you? and no, you're not invited."

"Don't tell me…I've finally fallen out of favour with the commander." It was an unfair comment but he felt like he had to say it anyway.

"No, that was Tates; the commander's second. He wants me to swot-up on oil rigs in the Irish Sea before I see Commander Gibbons tomorrow morning."

"Irish oil rigs? Who's ever heard of an Irish oil rig? No, don't tell me…..they stop when they reach Australia."

"Not even vaguely funny." She commented as she sat back down again having picked her laptop out of its protective case together with her notepad and pen.

"Well, you come up with a funny on the spur of the moment."

Pretending to ignore him, she went through the start-up procedure which included inserting her bespoke finger-printed security dongle and logged-on to the secure website, but before she explored it, briefly looked up at him. "Oil think about it."

It wasn't often that she got the better of him when it came to one-liners so she didn't give him the satisfaction of a smug look, but instead ploughed into her given task. It wasn't a topic that she knew anything about so she started with the obvious North Sea rigs and quickly discovered that in principle there was very little difference between them and other rigs around the world.

There were no run-of-the-mill rigs as each one was tailored to a particular environment. Those in the colder climes tended to have warmer facilities than those in the Caribbean where air-conditioning was prevalent. A small one in calm, shallow waters within easy reach of the coast might cost a mere fifty million dollars as opposed to the hurricane-proof, two or three-part behemoths found in the North Sea costing ten times that sum; or in some cases, more.

She concluded that the rougher the weather, the greater the cost, and the St. Georges Channel being quite a way into The Atlantic between mainland Britain and Southern Ireland certainly fell into the roughest weather category. Consequently, these off-shore rigs were designed to withstand hurricane-force winds in excess of one hundred and fifty miles per hour and waves which could swell to a hundred feet high. They needed to be capable of withstanding the nastiest aspects of mother nature's elements at any given moment, because typically, over a hundred souls' lives would depend upon the ruggedness of the rig upon which they worked.

Steel was the favoured construction material which despite its tendency to rust easily, nevertheless provided the rig with a stable platform and in heavy weather, would flex and twist depending upon the severity of the storm. Including the almost obligatory helicopter landing pad, several cranes, gantries, stack pipes, docks, and storage facilities, it could easily cover several football pitches. The working platform tended to be towards one end while the living quarters consisting of accommodation, galley, medical and control centre and other such vital essentials were at the other; this was for practical reasons in that if a fire should ever break out, escape would be theoretically easier. Lifeboats were easily accessible and regularly tested for immediate launch.

It was rare that a tanker would dock with a rig as it was more cost effective to lay pipes along the seabed and pump the oil into storage facilities on the nearest dry land. If the land was too far away then a temporary storage facility was located nearby; but out of explosion range. There were depictive charts showing the basic principles of how the oil, and often gas, was extracted, filtered, deionised, pumped, separated and stored. plus detailed information on cutting heads, tube types and lengths, flow rates and pressures; but she knew she was just scratching the surface.

She kept reading and quickly came to the obvious conclusion that an oil rig was a dangerous place to work; perhaps second only to a war zone as the most dangerous place on the planet. The mortality rate amongst the deep sea divers who tended to the underwater maintenance was ridiculously high but then again, if someone wanted to get rich quickly and legally, that was the place to go. Despite all efforts to make rigs safer, there was the very real possibility that a typical worker would suffer some sort of injury or other ranging from a broken finger to arm amputation. The odd death here and there was virtually expected and the oil companies had funds set aside to recompense the families of the deceased.

Her wide-ranging questions whetted her appetite as

she followed link upon link, forum upon forum, with far too much information to process in one sitting. Before she knew it, Justin was gently tickling her ear to gain her attention. "It's nearly two o'clock, and even if you don't want to, I'm going to bed."

She looked up at him with square eyes and nodded. "Give me five minutes."

Her bedside cabinet clock showed it was gone three o'clock by the time she laid her head on her pillow, and she went to sleep asking herself why there was a flame perpetually alight around a potentially explosive atmosphere.

Chapter 6

Justin Crawford reckoned he'd earned the right to a lie in and did exactly that. Surfacing, and through a half-opened eye, he was aware of Patricia trying to be quiet as she went about her morning ablutions before she left to join the thousands of others commuting into London. Certainly, there were a couple of fraud cases that he'd been looking into, but neither of them were urgent, and in any case, he suspected that the guilty party in one of them would own up straightaway when he confronted them.

Half-asleep, he tried to remember the last time he had managed a proper lie in and his mind wandered back to the time when he and Patricia had started their own detective agency; soon after Maurice 'bloody' Hamilton had had him fired from his old job as a diplomatic protection officer. He had easily fallen into a dogmatic routine during his time as one of the many Diplomatic Protection Squad officers, but there seemed something special being able to choose and pick one's own time as and when to have a lie in. A leisurely lie in was what he wanted and that was what he was going to get. He stretched out across the width of the double bed savouring Patricia's lingering scent and drifted off to sleep again with thoughts of doing something trivial once he got up; like washing the car.

By comparison, Patricia Eyethorne OBE was not enjoying her journey due to a concertinaing of underground passengers. Getting out of her car which she had parked at Hounslow police station, the brief shower caught her halfway as she trotted to the underground where she had caught the Piccadilly line, then changed to the District Line at Earl's Court. She wasn't wet; just slightly damp. Her position as an inspector in Special Branch required her to carry a pistol when on duty, but her problem lay with considering what constituted being on duty. Wedged upright by her fellow passengers next to one of the sturdy vertical poles, somewhere between Hammersmith and Sloane Square, she wondered if commuting counted as being on duty.

She was very aware of the holster under her left armpit that housed her Browning FN as it made her arm protrude just a little too much for total comfort. Suppose the person next to her discovered, even by accident, that she was armed. Would that cause a panic in the crowded carriage? That person wasn't to know that the Browning held seventeen 10mm cartridges, nor that her holster held a further two magazines; or even that she was part of Britain's security forces. She forced a return smile at the nondescript lady who mouthed an apology as they buffeted against each other.

On one occasion only a couple of weeks ago, she half-wished she had been back in her old job as detective inspector for Thames Valley police based in Maidenhead. The relatively simple task of catching criminals and discovering new culprits had been top of her agenda, but she also had to admit that she had enjoyed the limelight that went with her notoriety. Coupled with her stunning looks and hard-earned OBE, her sporadic visits at public events to promote policing had drawn admiring crowds and she thoroughly enjoyed the adulation.

Now her job was quite the opposite. Under the auspices of Special Branch headed by Commander Gibbons, she was one of a select few in The Diplomatic Information Section who were all under the strictest of orders never to reveal what their real task was. While members of the Diplomatic Protection Squad were highly visible, especially when protecting diplomats, ministers, foreign dignitaries and the like, those in the DIS were akin to ghosts. Those ghosts ferreted out plots and schemes and then passed on their suspicions or evidence to other relevant authorities such as the Diplomatic Protection Squad. Their anonymity was their foremost protection.

Security at the entrance of New Scotland Yard that day was more intense than normal and she had to wait while checks were carried out. An answer to her casual question of another passenger as she ascended the lift to the top floor revealed that there had been another bomb threat.

She knew that Commander Gibbons would not like to be kept waiting and it was with a sense of relief that a glance of her watch showed that it was just about nine o'clock as she approached his outer office. Opening the door, she saw Tates about to enter Gibbons' sanctum that overlooked The Thames; he motioned for her to follow him in. Before they had taken two steps, Gibbons indicated for them both to be seated while he finished jotting. She noted that Tates had a few files tucked under his left arm and presumed they would probably hold the topic of that morning's meeting.

Gibbons looked up and she thought she detected the beginnings of a new shallow furrow towards the top of his brow, but quickly passed over the conjecture as he looked directly at her.

"I understand that Tates has asked you to look into the workings of an oil rig, so you'll be up to speed with what goes on there. There's only one person in Special Branch who knows the ins and outs of oil rigs but he's indisposed at the moment which is why you've been asked to gen up on the subject, and I take it you've been doing exactly that. Am I correct?"

"Yes sir."

"Good." He was about to move onto the next matter when a thought crossed his mind. "What's your first impression of them?"

Her reply was terse, knowing that he liked direct answers. "They're bloody dangerous places to work but they pay well."

Gibbons didn't blink an eye while Tates shifted a little in his seat thinking that her response was a bit too tongue-in-cheek. When it became clear to Patricia that Gibbons wanted more, she continued. "It depends upon which aspect you're referring to. Almost without exception they work 24/7 as that's the safest and most cost-effective way. A normal shift will last eight hours with two other shifts on standby, but some run with twelve hour shifts and one on standby depending upon where they are in the world. A topside crew will typically remain on duty for two, three or four weeks while administrators and office engineers tend to stay longer. Staffing levels....."

Gibbons held his hand up. "I can see I need to be more specific." One of Gibbons' traits was that he didn't want to lead his investigators in one specific direction as he considered that a fresh, untainted mind led to alternative aspects to whatever the problem was. "What would I need to do if I wanted to divert some oil or manipulate the system so that some of it disappeared?"

It wasn't the sort of question she was expecting and it took her a couple of moments to gather her thoughts. "Well, that would depend if the oil was stored adjacent to the rig and collected by a tanker, or was piped ashore." She suddenly remembered that Tates had specified Irish on the phone. "Rigs in the St. George's Channel are normally stored because of the distance from dry land, either Southern Ireland or Wales, so a tanker would probably visit on a regular basis." A moment later she added, "Depending upon the weather of course."

She couldn't tell if this was the answer Gibbons was after as his face was deadpan, but he broke the silence. "It'll be a tanker then." He looked at Tates.

Both men were considering the consequences of her reply, and while they did so, she interjected. "I could be more specific if you told me what the problem might be."

As a relatively recent newcomer to the DIS and junior to both Gibbons and Tates, Patricia reckoned that they were reluctant to divulge almost any information; it was their natural instinct. It took Gibbons just a moment to make his mind up.

"I can see we need to complete your general knowledge with specifics. For over thirty years there's been an oil complex operating in The Irish Sea well off the southern coast of Ireland. It's referred to as The Douglas Complex and there's several rigs tapping into either the oil or gas reserves there. From time to time a new licence is granted to one operator or another and about ten years ago a financial consortium called The Blue Lizard Oil Company commissioned a new rig to extract crude oil. In all these years, and according to the company auditors, it's never turned a profit, yet every other oil company or rig operator you care to name manages such a turnover as to produce a very healthy tax return." He paused to let the significance of what he had just said sink-in.

It had.

"The first rule when running a business is to turn a profit, and so lucrative is the oil business that one would expect dynamic dividends within five years or so; but not in this case. According to HMRC, not only are they running at a loss but they are also claiming significant tax relief every year which is costing the treasury millions. Normally this would be a straightforward matter for HM Revenue and Customs who would appoint one of their own tax inspectors to investigate, but in this instance the oil field straddles the boarder of both the UK and Southern Ireland. Mainly because of that and other protocols, the European Union appeared to be the greater authority and assigned their own team to look into the company's accounts, and they declared that all was all 'above board'; nothing abnormal." He frowned just a little at this point. "Mind you, their own auditors have never declared even their own accounts as 'above board' so one instantly has to judge them in a similar light."

He leaned back a little further in his chair. "They also declared that under a previously agreed treaty, it was the UK government's responsibility to carry the burden should any of those licence holders become financially unstable; just to ensure reliability and so forth. This was particularly irksome to those in the treasury who could see millions being refunded to Blue Lizard, while they watched its shareholders rubbing their hands with glee as they lined their pockets at the expense of the British tax payer. Still, this was a matter for HM Revenue and Customs, and would have continued to be so had it not been for one eagle-eyed inspector who inadvertently came across an anomaly on one of his regular audits."

"Dynamic Digital Dials Ltd. is a medium-sized firm based in Newcastle who produce pumps and electronic equipment and it is they who supply and maintain Blue Lizard with their monitoring sensors and gauges that interface with the computers aboard the rig. These sensors monitor pressures, temperatures, humidity, flow, time, and all that goes with those types of devices. Naturally they're all connected to computers which are programmed to control, adjust and collect data etcetera. The inspector asked himself why Blue Lizard's rig was needing to replace certain components so often, especially the flow meters, when very little oil was being produced, and after a little underhand investigation, he came to the conclusion that they had somehow bypassed the system. They weren't declaring how much oil they were producing, and that raised an obvious question."

He purposely paused and was rewarded with the expected reaction from Patricia who had been following his narration easily, so she interjected "Where was that oil going?"

"Correct. But not only where, but how. The why we can guess at, as that'll be the usual greed story and following on from that, who. Now, rather than 'blow the whistle' and cry foul there and then which would have alerted our thieves, this inspector wisely completed his investigations on the quiet and presented his findings back to his head of department, who quite rightly passed it onto the treasury department. During the regular run-of-the-mill inspections by trading standards, health and safety, and OMAR - that stands for Offshore Major Accident Regulator - over a two year period, they arranged for these inspections to be accompanied by certain extra officials of their choosing, but nothing out of the ordinary that would cause our villains to raise an eyebrow. Those seemingly innocent extra officials were of course picked by the treasury for their skills in detecting fraudulent activity, and they too came to a similar conclusion that oil was going missing. But they couldn't prove a thing."

"The issue was then passed back to HMRC to see if their original inspector could get further than they had, and he pursued other possible angles as to what might be going on. There being a maritime element to all this, the insurers Lloyds of London were consulted and they passed him onto a liaison officer; a commodore in the

Admiralty. Between them, they came up with a plan to infiltrate a couple of personnel onto the rig and retrieve the data that couldn't otherwise be obtained, and here is where things started to go wrong."

Patricia questioningly cocked her head slightly to one side and started to gently nibble her lower lip; as was her habit.

He continued. "One gets a taste of how careful they were when one considers the length of time it took to set up this gently-gently operation. They didn't force any unwanted decisions, nor make any secretive enquiries, but let the natural process of enrolment take place. At different times, the pair of them applied for jobs through the employment agency that Blue Lizard had appointed, and the only contact they had with each other was to co-ordinate when they would be available to start their employment aboard the rig. One of those two personnel was an ex-mariner contracted by the navy as a resources manager, whose speciality was hacking into computers, and it was his job to delve into their systems to download anything of relevance. The other person was…shall we say… a current serving officer named Miles Glen who was sent along to watch the hacker's back." Gibbons paused again. "Three days ago, the pair of them flew out to the rig by scheduled transfer helicopter, along with some other relief crew, but it was only Glen who returned."

Gibbons' intake of breath was audible. "His report makes grim reading. Tates has the details." He nodded in his direction.

Tates opened one of the folders and although he

already knew most of its contents, before he recited from it, he took a purposeful stare at Patricia. "This is top secret information and I mean...top secret. You're only being told this because you'll be working with him."

Patricia successfully tried not to gulp, but a flush of awareness flooded over her.

"Miles Glen officially carries the rank of Lieutenant in The Royal Marines, 3 Commando which speaks for itself, so I think we can believe what he says." He looked down and turned a couple of sheafs. "I'll skip the preliminaries and go straight to the relevant part... and he says...

The locked compartment that housed the computers was opposite the passageway that led to the control centre and we hid in a store that housed hi-viz vests and life jackets for several minutes until personnel had ceased moving about. I picked the lock, beckoned him over and proceeded to keep a look-out while keeping the door open a crack while he accessed their mainframe. He told me it was encrypted and that it would take several minutes. I know it took him eight minutes because I looked at my watch when he announced that he had cracked it and was downloading the data onto a memory stick. That took just over one minute and he handed me the stick. I told him to get back into the store across the aisle while I reset the lock so that no one would know that we had been there. We went back the way we had come along a companionway through a watertight door and thought nobody had seen us as we went in different directions, but he cried out almost immediately. I heard running feet so hid round the corner and observed him being chased by a man. They went outside. I followed them without being seen.

Tates turned a page. "... He goes on to describe the gruesome details of how he watched our hacker have his throat slit and body thrown overboard, then how he hunted the assailants down and similarly disposed of their bodies; before they found him." He turned another three pages. "...He concludes by stating that the two murderers were professionals, possibly of Arabic or Eastern European extraction."

Tates closed the folder and looked up, so Patricia turned to face Gibbons who held a memory stick in his hand. "And here is the evidence retrieved by our hacker and Miles Glen. It has been analysed, and there are indeed some serious anomalies. The issue is not how much oil they are producing, which is around a thousand barrels a day, but why it's not all turning up at the refineries. Somewhere along the line they appear to be smuggling significant quantities out of sight and I want you to find out how, and where it's going. In view of the method of demise of our hacker, I've asked the admiralty for the loan of Miles Glen to accompany you."

The short silence was broken by Patricia saying "Thank you." She could think of nothing else.

"The Whitegate refinery near Cork in Southern Ireland, the Repsol refinery in Coruna North-West Spain are the usual recipients of their oil, but there are one or two others on occasion, like the West African coast in the Gulf of Guinea. Strangely enough, none of the oil ever seems to turn up at any of the refineries in Rotterdam; Europe's largest. I mention this as our thieves will by now be aware that someone is onto them, due to Mr. Glen's actions, but his report states that he had no other option than to do what he did as otherwise he too would be washed-up on a beach somewhere or other. So, it's likely that they'll have shut down their schemes as much as they can by now, but they'll find it difficult to do so at the drop of a hat as they'll have contracts to fulfil, etcetera. For example, if a vessel is due at such-and-such a refinery a month or two from tomorrow, they can't just let it motor round in circles while our investigation blows over. The oil on board will be worth a small fortune and their buyers will want delivery. There must be a paper trail somewhere and there's bound to be those who have seen what's been going on, so I've suggested you start with a visit to Blue Lizard's rig."

Gibbons held her gaze and offered the memory stick for her to take. "Be swift."

Tates held the door open for her and closed it quietly behind them. "I take it you still have your Thames Valley Inspector's badge because you can legitimately claim that you are investigating the disappearance of personnel? And I've warned Blue Lizard that you're coming. I'll give you the name of the hacker together with his background, both real and imaginary; you already know of Miles Glen and I've arranged for you two to meet in our secure room in..." He glanced at his watch. "At eleven o'clock." He handed her a pile of files. "Take these there and familiarise yourself. The Irish Garda are already interviewing those aboard the rig, so you'll need to have the facts at your fingertips."

Patricia was already thinking of what lay ahead and

asked "If I'm an investigating officer, what role is Miles Glen playing? Won't they recognise him?"

"I shouldn't think so as we've already thought of that. You see, he's from Jamaica, of Rastafarian extraction, and he'll be in disguise." He let her mull on that while they walked along the corridor towards the lift. "I won't spoil the surprise, but you'll see what I mean when you meet him." The lift door opened and once inside he added "This'll need fast work and I've arranged for you both to be on a helicopter out to the rig this afternoon. It's all in the green file." He glanced at the files under her arm.

She left him in the lift, turned left and showed her pass to the armed sentry who guarded the secure room. She'd been in the small theatre-like room once before and after she fully-closed the door, she just stood there for a moment listening to the dead silence. She marvelled at how quiet it was compared to the bustle outside in the centre of London. Not even a vibration attesting to its insular structure. Putting the files on one of the cushioned seats, she sat in an adjacent one and opened the green file.

The only page on Miles Glen was scant to the point of being virtually useless in its description, to such an extent that there wasn't even a photograph of him, and thus impressed upon her his top secret status. What there was took her less than thirty seconds to digest.

The next few pages were in a separate clear plastic folder and detailed the crew manifest aboard the Blue Lizard rig, whichought to have been one hundred and eight, but fell short by four..

Further to her swotting-up the previous night when she learned that there were a remarkable variety of positions aboard a rig, she now had a chance to put names to those postings. It seemed that the Americans had cornered the market when it came to who was responsible for what and she had gleaned that generally, worldwide, those names had stuck. Top of the hierarchy came The Company Man who was not required to be on the rig at all times; he carried more of an executive role. There were managers for each aspect of the rig. Most senior was the Toolpusher, then the Driller, after that each position was very specific with no seniority over another. Chief Mate, Chief Mechanic, Chief Electrician, Coxswain, Welder, but near the bottom were the Roughnecks.

After the first few, she gave up trying to analyse the individuals as otherwise she'd be sitting there past midnight and still be none-the-wiser, but it was a very cosmopolitan mix of individuals. Dutch, Germans, English, Irish, French, Guyanese, , Nigerian, and naturally some Americans. Knowing that she might well confront some of these men in a few hours, she memorised some of the names in positions of responsibility. What did pique her interest was that there were no women on board, but she brushed the whys and wherefores of that question aside..

"Shit. Only half-an-hour before Miles turns up." She muttered to herself and reached for her laptop. Before she could access it, she inserted her own designated security dongle that required the prints of her thumb and finger to squeeze it into its slot. As the screen verified it really was her, she wondered if there was someone, or even another machine at GCHQ, monitoring her and noting what she was up to. She cast that notion aside as well. She inserted the memory stick and up came files pertaining to The Blue Lizard. Immediately, the thought struck her that this was going to be an impossible job without some kind of help as there was just too much of it, but she started to mentally discard batches of files whose names indicated irrelevance.

She created her own folder so that she could copy those seemingly unimportant files into it and managed a serious reduction; what was left, in alphabetical order, looked more manageable. In the background she saw a programme by the name of Geniesym being downloaded automatically, and once it finished, she clicked on one of the folders. A colour 3-D schematic of the rig appeared. Hovering her mouse over a particular section produced an enlarged diagram which could be zoomed-into; the relevant reference box off to one side depicted a series of alphanumeric links to sub-files.

It was an easy program to use, but aware of how long this might take, she didn't follow the files all the way down to their nth degree, preferring to concentrate on the corporate workings of the company. There was still a copious number of files, but she persevered.

The Blue Lizard Oil Production Company had listed on the Irish stock exchange over a decade ago. Being the equivalent of the London Stock Exchange, Euronext was located in a grand building in the historic heart of Dublin and traded in worldwide shares and bonds; including BLOP, which it had been shortened to. It then swopped its listing from Ireland, opting instead for the London Stock Exchange where trading rules were easier than from within the European Union. The register's balance sheet showed that it had a capital worth of nearly quarter of a billion US Dollars yet it had been running at a significant loss for the past three years. She assumed Gibbons' comment was correct in that it had never turned a profit so didn't look back to earlier years. She trawled through various associated documents and discovered that BLOP was actually registered in Riyadh in Saudi Arabia but had its headquarters in Baku; the capital of Azerbaijan.

She raised an eyebrow, sat back with speculation that this was an extraordinary set-up and made a mental note to ask someone in the oil industry if this was normal. It seemed to her to be awfully convoluted, and she cynically wondered if this was just a very expensive exercise in tax avoidance. In her limited experience, this would also include bribery, corruption and all that went with it.

She read on. The Amsterdam-based auditors' report was boring and the directors' report even worse, and, unusually for her, she skipped most of it but did take on-board the general optimism for a return to profit at some time in the future.

The list of directors included some unpronounceable names, and she started to scroll down to the pages which showed a list of major shareholders.

"Good morning."

A dulcet baritone voice immediately behind her made her jump a little as she had not heard or felt anything in the still air. She belatedly tried not to react, as in that same micro-second she realised that it must be eleven and that the voice belonged to Miles Glen.

"Come and join me." She responded as nonchalantly as she could muster.

"Pleased to meet you. No need to get up." said Miles as he moved sideways between the row of seats to sit next to her.

She watched him glide with ease in between the seats and now she frowned lightly, trying to comprehend his second comment. Before she could manage a smart retort, he added "Only kidding. I can see you're busy." He referred to her laptop; where else but on her lap. He leaned over and offered her his hand. "Can I call you Pat, or would you prefer Patricia?"

Her thoughts were still taking in oil rig material and she hadn't retuned herself to meeting Miles just yet, but she was aware that he'd offered her only two options. "Either, if I can call you Miles."

He motioned at her laptop. "How far have you got and how will it help us?"

During their brief handshake she'd felt the cool hardy texture of his palms and fleetingly wondered about the rest of the man. His questions caused her to stop thinking about her task and spare a few seconds for an introvertial moment. During just the first ten seconds of meeting Miles she'd realised that he was silent, as a killer should be, had a sense of humour, was polite and asked pertinent questions. Oh, and she loved his voice. She hadn't previously tried to imagine what he looked like in the flesh but his well-proportioned body didn't disappoint. This dark-skinned man of above average height had the hint of a smile on his face that somehow accentuated his near baldness; a bit like a smiley face.

"Rigs are extraordinary structures and so are the people who man them. They're like towns in the middle of nowhere with a life of their own and not the sort of place I'd like to go on holiday to." Just in time she stopped herself from asking if he'd ever been on a rig.

"You won't get an argument from me over that one, but what I meant was do you yet know who to interview when we get there? If not, I have a suggestion."

"Go on."

"The head of the operations on board is Jorge Arlesson, a seasoned Norwegian from Bergen and his right-hand man is Matt Hewdy. He lets you know he's from Texas... naturally, with a name like that. They're probably the only two worth talking to as the others, as far as I know, work on a shift basis. Either one of those two will be found on the rig, often at the same time, and they have overall control of what goes on, and they answer directly to Jason Donnelly who's the company man on the mainland in Cork, Southern Ireland. If there's any skulduggery going on, and if anyone knows about it, it'll be Donnelly or that pair. There is one other chap who I haven't found yet as he's their computer operator, and it'll be interesting to see their reaction when we ask about him."

"You've done your homework and thank you for saving me quite a lot of time, but have you come across any skulduggery linked to those three?" She used his expression of foul play.

"No, not yet." The slight dejected look on his

face wasn't obvious. "During my short time on board as a roughneck I only caught a glimpse of Matt in the distance, and remember, I was supposed to be bodyguarding our own computer expert not mixing with the high and mighty. You're quite right in that I did do some homework before I left for the rig, but finding out about a well-hatched smuggling plan from the comfort of a computer screen is almost impossible for me, but I am rather hopeful that our face-to-face interviews may bear results."

She reached out, lifted it up so that he could see the memory stick. "What I have here is next on my agenda to look at once I've finished with this report." A thought crossed her mind. "I don't suppose you know what's on it?"

"Haven't a clue. You don't mind if I look over your shoulder, do you?" He said and without waiting for her response easily hopped over the row of seats and looked down on her screen from behind her. "I might spot something."

Patricia's eyes flitted back to her screen. "Let me finish this first. I'm nearly done."

Her initial thought was that he might not have security clearance for what she was looking at, but an instant later realised that what she was browsing at was in the public domain. Only eight more pages to go and after she picked up where she had left off, she scrolled quickly down the list of interested parties, and nearly missed his name.

Maurice 'bloody' Hamilton.

"Bastard." So much did her exclamation carry a

venomous edge to it that Miles was taken-aback. "That bloody shithead's up to it again." She added.

"Who's a shithead?"

"Maurice bloody Hamilton MP and Northern Ireland secretary, that's who." Without turning her head she retorted. "Oh, you might have heard of him or seen him on the telly, but you won't know him like I do." She shifted round in her seat so that he could see the look on her face. "That bugger did all he could to set me up for a sting that would have landed me in prison for a long time. He's had people murdered. Blackmailed his way to the top. He was hated by all when he was a captain in the army, and not just by the IRA when he was posted to Northern Ireland during 'The Troubles', but also by his own men. I've even heard a rumour that they tried to kill him; on more than one occasion. He's beaten children and he's a whoring philanderer who fucks his way through life. God knows how he gets away with his abuse of power, and as a senior cabinet minister he exploits everyone he comes into contact with, to extort money out of whoever he can. Earlier this year Justin and I were involved with a bogus platinum mining operation and guess who was at the heart of it? He's the worst kind of immoral person you could possibly meet."

She watched his face reflect the gravity of her jaundiced comments and with a more bitter tone to her voice added. "That arsehole tried to rape me once… he's a right cunt of the first order."

Miles had never heard anyone describe another person with such rancour. "I take it he didn't succeed."

"I kicked him in the balls so hard he could hardly walk for several days. Make no mistake, this man is evil and it's about time he was put down like a dog. If his name's connected with this rig, then you can bet your bottom dollar that he's part of it."

"Then we'd better add him to our list of interviewees."

"Oh no...not if you value your career you won't. He'll lure you in with some cock-and-bull story which you'll follow, then just when you think you've got him, he'll contort the truth to suit his own ends. He uses his authority to twist the facts and if that doesn't work, he won't care who he has to bribe or blackmail. You'll be lucky if you manage to hang on to your pension at best, and at worst you'll spend the next twenty years in prison. No, we need to investigate all those around him first without them raising suspicions, because if he finds out that we're on to him, he'll move heaven and earth to wriggle out of it."

"Are you sure you're not taking this too personally?"

"Of course it's personal and I'd take great delight in seeing him hang, but more importantly I have a reputation to uphold and that's something I value above almost all else. I'm proud of my OBE and I'm proud to be a detective inspector in the police, but I won't let my desires distract me from doing the job properly." She lowered her voice. "And yes, I am bloody good at digging out subterfuge and hidden facts, so let's get on with finding some, shall we?"

Miles looked at his watch and shuffled to the aisle between the seats. "We'd better get going as the helicopter is due to leave Northolt at one. I'll see you downstairs in the lobby in fifteen."

"Why not now?" She too had noticed the time on her laptop.

He paused and turned back to face her. "I need to change."

As he exited, she noticed his attire for the first time and that he carried a holdall. She agreed that he'd need to smarten-up if he was going to pass himself off as an official. She started to pack up her own bits and pieces, and paused, wondering what kind of official he was going to be when they confronted those on the rig.

Chapter 7

Dressed in his quilted jacket, Maurice Hamilton gloated over his latest conquest as she finished dressing in front of him. The bedroom was a bit of a mess due to her extraordinary cavorting performance prior to their love-making, and reminded him of someone he once knew from the circus. It wasn't quite a case of 'the-bustier-the-better', but he'd have to find another painting to replace the damaged one that, up to half-an-hour ago, had hung above the bed.

As she went to open the door to leave, she made some comment about hoping that the tribunal currently convened would find in her family's favour; but Hamilton wasn't really listening and just nodded with a smile. Before he closed the door firmly behind her, he noticed that his security detail from the diplomatic protection squad was seated outside in the corridor in his usual place. He made a mental note to remind the young man about discretion.

He jaunted over to his desk, unlocked one of the top drawers where he kept a list of his paramours, as he liked to call them, and scored her out of ten with an appropriate comment in the last column. His love list was one of his treasures which he liked to croon-over now and again. He turned a couple of pages to remind himself of past deeds, but frowned when one name reminded him of that bitch Miss. Patricia Eyethorne. That was why he now kept his list under lock and key, as she and her boyfriend had somehow purloined it and scuppered his plans for them. He slammed the drawer shut, almost forgetting to relock it as he conjected what he could do to the pair of them should their paths ever cross again.

He looked at the wall-mounted clock and decided he'd have time for a leisurely snifter of Irish whiskey from his arm chair in front of the window that overlooked The Thames opposite the Houses of Parliament.

What he wasn't looking forward to was having to return home later that night. His wife Caroline had been adamant that he attend their daughter's eighteenth birthday party the following evening, and anyway, she had argued that it was his duty as her father. Georgina would soon be leaving Cheltenham Ladies College and had persuaded her mother to let her hold a party; only a small one for about fifty people; with a band. Caroline had also reminded him that Elkins their gardener had just retired, and that the gardens were reverting to their natural verdant state far too quickly; especially at this time of year. In answer to her urgent enquiries as to his replacement, a couple of chaps would be available to start immediately and were expecting to be interviewed by him tomorrow morning.

As he rotated his crystal-cut glass tumbler of whiskey to catch the light, he relished the fact that the entire case of Bushmills had been a free gift from a man called Dougal who had curried his favour. He couldn't recall what Dougal wanted, but for some reason his mind wandered back to the Eyethorne woman; perhaps it was because she had been sitting in the chair opposite him a few months earlier. By God, if the chance to get even ever arose, he'd take it... and maybe her at the same time. Even though he had just enjoyed a rough round with 'busty' he felt a stirring, lusting after her gorgeous body.

He started to picture how it might pan out when he was bought down to earth, his carnal thoughts interrupted by his phone ringing. He downed his glass in one and answered the number which he recognised as belonging to one of the party whips, and was reminded which way to vote in the division chamber in half-an-hour.

* * * * *

The daylight that escaped round the edges of the bedroom curtains woke Hamilton who stretched out in his voluminous bed. As usual, he couldn't remember his dreams, but he didn't care as his conscious mind took over command and started to create order for the forthcoming day. He frowned lightly as he realised he was in his own bed at home and not in his luxurious apartment on the south bank next to Westminster Bridge, and would consequently need to assume his role as a husband and father to his family.

He let his arm flop across the king-sized bed to where Caroline ought to have been to establish that she was already up and about, threw back the covers and sauntered over to the bay window in his pyjamas to draw back the curtains. His wincing eyes quickly adjusted to survey the tennis court and croquet lawn just below him, and a little further on off to one side, the tall wall that surrounded the Victorian vegetable garden.

It reminded him that he was supposed to be interviewing a pair of replacement gardeners shortly and he looked down at his expensive watch. Late last night when he had returned home, she'd told him that one gardener wouldn't be enough to keep the estate in order. Quite simply, now that they had just bought an extra twenty-eight acres of adjoining fields to cater for the ponies that their children had wanted, that acquisition had nearly doubled the size of the entire property and included three, empty terraced cottages. It all needed upkeep.

He decided that life was rather good right now, and accentuated his sentiment with a classic stretch and yawn, then hoped something would crop up during the day to make it another memorable one. Looking in the other direction, he saw one of his security detail accompanying a pair of men from the direction of the gated entrance. Probably the new gardeners, he thought to himself. While he was getting dressed, he chuckled with the knowledge that he warranted as much close protection as the Prime Minister.

Taking the back staircase treads two at a time, he emerged into the corridor that linked their utility room to the kitchen and nearly tripped over Caroline's two Boxer dogs as they competed with each other in greeting. One sharp 'Oi!' sent them scuttling towards the kitchen ahead of him, where he was met with a pleasant domestic scene of mother and daughter, both dressed in their silk dressing gowns, discussing that evening's forthcoming party. Georgina jumped-up and gave him a great big hug, thanking him for allowing her to hold her eighteenth birthday party at home. He wasn't aware that he had agreed to that, but didn't let on. What he was aware of was the way her ample bosom pressed against him through the flimsy gown, and he succeeded in quickly dismissing bodily thoughts.

His wife had no such urge to cease enjoying her marmalade on toast. It wasn't that they didn't get on as a couple, it was just that they left each other to their own devices. She was happily ensconced in the family home in Worcestershire while he revelled in the parliamentary world in Westminster, over a hundred miles away.

Hamilton went to open the fridge when she reminded him that the two new maintenance men were outside in the covered loggia, waiting for him to endorse her choice.

"They seem a nice pair of chaps who moved into the village a few years ago. Middle-aged. Both married. Families, and I've provisionally offered them two of the three new cottages. Good help is a bit thin on the ground round here, but I think they'll fit in well. Oh, by the way, our local postman may be interested in renting the last one as his wife passed-away not long ago and he's on his own now. I've left the final decisions down to you, but what with you being away in London most of the time, thought they would fit in nicely." He knew it was her way of telling him to agree with her choice, and he moved off through the back door of the kitchen.

He did a double-take as the two men stood side-by-side at the entrance to the loggia. Twins; if not they ought to have been. Not quite in unison, they offered their good mornings, and waited for Hamilton to make his mind up.

Eventually he did, and in a sarcastic voice said. "I suppose you two fellows are twins."

"Yes sir."

"My wife didn't tell me you were." As though it was their fault that he hadn't been told.

There was an understanding between Eric and Ernie that Eric would speak on behalf of the both of them. Neither of them minded nor blamed their mother for being named after the infamous TV comedians of the previous century; Morecambe and Wise had been her favourites. Eric told Hamilton, who really didn't care much for that kind of humour.

"So, you two are to be our new gardeners, eh? What makes you think either of you is qualified?" Hamilton wanted to stamp his authority from the outset.

"Before we moved into the village a couple of years ago, we were working in a garden centre for nearly twenty years. Ernie and I ended up running the place in the end as the owner became so unsteady on his pins. He couldn't manage it himself. He eventually sold the business to a developer who included our bungalows in the deal, so we rented a house in the village down the road here, and have been helping out in the local builders merchant's part-time ever since. You want anything planted or a fence repairing....."

"Grass mown." Interrupted Ernie.

"Walls rebuilt, gutters mended."

"Ditches cleared."

"Tennis courts kept clear of weeds." Eric had

spotted that the tennis court was beginning to sprout a few weeds where the link fence met the tarmac.

"Then we're your men. Day or night." They had taken it in turns.

If nothing else, Hamilton was shrewd when it came to business, and he instantly recognised that the pair of them would be ideal, and not wanting to be shown up by his ignorance of rural matters such as how to mow grass, decided he'd pass the matter back to Caroline.

"Right then. Looks like you can start immediately. Sort the details out with my wife." He still felt he needed to let them know who was the boss, so he added "But whenever you address me in the future, you call me sir. Clear?"

"Yes, sir." Their response was instantaneous.

He took one last look at them, trying to spot any difference between them, before about-turning and heading back to his house with breakfast in mind. Somehow, they looked familiar, but he couldn't place them.

Hamilton's close protection officer had been standing to one side, just about in earshot, but now came up to the pair of them. "He must like you 'cos he's never been that civil to me."

Eric and Ernie walked back towards the village but waited until they were well out of hearing range before uttering a word.

It was Eric who broke the silence first. "How about that, then. We didn't think he'd recognise us."

"He doesn't care, does he? I'll bet he's not even kept in touch with his fellow officers of the Welch." Ernie was referring to their old infantry regiment when they had first enrolled together, during The Troubles in Northern Ireland. Maurice Hamilton had been their captain then and had turned out to be a right bastard. While out on patrol, the twins had prevented him from beating a child senseless, and that confrontation had led to a severe Company punishment. On another occasion, on the eve of their simultaneous weddings, he had revoked their passes, forcing them to delay their marriage plans for over six months until their tour of duty was over. Their wives, Melanie and Mandy, were also twin sisters.

The kindly character of the twins was constantly tested to the limit by Hamilton while they were under his command. Although they were not the type of people who held grudges, what Hamilton had done to them was etched into the basement of their memories. The regimental chaplain had sympathised with their predicament and had given them some words of wisdom at the time. 'Never forget, but don't remember'.

His sound advice was well received by them, but they had agreed that if ever the chance to get back at Hamilton arose, they would take it. The postcard pinned to the notice board in the builders' merchants advertising for Elkins' replacement was like a bolt out of the blue. The terms of employment sounded generous and they reckoned that they had nothing to lose by applying. Hamilton was no longer their commander and as civilians, they were their own men.

"He certainly doesn't care. Not like us." Eric replied proudly. The twins made it a point to attend the informal Company reunion on an annual basis.

"Recognised him as soon as I clapped eyes on him. What with his receding hairline, that birthmark on his head is a dead giveaway."

"Just so long as he doesn't remember us.."

"Let's not give him reason to. From what we've heard in the village, he's never here, so as long as we keep out of sight, he won't remember. You could hide our old Company in this place and he'd never see any of them." Ernie commented.

"So now, let's see how we can screw up his life like he screwed up ours."

* * * * *

Hamilton had spurned his former life as a captain in the Royal Welch Fusiliers, considering it merely as an old springboard to his current position. He didn't maintain contact with any of his fellow officers, except on the odd occasion when it suited him. The Company that he had commanded forty years ago had consisted of some eighty men, mainly from Wales, and he had absolutely no desire, or need, to maintain contact with any of them. Naturally, he had forgotten what the Cartwright twins had looked like, and it never crossed his mind that that was where he had first come across them.. He was oblivious to their identity.

Right now, all he wanted was to retreat to his study to open his pile of mail while enjoying his duck liver pate on toast, but Caroline cornered him into sitting down at the breakfast table to outline some details of Georgina's birthday party. He was only half listening as he spotted the news headlines on The Times front page while cutting through a piece of buttered toast.

He vaguely gathered that later in the afternoon, the disco chap would set up at one end of their living room about the same time that the caterers did likewise at the other end, and that a barman from the local pub had been drafted in to organise alcoholic and non-alcoholic drinks. She made it clear that he was expected to make an appearance, if only for a short while, for the sake of their only daughter. Inevitably, she quizzed him about the two new gardeners, and after a brief discussion, he left the employment and housing details up to her.

He eventually made it to the sanctuary of his quiet study and sat down at his desk which supported several stacks of unopened post, but before he attacked them with his silver-plated letter opener, he attended to his computer. Once through the security protocols, he was expecting one message in particular, and was not disappointed when he opened it. He sat back as far as possible in his chair, closed his eyes, and smiled in gratification. Just to make sure he hadn't misread it, he opened his eyes and re-read the message that stated that his new bank account in The Caribbean had been credited with another two hundred and fifty thousand pounds from the Blue Lizard Oil Company.

"Ha ha. This is what it's all about." He exclaimed out loud to himself. He did a mental calculation and reckoned he had ample cash to afford that replacement Bentley he had ordered the previous year. He looked up at the shelf opposite where a large, heavy gold-plated model of a Bentley Continental GT sat. It had been a gift from his Blue Lizard contact in Azerbaijan, and he loved it so much that he had ordered the real item.

It took him some hours to wade through the many letters and documents in front of him, and by the end of it, his previous sunny disposition had dampened only a little. He decided to stretch his legs round his newly expanded estate. For all of two seconds, he thought about taking the two Boxer dogs for a walk before discarding the idea of having to control the unruly animals, and to clean up after them.

* * * * *

Hamilton's close protection officers from the diplomatic protection squad usually went about in pairs, but once they had reported to headquarters that there were many teenagers being dropped off by their parents at the Hamilton household, they were told to remain in the background. It would have been an impossible job to vet each and every one of them in time.

Georgina was naturally over excited at the prospect of holding her birthday party in the family home, and her friends started to arrive from midday onwards. Most of the early arrivals were her girlfriends, and they mainly disappeared upstairs to the bedrooms to try on and show off various outfits. The later arrivals would swell the party numbers to over seventy; the majority of them being girls and all about the same age as Georgina.

"How about this, then." 'Leggy' Laura exclaimed as she turned round to face the other two girls, but she was still trying to lower the hem of the singlet that revealed far too much of her legs.

"You grew out of that three years ago, and anyway, that doesn't qualify as a cocktail dress." Commented Simone who looked up from the mirror she was holding in front of her face.

"I know. But I just wanted to try it on for the last time." Laura reluctantly admitted that Simone was right. As she bent over her overnight bag to retrieve the dress she was going to wear, the three girls heard the beginnings of a rip of the stitching. They all stopped as if frozen in time for half a second, before bursting out loud with laughter. The incident typified their close-knit friendship.

The gaiety of the occasion pervaded once the party got going at around six o'clock with background music, champagne and canapes to accompany the growing throng. Georgina's younger brothers produced a drone with a camera attachment and the machine sporadically darted in and out of the open French windows. Exclamations flew when a couple of young chaps managed to snatch a bottle of champagne from the bar and fired off its cork at it as it hovered just outside. A small group were randomly dotted around the croquet lawn as they tried out the balls and mallets.

Caroline had naturally invited her close family and some of her own friends, and they tended to congregate around each other since they were severely outnumbered by the youngsters. It wasn't a case of 'us and them' but there was a noticeable disparity between the two age groups. Nobody seemed to mind.

Maurice Hamilton made an appearance, more out of curiosity than duty, and found himself actually enjoying himself as he cuddled a tumbler of scotch. He found himself standing in a circle amongst those of a similar age, including his wife, and he was careful not to be seen admiring the plethora of teenage girls who flitted back and forth. Most of the youngsters were aware that they were in the presence of a leading member of the government and a few of the braver ones attempted to engage him in meaningful conversation; they were generally disappointed. One young man's probing comments piqued him, but another called William earned himself a pat on the back when he mentioned that his father was one of the influential investment bankers who Hamilton had been trying to butter up recently.

With the onset of night, the music volume increased and it became more difficult to hold a quiet conversation. Hamilton was thinking about retiring back to his study when he was approached by a particularly tall brunette who nervously introduced herself as Laura. She started to describe her friendly relationship with his daughter Georgina while at college, and told him that they were thinking of touring parts of South America together later that year. She had aspirations to become a racing driver and had already been offered a day's course at the UK Motorsport's circuit near Bicester.

His sensual interest in her began to increase as he appreciated her sleek frame, accentuated by the hugging black cocktail dress which fitted loosely over her shoulders and had a rather high side split on one side. She led the conversation towards her love of motor racing and how the throbbing of engines excited her, but cut it short when another girl tapped her on the shoulder and announced that she was wanted for a group photo. He ogled her rear end as she mingled with the crowd, and tentatively wondered if there'd be another opportunity to see if there was more to this girl.

He wandered over to the table of canapes which had grown into a fine display of larger finger foods and helped himself to a cold chicken leg.

"Wonderful isn't it." Caroline appeared at his shoulder.

"The food's excellent. Where did you find the caterers?"

"Not just the food, silly. The whole thing. It's nice to see today's kids growing up and enjoying themselves. Don't you think?"

"I can't remember us ever doing anything like this. Can you?"

"No. In our day we'd end up in a stuffy restaurant somewhere, surrounded mainly by your friends who talked about high finance and the cricket score. We never let our hair down like they are." She motioned towards the centre of their living room that had become the dance floor. "I think the last time we danced together was on our honeymoon."

"But that was more like ballroom dancing... not this." He remarked as he turned back to the table for a second chicken leg. He didn't want his wife to see him enjoying the lithe movements of supple young women cavorting to the music; she might get the wrong idea. "I thought your brother and his family were coming."

"They were, but he phoned this afternoon to say that they had gone down with food poisoning. I'm always telling him to avoid that Chinese they keep going to. Hey, mind your back. Here comes the trifle." She gently nudged him to one side as a waiter approached with a large plate, and shuffled some of the smaller dishes to one side to make room for it. "I'm just going to check if they managed to get some black forest gateau." She left him standing there.

Hamilton edged around the periphery of the heaving dance floor towards the bar, ignored the barman, and poured himself another decent measure of whisky. He then picked one of the niches next to the fireplace as an unobtrusive observation point to admire the young fillies. Safe in the knowledge that nobody would be able to see where he was looking, especially as the flashing disco lights distorted vision, he feasted his eyes hungrily on the young girls as they flaunted themselves. These females were a far juicier selection than the stream of older women he had had the pleasure of in his London apartment.

Five minutes later he returned to the bar to refill his glass yet again. Back in his niche, he noted that the older guests had vacated the noisy room, probably in search of somewhere quieter to carry on their conversation. He resumed his ogling, spotted Laura who was exposing plenty of thigh, and admired the way her physique gyrated in time with the beat.

Considering their earlier conversation about throbbing engines, he reckoned she might just agree to a private liaison. His thinking went along the lines that she was just another female who had desires like any other; and why not with him?

Absent-mindedly, he gulped down half of his glass,

formulated a plan, and stepped to the edge of the action. It didn't take Laura long to notice him standing there, so she came over, but whatever she tried to say to him was lost on the waves of music. He motioned that they should go to the hall.

Their initial conversation revolved around what a nice party it was, and how everyone was enjoying themselves.

Hamilton nudged the topic towards cars. "You mentioned to me earlier about motor racing, and it just so happens I may be in a position to help. Which discipline are you particularly interested in?"

"Oh, saloon car racing, and my brother has a friend who races in the BTCC. That's the British Touring Car Championship. He said I might be able to have a go in one of their test cars at the end of this season. If you've ever been up close to one of those cars, you can really feel the power when they rev the engine. Gets me excited just being there."

"Well, that sounds promising, but what I had in mind is something a bit more potent. Come with me to my study and I'll show you." Before he moved off, he downed the rest of his scotch, and on the way placed the empty glass on an occasional table.

Laura felt honoured to be asked into his study and made the appropriate 'wow' noises as she looked round at his photographs and memorabilia. Hamilton reached up and managed to fetch down the heavy model of his Bentley which he placed squarely on his desk in front of her. The gleaming metallic model was almost three feet long and had the desired effect.

Laura went to reach out but paused. "Can I touch it?"

"Oh yes... and before you ask, yes it is real gold." Hamilton moved to one side and stood behind her.

She placed just one finger on the roof, then ran it along its length towards the rear. A chill of excitement shivered down her spine as she took in its beauty and exquisite detail. The sheer size of it had her in awe, and she stretched out her other hand so that both were in contact with it. She closed her eyes for a moment; her imagination running away.

Hamilton stood directly behind her. "Try and lift it. Feel how heavy it is."

She stretched her arms out wide to curl her fingers under the front and rear bumpers, and tried to raise it. Only then did she realise its weight and as she leaned over it further, felt Hamilton's body press hard against her back. His arms came round her sides and he wrapped his hands over hers so that together they lifted it a few inches.

"You can almost feel the wind rushing over its sleek body. Its engine throbbing as it cleaves its way through the air; surging down the road and eating up the miles."

The dulcet tone of his voice in her ear was unexpected, but she didn't alter her stance as he slowly removed his hands, leaving her holding the hefty model in mid-air by herself. From the close proximity of his mouth, she caught a whiff of whiskey on his breath. Engrossed in admiring the magnificent car in her own hands, she hardly noticed his fingers stroking their way up her arms and up to her shoulders, but she did notice when those fingers started to worm their way past her armpits and ended-up circling her breasts under her flimsy dress.

She was gobsmacked. At first, she didn't know what to do or say and it took a couple of blinks of the eye before she realised that the car was making her muscles ache, so she put it back down on the desk. Comprehension of what Hamilton was doing kicked in. She controlled her initial shock and took time to consider what was best to do next, just as his fingers neared her sensitive centres. Still uncertain, she clamped his arms between hers and her body.

"A man in my position could be very influential… given the right motivation."

She'd not encountered such a situation before. As her mind raced to arrive at the obvious conclusion, she immediately realised that she had only two options. Either to give her virginity away and hopefully further her racing aspirations, or to spurn him.

She chose the latter, on the principle that Hamilton was nothing like the perfect man of her dreams; racing could wait. She controlled the revulsion that began to well up in her, thinking how best to handle the strength of the man whose body was now pressed tightly against her. Again, she calculated that she had two choices, and was certainly worried that if she rejected his advances, he would then try to force himself on her; violating her virginity in his own home while his family were in the next room. Her heart was in her mouth, but she succeeded in not gagging, and calmed down enough to work out what she had to do to extricate herself.

Without flinching, she slowly turned round to face him, and was appalled by his evil grin that accompanied his smugness. He had taken half a pace backwards to allow her to turn, and that was all the space she needed. Involuntarily, she kneed him square in the groin as hard as she possibly could.

In her own mind, when she was alone in the cloakroom a short while later, she had a quiet moment; reliving the incident without being sick. Holding her head in her hands, she tried unsuccessfully to analyse why she had done that, rather than try to walk away, but she felt glad that she had done so. Her solace was that she had done the right thing morally. Her next dilemma was should she tell anyone; in particular, Georgina? She knew she wouldn't be able to face him again, but then she considered that he wouldn't be able to face her either; could he? Perhaps it would be for the best if she phoned for a taxi and left.

Doubled over and gently clutching his groin area, Hamilton watched her hurry out of his study, then shuffled around his desk to sit on a soft chair. It wasn't soft enough in the right places, so he perched on the edge of a wooden stool so that his swollen genitalia could dangle without interference in his trousers. It bought back memories of being in such a position after that Eyethorne bitch had kicked him in the same place the previous year. He had sworn vengeance then, but now he just swore.

Chapter 8

In a Fleet Air Arm Merlin helicopter and with Peltor headsets sitting comfortably over their ears, thus cutting out most of the helicopter's noisy mechanisms, they found that they could converse normally through them. The co-pilot obliged them by flicking a switch, which meant that Patricia and Miles could talk to each other without the pilots hearing their conversation.

"I presume you're used to this sort of thing...I mean, getting around by helicopter." Remarked Patricia.

"I've been in a few."

"Can you fly one?"

Miles looked at her a little strangely. "Have you ever tried to fly one?"

"No."

"I had some brief instruction once, and I can tell you unless you've been properly trained, you don't stand a chance. Hovering is the most difficult."

Patricia decided to steer the subject away from something she knew absolutely nothing about. "I have to compliment you in your change of appearance." She referred to the look of his newborn character. Whereas before he had been unshaven and dressed in a grubby-looking sweat shirt and holed trousers, now he was dressed in a dark suit complete with a tie under his overcoat, and looked like someone ready to attend the City office. The dreadlocks looked real and helped hide his kindly looking face.

"Nobody on the rig will recognise me, especially the management, but they'll naturally be wary of us; being police officers."

Patricia knew what he meant as she had often come across similar scenarios before. Once a member of the general public found out who she really was, their whole demeanour changed, and if they were remotely guilty of anything, they tended to be more guarded with their responses. It would distract them from peering too closely at their inquisitors.

"What rank have you appointed yourself?"

"Detective Sergeant with the City Police, so I'll let you take the lead. After all, I'm really here to watch your back."

She considered her next words with care, knowing that they might influence their new-found relationship. "I'm naturally aware of my predecessor's demise, but now that it's all official, I don't suppose they'll try anything like that again."

"That was most unfortunate and I can guarantee that I won't let the same thing happen to you. You see, we were undercover and had to tiptoe around their security without them knowing what we were up to. What we discover today will form part of an authorised investigation, and if there's even a whiff of a threat from them, they know that they'll be shut down straight away. In any case, I doubt they have had time to replace that pair of heavies." He let her consider his assessment for a moment, before adding. "I'll be right behind you all the time, so don't let it worry you."

Something in the tone of his voice reassured her, but she knew she would have to keep her wits about her. "I hope we'll be able to interview Jorge Arlesson and Matt Hewdy at the same time without interruption, and if so, I'd like you to make a note of their reactions with each other to certain questions. Don't let them know that you're doing so, as that'll put them on the defensive and they'll just clam up."

In response to his quizzical expression she explained "Watching suspects' interactions often leads to a parallel line of enquiry. It's an old detective trick I was taught. For example, if one of them says he was at such and such a place at nine o'clock, I can bring up the time factor with the other one further on down the line, but alter it by, say, quarter of an hour to suit. When I point out the discrepancy and challenge the difference, collaboration of their story ought to produce a natural reaction if they're innocent. If they try to eye each other for confirmation in a certain manner, then it's a sure sign that one or other of them is lying."

Miles nodded his head in understanding and remarked. "That's a bit sneaky isn't it?"

"That's us detectives… we're sneaky through and through."

He thought about that for a moment. "Do you practice on your boyfriend?"

She laughed. "Ha. Chance would be a fine thing. Not only is he ex-diplomatic protection squad with keen powers of observation, but he usually outguesses me... most of the time."

It was Miles' turn to laugh. "It must make for a wonderful relationship."

"It does. We're engaged to be married, but somehow time always seems to get in the way."

"I know what you mean."

They fell silent, each reflecting on their own circumstances.

Mercifully, the weather was showing its more clement side as they crossed the Cornish coast and flew out into The Atlantic Ocean. It wasn't a crystal clear day, but after a while they could see the rig in the distance. As they neared it, they saw another helicopter take off from the designated landing platform area. They instinctively assumed the crouched position when they alighted, and followed the man sent to guide them to safety.

Once inside, they immediately appreciated the lack of chilling wind as well as a serious reduction in the level of noise. They were led through a series of what they presumed to be either waterproof or fireproof doors, due to their thickness, down a flight of stairs, and along a corridor. As they passed one particular pair of doors opposite each other, Miles nudged Patricia and indicated their location. The corridor dog-legged to a longer one, at the end of which was an emergency exit sign. Before they reached it, their chaperone knocked on another door and entered without waiting. They heard him address the person inside with something like '... more visitors for you.' He held the door open for them before leaving it to slam shut.

There were two men at desks, perpendicular to each

other. The grubby-windowed room was clean, odourless and surprisingly quiet, except for a background hum which betrayed the presence of air conditioning. Filing cabinets were in the far corner, while a couple of charts and an aerial photograph of an oil tanker completed the decoration along the adjacent wall.

Patricia fervently hoped that the two men would be Messrs Arlesson and Hewdy, since otherwise it would probably take some time to fetch either of them on such a large rig. Her first impression of them was that they looked tired. Her second impression was that they were very tired, as the bearded one rested his head on his left hand while his right hovered over a keyboard; he eventually looked up.

The other gentleman rose from his seat, came round the side of his desk and approached them with his hand outstretched. "Jorge Arlesson. You must be the two policemen from London." It was not a question.

Hand-shaking introductions were made after the bearded one stood up and let them know that he was Matt Hewdy from Texas. As expected of a Scandinavian, Arlesson was a head taller than Hewdy, whose frame portrayed him as an archetypical roughneck, and he even wore a faded chequered padded shirt.

Arlesson suggested that they pull up a seat from the half-a-dozen metal and plastic chairs parked against one wall. Patricia was careful to grab one before Miles so that she could place herself in a position where she could see both men simultaneously without having to crane her neck. She knew that the worst scenario would have been akin to her watching a tennis match from the sidelines, and she motioned for Miles to seat himself next to her, but slightly behind. From the way he positioned his seat she surmised that he might have done this sort of thing before.

Laptop on her knees and voice recorder on Hewdy's desk, Patricia started off the interview with some of the usual mundane questions, managing to surreptitiously include a time reference quite early on. She wanted the two men to relax, as this was her style, and she felt comfortable with her well-founded method of extracting information. It also gave her a chance to gauge their normal tone of voice so that she might be able to compare it when her questions became more awkward.

She quick-fired a mixture of easily answerable questions with some more probing ones, but they were mostly of a mundane nature. "So, these four men that just disappeared, did they know each other?", "How can you be sure that they didn't?", "How long had they been aboard?", "What length of contracts did they have?" Similar dull questions continued for a few minutes.

From the speed of their replies, it was clear that they were in agreement without having to refer to each other.

Hewdy was the first to break the question and answer session with his slight Texan drawl. "Look, we've already told all of this to the others. First we had the Irish Garda, then a team from the Health and Safety Executive, a man from OMAR who took great interest in the structure, and after them came a pair of union officials, and just before you arrived, a helicopter all the way from Brussels dropped off a couple of chaps from the European regulators. They're being shown round now if you'd like to join them." His inference was clear in that they ought to be asking their questions elsewhere.

Miles spoke for the first time. "I see you ceased operations."

"Damn right we have, and it's costing us a fortune, so the sooner you lot finish up here, the sooner we can get back to extracting crude."

It was just the opening Patricia wanted. "And how much crude do you extract on a daily basis?" From what she had previously read and from her own calculations, she knew what the answer should have been. It wasn't that it was a trick question, but it was exactly the sort of thing that she thought he ought to have had on the tip of his tongue.

He hesitated, and she didn't miss the flicker of his eyes towards Arlesson. "What's that got to do with it?"

She inwardly smiled to herself without altering her visage, knowing that her ploy had worked, and that she had chosen the correct person to needle. She had already considered that Hewdy would look on her as some sort of blonde bimbo, and one that could be brushed to one side easily. She now knew that, if aggravated enough, he would be likely to accidently divulge something along the line. Now was the time to apply pressure and to let him know who was boss.

"Four of your employees disappear and you don't know where they are. You're responsible for their well-being while they're on this rig, and for all we know they might still be on board. If they're not here, then how did they get off? Did they fall off en masse? Did they have an argument and fight each other to death before throwing themselves into the sea? Did a helicopter spirit them away without you knowing? Perhaps a passing fishing vessel decided to give them a lift to the nearest port, or did they just lock themselves in a lavatory and lose the key? How about they were working on some part of the platform which collapsed and dragged them down into the depths? I'm asking you any question I like in order to find out what you obviously don't know, and if I suspect you're holding anything back, then we'll continue this conversation from the comfort of a cell on the mainland. Clear?"

Initially, Hewdy had maintained his posture in his arm chair, but now he sat up.

She wasn't finished. "We'll want to interview their fellow workers, inspect their quarters and lockers, visit where they were last seen, and look closely at their duty rotas. I want to know if they left their phones behind, and if so why, and we'll be requisitioning phone records from this rig to see who they've been contacting."

She paused. Hewdy and Arlesson looked at each other with concern on their faces.

"If we establish that they are missing persons, their families will be notified, and at that point we decide if charges of manslaughter or murder should be bought. So I ask you again, how many barrels of oil are you extracting each day?"

Before Hewdy could reply, Arlesson butted in; his voice was calm. "I'm probably the best person to answer that question."

Patricia didn't want Arlesson's input while she had

Hewdy squirming, and looked pointedly at him. "I asked Mr. Hewdy. Not you."

Arlesson tried again. "Matt looks after the day-to-day operations which includes duty rotas, machine operations, mechanical continuity, maintenance, etcetera, while I attend to the more corporate side of things, such as production volumes, shipments, finances. It's too much for just one person to handle. We don't tell each other how to do our jobs, which is why I am more qualified to answer that particular question."

Patricia had to concede the point. "Well?"

"At the moment our target is five hundred barrels a day, but we're hopeful of reaching nearer eight hundred soon." Arlesson's voice held no trace of nerves.

"Why the variation?"

"Matt is better qualified to answer that one."

She quickly worked out that Arlesson was hoping to unbalance her by deflecting the questions from one to the other. She surmised that he had more of the brains; less of the brawn. She pointedly looked at Hewdy for an answer.

He smiled before answering, and Patricia suddenly realised she was forcing an issue about which she knew very little. "You need years of experience to know why, and even us experts don't always know the answer, but the latest thinking is that it could be down to geothermal activity. It could also be because on occasion we scour out the extract pipe which means we have to stop sucking and start blowing, and that sometimes the release valve needs clearing out, and then we have to send the divers down. A few hundred feet below us. Then…"

She could tell he was growing in confidence as he spoke on a subject that he clearly knew well, and she could also tell that she was going nowhere if she pursued this line of questioning, so she stopped him there. But she didn't want to let him off that easily, so hazarded a guess.

"Other rigs don't seem to have that level of variation."

She was glad to see that that made him pause. "It's complicated…"

"Well, I'll come back to that later if I have to. Now, I want to see your personnel files on the four missing men and after that we'll inspect their lockers."

As Arlesson handed them a tablet, he added in a flat tone of voice "The Irish Garda already have this information."

Patricia and Miles shared the screen and were careful not to be seen skipping over the information about him and their hacker, instead concentrating on the two murderers. They didn't need to suggest to each other that whatever names appeared were probably as false. Carnegie McFearson from Scotland and Daniel Dougan from Eire were their supposed names and the rest of their details were therefore hardly worth reading. Patricia was about to swipe her finger up the screen to dismiss one page when Miles stopped her, and pointed at the 'next of kin' mobile number for Daniel Dougan. He made a note of it.

"Living quarters and lockers next, I think." Patricia rose first.

Hewdy consulted the register on the inside of the key cabinet door and collected a bunch of keys. "Follow me, then."

They re-traced their steps along the corridor and as they passed the pair of doors, Miles decided it was time he contributed to unsettling Hewdy and to see how truthful he was being. "What's in these rooms?"

Hewdy finished taking the next step then half-turned around. "Oh,,, er... one's a store cupboard and the other's for computers." Without waiting for another question, he continued, turned the corner of the corridor, and opened another door which led to an internal metal staircase. "Fire doors have automatic closers." He added.

He led them through the door to the changing and shower rooms, paused, and took the aisle between the left hand banks of lockers. The spacious layout was quite typical of changing rooms the world over, and the strong mixed odour of soap, damp towels and human ablutions intertwined with the steamy atmosphere. There were two almost naked burly men at the far end but Hewdy didn't, or wouldn't, notice them. To him this was a perfectly natural activity. Patricia wondered if he had chosen this bank of lockers on purpose, knowing that there'd be naked men on view there, and her suspicion was confirmed when he reached one particular locker, but before reaching for the lock with his keys, he turned to look Patricia in the eye just for a moment too long. She felt certain that he wanted to see her reaction. She didn't even blink.

Miles knew that this was his allocated locker when

he had been on the rig before, and that the one almost opposite had been the hacker's.

Hewdy told them which belonged to whom and volunteered "A bit strange, but these two were never used. These two men joined us only a day before they disappeared and it looks like neither of them got round to putting their things in there."

Hewdy took them past where the two men had been undressing a few moments before, in the direction of the open showers where they now stood soaping themselves under the steaming hot water. Patricia assumed that this was another of Hewdy's attempts to embarrass her, but it turned out that the other pair of lockers were right next to the wall that divided the wet area from the dry.

Hewdy stood back while Miles inspected first one then the other and Patricia took the opportunity to continue her questions. "Where do all your employees come from?"

"Eh?"

"It's a simple enough question."

"Well, apart from a few Texans, quite a few are Scottish. That's where the skilled workers are. Ex North Sea oil rig workers, but we've a few Irish, and then the usual few Scandinavians as well as Middle Eastern types, but recently…"

"No. What I meant was how do you find them? Do you advertise for workers or do they apply directly to you?"

"Oh, I see what you mean. No, we use an agency most of the time, but as it's a pretty small community, word gets around."

"What's the name of the agency?"

"Er... Cane Global, mainly."

"Mainly?" Patricia inflected her voice to show surprise that he thought it was only mainly.

"Well, er... yes. But occasionally we get people in through other agencies."

"Why's that?"

"Depends on what type of skill you're after." He said glibly.

"I'll need a list from you."

Hewdy was about to challenge why she would want such a list when Miles stretched out his hand between them; it held a small brown plastic bottle and a light brown packet. "Did you know Mr. Dougan was on medication?" he asked.

Hewdy was nonchalant in his reply. "Most of the guys round here take pills. It's part of the job"

Neither Patricia nor Miles said anything; Patricia looking at the meds while Miles looked at Hewdy.

When it became clear that his explanation wasn't going to appease them, he continued. "Look, these Roughnecks work hard and need pills for their aches and pains, and some just need them to keep going until the end of their tour. Ask our doctor and he'll tell you that some visit him nearly on a daily basis. It's common practice on any rig." He shrugged in an attempt to convey standard practice.

"But these aren't for aches and pains, are they?" Miles stated as he moved his open hand closer to Hewdy so that he could see them more clearly. "These ones are Barbiturates; Zopiclone. When taken with Diazepam there's a serious risk of addiction, and together, they've been known to lead to suicide."

"You can't expect me to know what every guy brings on board in their own bags." His defensive attitude was a natural reaction.

"Why's McFearson's locker totally empty?" Miles turned to Patricia. "How about we call in the drug squad?"

"Now wait a minute." Hewdy's voice carried a definite anxious note. "If you do that we'll have a walk-out on our hands. A riot. Our gangs might not be squeaky clean, but when it comes to their jobs, I can guarantee that none of them are on any drugs while they're working. We have a strict non-alcohol and drug policy and if they're caught, they're back on the next transport. They value their private time and while a bit of dope is ok on the mainland, it follows that it's ok on this rig... just so long as it doesn't interfere with their duties... and I know it doesn't."

"You didn't know Mr. Dougan used these."

"Like I said, I can't be responsible for what they bring on board."

"Might it be worth looking through some of the other lockers? Who knows what we might find?" Miles looked at Patricia.

She stepped half a pace to one side so that she was standing directly in front of Hewdy. Despite being a few inches shorter, she managed to carry the necessary authority.

"I think it's about time you cooperated with us a bit more, Mr. Hewdy." The threat was clear. "I want to know where these two characters came from, how long they were here and I'd love to hear your explanation as to where they are now. They must have known each other; their lockers being opposite. Then we'll start asking the same questions about the other two." She inwardly smiled to herself knowing the answer to her latter comment.

Miles chased up. "How closely do you scrutinise potential employees?"

"Ok, ok... let me see." Hewdy had shuffled half a step backwards against the bank of lockers. "Can we go outside so we can let them get changed in peace?" One man emerged from the steam of the showers and was heading in their direction, so they headed back to the door and out into the corridor.

They re-congregated in the empty passage; Patricia noting that Hewdy surreptitiously looked both ways. "Dougan and McFearson were sent to us a couple of weeks ago by Mr. Donnelly. He's the man in charge on the mainland,"

"Where on the mainland?" Asked Patricia.

"Cork."

"Why?"

Hewdy hesitated. "We've been having one or two problems with a couple of trouble- makers on the union side and there was talk of sabotage, so I asked him for some extra help."

"What kind of help would that be?" Asked Miles.

Hewdy was cornered and he knew it. "Look, some of these guys can be kind of rough when it comes to putting their point of view across, so Dougan and

McFearson were here to make sure none of the regulars were being leaned on."

"Don't you mean they were here to identify the ringleaders?" Miles countered.

"Er... well, er... maybe that as well."

"Perhaps the other two who went missing were the ring leaders?"

"No way." Hewdy retorted a bit too quickly.

"How can you be so sure?" Pressed Miles.

"They'd only just arrived and wouldn't have had a chance to get to know the others well enough. And anyway, one of them wasn't a roughneck. He was just systems analysist."

"How about the other?" Patricia interrupted in an attempt to divert Hewdy's attention away from Miles.

"I dunno. I only met him once, but he was supposed to be one of the derrick hands."

In comparison to the quick-fire question and answer session, only the background thrumming of machinery could be heard, and felt.

Patricia broke the relative silence. "For someone who's in charge of a lot of men, you don't know much, do you?"

"Look lady, I've been on oil rigs ever since my Dad thought I was strong enough to lift a four-foot monkey wrench, and I've been running operations on rigs for the past ten years without any problems. I know how to handle men when the going gets tough, but I also reward them when we get the right results, but this is the first time anyone has gone missing, so I'm not exactly up to speed with what happens when somebody disappears."

"When four people go missing." Miles corrected.

"Yes, even when four people go missing." Hewdy acknowledged. Miles detected a hint of anger in his voice, while Patricia sensed a touch of anguish. She thought it might be genuine anguish, since he'd probably answered the same questions put to him over and over again, by earlier officials, ever since the disappearances had been notified.

"Right then, let's get the names and addresses of those agencies and tell Mr. Donnelly that we'll be interviewing him right after we leave this rig."

She suspected Hewdy was still holding back, and also knew that she was unlikely to be able to prise that information out of him, until after they'd spoken to Mr. Donnelly.

After donning the Peltor headsets in the helicopter for the flight to Cork airport, Patricia adjusted her microphone and flicked the switch to cut out the pilot. "If we receive the same sort of reception from Donnelly, then we'd better change tact."

"What are you suggesting?" Asked Miles.

"These male chauvinistic types tend to look down on blondes as all being dumb, so when we confront Donnelly, maybe I'll nurture his suspicions and act accordingly. Once we've established if he's likely to cooperate, you cut in with the more salient points, and I may or may not pick up on them. OK?"

A smile crossed his face. "Are we trying to catch him out?"

"In my experience, all criminals have a secret desire to be caught out, but let's see if he's a genuine criminal or just the belligerent type."

"Or both."

"That's when it gets interesting." They smiled at each other.

Chapter 9

A pissed-off Jason Donnelly slammed his desk phone down for the second time in as many minutes. The first of the two calls had been from his second wife who shouted and swore at him, while rattling off a list of his misdemeanours, and ending up stating that she was divorcing him. He knew what most of those misdemeanours were, but couldn't understand what some of the more trivial ones were all about. Some of them sounded familiar, being a repetition of those reasons as to why his first wife had left him. He thought that that had been cleared-up at the outset of their marriage, but obviously not. No sooner had he hung up than the phone warbled again, and he half-expected it to be a continuation of all his faults from his current wife. Instead, it was from Arlesson telling him that a couple of policemen were on their way.

The week was now turning out to reveal nothing but bad news. Forty-eight hours earlier he had been enjoying himself to the full in Palm Island's Atlantis Hotel in Dubai, and he didn't give a thought of the cost of a mere two thousand pounds a night for one of the more modest suites. Nor did he care about the expensive wines and sumptuous menu prices that he shared with his shapely female 'chaperone' that had been organised for him. The company would be covering all costs;

as usual. While enjoying a breakfast of eggs benedict with the finest smoked salmon, with her, on his private terrace, twenty-one floors above sea level, he received a text from Arlesson.

His five day utopian visit, ostensibly on business, came to an abrupt end.

The text was swiftly followed by a concise phone call from his secretary in Cork telling him that several employees had apparently gone missing from the rig in The Irish Sea, and that the local police were asking for him. Annoyingly, he'd had to cut short his stay and make calls to book a non-stop flight back to Heathrow, and then catch the connecting flight to Cork International. Just as annoying was the loss of his 'chaperone' that he had planned to spend the day with, but he did use the wait of nearly two hours wisely before leaving his room.

His host in UAE had been difficult to contact, and when he did manage to get an answer on his mobile, he was told by his assistant that he was off-road driving in a new Range Rover over the dunes. He left a message to the effect that he was heading back to Ireland.

Having been raised in the outskirts of Killarney not far from the brewery, Donnelly preferred the green landscape of his home country to the arid sands of the Middle East. But he also enjoyed the decadence, the temperature and the lifestyle of Dubai. These were things that couldn't be found anywhere in the whole of Ireland, where it seemed to rain more often than not; hence its affectionate name of 'The Emerald Isle'.

Straight after leaving school for the last time, his uncle had taken him under his wing on his first job on one of the North Sea oil rigs, where he learned how a rig works. His quick wit and intellect soon taught him how to manipulate those around him, and it didn't take him long to work out that there was easier money to be made by swindling his employers from the mainland. He soon built up a network of those who would buy oil at a 'discounted' rate on an ever-increasing scale.

He found himself being confronted by officialdom in the form of two policemen from London. He had already been interviewed by a sergeant from the local Garda who he had considered to be a mere functionary from the number of simple questions he had been asked. This pair were a different breed and were asking far more pertinent questions. They sat abreast on uncomfortable chairs, across his functional desk in an office above one of the many shops just off the high street. The slightly grubby carpet competed with the ceiling and windows as to which needed cleaning first, and pinned to the walls were a selection of photographs of tankers, ploughing their way across the oceans.

"I understand you use Cane E-Global to find workers on the rig. Why that agency, how long have you been using them, and did the missing persons all come through them?" Asked Patricia in her opening gambit. Other questions from one or the other followed in short order and while he did his best to maintain an impassive face, he was finding it increasingly difficult to provide straight answers that could be corroborated. In between two of the simpler answers, he found a little time to wonder why they were asking about the corporate side of the organisation, but didn't really have the opportunity to work that one out.

"Tell me, is it normal for an oil exploration company such as Blue Lizard to be registered in Dubai, yet have its headquarters in a different country?" She already knew the answer to that one, but it was one of her ways of testing how truthful and overt he was being.

"Oh sure, Blue Lizard operates on a global basis and has interests all over the world. That's normal for companies like ours."

She waited for him to expand on his answer but nothing was forthcoming, so she continued. "Originally quoted on the Irish stock exchange, de-registered, and now listed on the London stock exchange. That doesn't sound normal to me."

At first he blanked her as it seemed to him that she had made a statement rather than ask a question, but then he relented. "I'm not sure I can answer that one as I'm not part of the executive that decides these matters."

"Would I get an answer if I asked your employer, and by the way, who is it exactly who pays your salary and everyone else's round here?"

For less than two seconds, Donnelly wondered if it would be worth bucking against such questions; just to let them know that he wasn't going to roll over easily. Before they had arrived, he had decided to see what calibre of policemen they were, and what sort of questions they would be putting to him. He'd answer the easy ones honestly, but be guarded with those that required a bit more subtlety. On the face of it, this question was a simple one.

"Oh, I and the other staff get paid in Euros through

Imnibank, but there's only four of us here, and I'm away quite a lot of the time. I don't actually know who holds the purse strings, only that my account gets credited every month."

"Is there an Imnibank here in Cork?"

He was ready for that one. "No, they're an international bank apparently specialising in off-shore enterprises such as ours. I think they're based in Baku... Azerbaijan. That's where crude oil was first drilled on a commercial basis back in the late 1800s but it's generally referred to as the birthplace of oil, as it was discovered there generations ago."

"So, who decides what level of salary you receive?" Patricia ignored his sidetrack, wanting to focus on the salient issue.

Donnelly suspected this question also would be coming his way, and he tilted his head just a little, hoping to depict an honest answer. "Do you know, I've never known his full name, only that he's based in Baku. You see, I report straight to the company board on a regular basis by email and they instruct me by the same method."

She didn't sigh at his evasive answer, but tried to portray a sense of frustration. With hardly a pause she continued. "So, Cane E-Global acted as agents for your employment, and presumably you know what kind of contract you have."

"Oh yes, but I haven't the faintest idea as to what's in my contract." He let his statement hang, hoping that it would goad her.

It didn't, but Patricia was mighty tempted. She

decided to play his game a little longer with a rhetorical question. "That oversight will be due to your massive salary then... not knowing what's in your contract?"

"Oh, they certainly pay me well, and it's certainly not my place to ask petty questions like what's in my contract. This is the oil business, and around the world it boils down to one thing and one thing only: Deliver or be fired. If I don't deliver, I'll be out of a job. Simple as that."

"And does that attitude extend to your employees?" Before he had a chance to respond, she added. "Including those who go missing from you rigs?"

"Oh, no, no, no. They're all on standard contracts through Cane. We might be classified as employers as far as statistics go, but we don't go interviewing them from here. That's their job."

"So who at Cane interviewed you?"

"I was head-hunted," He let a brief smile out, but she detected the smugness behind it.

A light cough came from Miles beside her, so she canted her head sideways to approve of his interceding. His deeper voice was in total contract to hers.

"What is the process of becoming employed by Blue Lizard? For example, how would I go about finding work on one of your rigs?"

"I don't get involved in the daily hiring and firing of personnel. That's all down to Cane. But I imagine you'd need certificates and a track record to become a Derrickhand, and I believe there's quite a long waiting list as it's a well-paid job, due to the inherent dangers that go with it."

"So you wouldn't know what qualifications I would need to become a derrickhand, for example? You see, what we're trying to get at is how these men came to be aboard the rig, presumably in their respective job capacities, and how they suddenly disappeared overnight. Were they qualified to do what they were doing at the time, and what exactly was that? One man falling overboard during a storm is believable. Two men most unlikely. But four on the same night sounds like corporate negligence."

"No. You've got that all wrong. There's nothing corporate about this unfortunate accident. I'm told that the storm winds came from differing angles and that the four men involved must have been blown off. I wasn't there so I cannot expand on that any further, but if you ask Arlesson or Matt Hewdy, they'll be able to tell you."

"They have told us." Miles stated in a flat tone of voice. "And what you are now telling us is commonly known as the run around… passing the buck. But it's your name as managing director which is listed at Companies House, and it is you who is responsible for every aspect of operations, so unless you are more forthcoming with your answers, we'll be requesting that The Crown Prosecution Service initiate a negligence investigation." He turned to Patricia. "I believe the maximum fine for each offence is twenty million pounds for corporate manslaughter, and in the more blatant cases, the responsible person would end up in prison for five years… or twenty in this case as there were four of them."

"Now wait just a minute…"

"I can obtain an international arrest warrant in minutes." Miles extracted his mobile from his jacket pocket and held it in readiness. "Negligence is just the start."

"Obstruction." Added Patricia.

"Manslaughter for certain." Miles retorted.

"And that's before the insurers delve into the corporate side of things, which you will be accountable for."

"Then no doubt your employers will become personally liable for recompense from the lost personnel's families."

Their unrehearsed routine appeared to have some effect on. Donnelly. "Ok, ok, ok,ok. I get the point, but the point is that I am only a figurehead and I really don't know the answer to everything."

"Then tell us the name of the individual who employed you and who authorises your salary." Patricia edged a little closer on her chair.

His eyes briefly flickered to his own mobile phone on his desk; the action unmissed by Patricia. "I'll need to contact head office in Baku and ask them, but they'll be closed as they're four hours ahead us here and it'll be the middle of the night… but there is just one person who I might be able to reach at this time of night. Erm…". Donnelly rubbed his chin with one hand while the other handled his mobile.

They all waited while he attended to his mobile rather than the cordless on his desk.

"There's no reply… so… "

"Who were you trying to contact just now?

His name please, and what does he do?" Patricia pressured him.

Donnelly could hardly avoid a direct answer. "A... er... Mr. Huseyn. He's the... er... man in charge of the Baku office."

"So, if we were to attend this office at say, eight o'clock tomorrow morning, he'd be available would he?"

Again, Donnelly paused before replying. "I suppose so." He hurriedly added. "I don't speak to him every day."

Both Patricia and Miles sensed his anxiety. His entire demeanour shouted at their trained eyes that he was hiding as much as possible, and it was clear to both of them that they weren't going to get much more from him by mere questions.

"Right, then." Patricia stood up just ahead of Miles. "We'll be back at eight o'clock in the morning."

"Just make sure you're available, as otherwise we might have to contact the local Guarda to find you."

They saw themselves out as Donnelly remained seated. Patricia purposely didn't close the door all the way behind her, and indicated to Miles to continue down the stairs while she waited to one side. She stamped her feet to feign departure but stayed by the partially open door to eavesdrop. Listening as hard as she could, she initially couldn't hear Donnelly doing anything, but she risked craning her neck right up to the slight crack on the hinge side, and deduced that he was using his phone to text.

She smiled to herself as she silently tip-toed down the stairs.

Miles was waiting for her in an adjacent doorway in the deepening onset of night, and half-startled her as she was passing. "Are you thinking what I'm thinking?"

She turned and cocked one eye at him. "I suspect we're both of the same mind. I reckon he could hardly wait until we were gone before getting in touch with whoever."

Miles' white teeth betrayed his smile. "I hoped you would say that. Why don't you find us a hotel for the night while I do what I do best."

She tilted her head slightly to one side. "I'm not bad at doing what you do either, but I bow to your manly attributes, and accept your offer." She grinned back at him.

"That'll mean you might need to take the second watch." He jested.

She hadn't quite thought that one through, but conceded to herself that Miles was probably far better qualified.

She watched him as he removed his tie and jacket, followed by his false dreadlocks, then delved into his backpack. Once he had donned a dark woolly hat and covered his white shirt with a nondescript sweatshirt, he was all but invisible in the shadows. "See you shortly."

"You don't reckon he'll be that long then?" Asked Patricia.

"Nah. Once he's contacted his boss, he'll either head for the local pub, or go home and down a few whiskeys. Maybe both."

"I don't need to ask what you're going to do. I'll let you know where we're staying tonight when I've found somewhere. Oh, and any ideas as to which direction? I've never been to Cork before."

"That's simple. Just follow the road downhill to the seafront. There's always a hotel or two on a seafront."

She mulled his last comment for a moment before leaving, and thought to herself how right he was. This was a man of logic and experience. It didn't take her long to reach a bridge spanning a river, the sign advising the tourist that it was the River Lee. It took even less time to spot a sign on the wall advertising the Hotel Metropole, with the promise of good food there promoting its whereabouts at the other end of the alley.

She faced her first conundrum of the evening at the reception desk; what type of room to book as they only had one twin available. All other rooms had been taken and there were no singles left. Rather than traipse around Cork looking for two separate rooms, she took the twin on offer, and surmised from its layout and décor that it was a typical Victorian type hotel, which indeed it was. Its high ceilings with ornate coving and strange-shaped rooms off rooms, like the en-suite in her twin-bedded room on the first floor, attested to its age.

She used her mobile to text Miles that they were booked into room number 125, and pointedly didn't ask how he was getting on. She knew he would appraise her when he eventually did arrive. Half an hour later, she felt more woman-like after enjoying a hot shower, and decided to see what was on the menu downstairs.

She felt at home in the lounge next to the hotel's restaurant, and had chosen an inconspicuous round window table to sit at while she sipped a pint of

Guinness. It wasn't crowded but she didn't want to perch at the bar and possibly attract the wrong sort of attention. She wasn't particularly vain about her attractiveness, and didn't over-pander her natural stunning looks with unnecessary make-up, but she was well aware that her figure had a certain effect on some men. Several of her female colleagues from her previous job as a detective inspector had told her as much; in their own particular manner.

Catching up with her phone messages, of which there were very few, she responded to Justin's by telling him where she was staying, and that she hoped to be back tomorrow; via another noisy helicopter. A thought then struck her that she hadn't advised their pilots what time they expected to take-off tomorrow, so was side-tracked while she used text to advise them. Being Royal Navy, she presumed that they would be billeted nearby, or had booked into a known hotel.

Halfway through her Guinness, she noticed a rather windswept and scruffy-looking middle-aged woman enter the lobby, and before she realised it, she had approached her table and sat down in the chair opposite; placing her large bag on the floor next to her. Patricia had only read about Irish friendliness and surmised that this might be one of those occasions, and trying not to show too much surprise, she asked herself if this was typical of how the locals got to know other people.

The woman spoke first with the archetypical accent that comes with the southern Irish; soft clipped 'Ts' and inflections. "I can tell you're troubled." She said with a half-smile.

Patricia took a brief moment to make her mind up whether or not to dismiss the woman, but as she was passing the time, decided to indulge her. "And what makes you suppose that?"

"I can tell." She let her statement hang. "I can always tell." She paused. "It's the aura that surrounds you, but not to worry. It's not all bad." She paused again. "In fact, you're giving-off signs of benevolence, and if you give me your hands, I can tell you more."

Patricia quickly picked up that this woman was a fortune teller cum palm-reader, trying to make a living by visiting the local bars and hotels and catching unsuspecting travellers unawares. She'd never had her fortune told before, not even at a fun fair when she was much younger, and despite her natural scepticism, she moved her Guinness to one side and stretched out her arms so that her elbows rested on the table.

There was no electricity or buzz on first contact, but she immediately sensed the smooth coolness of the woman's surprisingly delicate fingers as they gently massaged and kneaded her hands. She looked into the woman's bluish green eyes and felt as if she was opening a door into another world. The kneading stopped but thumbs pressed down gently into her centre of her palms.

"You've a very interesting past... and it's catching up with you... that's why you're here, and that's why you're troubled."

To Patricia's mind, anyone could have made such broad statements, and she congratulated herself on being suspicious about the veracity of the woman opposite.

"You're a brave lass at heart with a willingness to

help others... it excites you... makes you feel alive." Ever so gently, the lady started a circular motion across her palms with her thumbs, and all the while Patricia looked into the pools of her eyes; as if held by some invisible power.

"Your past is not an indication, but has laid the foundation of your future." Her thumbs came to a rest back in the centre of her palms but with a little more pressure this time.

Patricia was expecting to hear that she would meet a tall dark stranger, as told in all story books about fortune tellers, but what came next took her by surprise.

"You're going back to your lover at home tomorrow, and when you do, you'll conceive children."

It took her a moment to take in such a shocking statement. Her first reaction was to take her hands away, but they were held in such a way that in her stunned state she just left them there.

"You'll return back here soon and when you do, you'll be stepping into jeopardy." The lady's eyes seemed larger than when she first looked into them. "Beware of the water... and of a dark man."

She was so was shocked at her comments that she didn't realise that the lady had released her hands, and it took her a few seconds before she placed them back on her own lap.

"Don't worry girl... you'll probably live . Now, would you be kind enough.....?" The lady was holding her hands together forming a cup in the centre of the table, and Patricia realised that this was the 'crossing the palm with silver' bit, so she reached into her own bag and offered a twenty Euro note; she had nothing smaller. "That'll do nicely thank you, oh, and when you do come back, I'll be here for you."

"How do you know I'm coming back?" She asked as the lady rose to leave.

"I can tell... I can always tell."

In the blink of an eye, the lady had gone, leaving Patricia wondering. Wondering what had just happened and if she ought to heed any of it. She looked around to see if anybody had paid any attention, but it might have been as though it never happened. She sipped at her Guinness, started to read through the menu and decided to go through to the restaurant immediately; optimistically telling the waiter to lay the table for two. She took her time over her choice, hoping that Miles might make an early appearance.

Casually looking around at her fellow diners, she played her usual game of guessing what they were doing here and what they might do for a living. She savoured a glass of white wine with her prawn cocktail and made it last far longer than she normally would have done; occasionally glancing at the entranceway. A slight feeling of guilt began to creep in as the waiter removed her empty starter, because she hadn't ordered anything for Miles, but for all she knew, he could be out the entire night.

Before she tucked into her rump steak course with a glass of house red, she decided she was going to enjoy it to the full. After all, it was Miles who had suggested she find the hotel, while he pursued his own nocturnal activities. And then she remembered that she might have to get up in the middle of the night to relieve him. Whatever he was doing. It was getting late and the restaurant was beginning to thin out as she tucked into a small glass cup of ice cream, and before the kitchen shut, she had the consideration to order a couple of sandwiches to take up to their room; for Miles.

She chose the far bed, thinking that when Miles did appear, he wouldn't disturb her; unless he needed to. Before drifting off to sleep, her mind started to dwell on what could-have-been if they had gone to bed at the same time, and her thinking revolved around the fact that she was engaged to Justin, and should she remain sexually loyal to him. Certainly, she had shared beds with other men prior to meeting him, and had dreamt of meeting 'Mister perfect'; which Justin seemed to be. She questioned herself if she was 'Miss perfect' in his eyes, and if so, she ought to behave accordingly.

She wondered if Miles might have propositioned her and if he had, while her initial instinct would have been to rebuff him, she wondered what could have really happened. Lying on her back under the duvet and dressed in her underwear, she found that her fingers had been circling in the vicinity of her upper thighs and were now starting to explore the surface of her knickers. Half-asleep, she consciously bought her hands to her sides and decided not to continue down that path.

It felt as though she had been asleep for only a few moments. Surfacing from slumber, she wondered what had disturbed her dreams, and why the jetty she had been lying on a few seconds ago was rocking so violently. Opening her eyes, she saw Miles' shadow bending over her as he gently shook her awake.

"It's nearly six o'clock." He said before disappearing into the en suite.

Only just half-awake, her first question she asked herself was 'morning or evening?', but a couple of seconds later she realised it must be the morning. From the slight chill outside of the duvet, it felt like morning. It wasn't that she was unused to getting up early, but the question she asked herself was 'why?' Why six o'clock?

She briskly got out of bed and shook herself awake while searching for her clothes on the chair which was against the wall by the window, and decided she needed something like a splash of water in the face. That would have to wait until Miles had finished in the en suite. The cogs in her mind started to turn faster as she buttoned up her blouse, and she worked out that Miles had woken her because of what had transpired during the night. She had just finished tying her shoe laces when Miles reappeared, and without a word between them, she took her turn. All very business-like and platonic and when she emerged, she saw him peering into his mobile as he stood by the now opened-curtained window.

"Good news, I presume?" Not even a 'good morning', but she did notice that the sandwiches had been eaten.

Miles dragged his eyes from his screen to briefly look at her. "Certainly good news, but as usual there's some bad news to go with it. Come and have a look at this." He adjusted his arm a little so that they could both see. "What you're looking at here are the contents of Donnelly's mobile and it's a small mine of information." They looked on as Miles scrolled through various screens.

After a few seconds Patricia asked. "Does he know?"

"No. He never felt a thing."

She wondered if his turn of expression meant that Donnelly was still unconscious, or even dead, but doubted that Miles would have needed to go that far as it was unnecessary. "Is that the good news?"

"Um... The bad news is that I can't break through his security code. I believe you know someone who can."

Patricia mulled on this for a moment. "Do you reckon you can copy Donnelly's to my laptop, or better still, send it directly onto someone else?"

"I don't see why not as there's 5G round here."

"Just hang on a mo while I get hold of that someone." She opened her laptop and once it was ready, she inserted her fingerprint security dongle, thus enabling secure communication with DIS centre; manned twenty-four seven. It was a routine she had got well-used to ever since she had been enrolled into the Diplomatic information Service by Commander Gibbons some months ago. Indeed, she had been instructed to initiate contact through her laptop every forty-eight hours as a security precaution, so this was one of those opportunities. After a series of security Q&As, she posed the problem of code-cracking a passcode and what went with uploading mobile phone info, and was advised to wait.

Her laptop came back to life as the unknown person on the other end probed her as to what exactly she wanted, and it took less than three minutes before she indicated to Miles to start the upload to an address somewhere in the UK. She asked the person on the other end to respond within the hour as to the most used names and numbers, if there were any linked to terrorism or other crimes, and as an afterthought, if there were any VIPs or other such luminaries.

While she waited for an answer, "Come on then. Do tell as to how you obtained this without Donnelly knowing."

Miles gave a half-laugh before replying. "It was all too easy. As I predicted, after nearly an hour he left his office and went straight into a bar where he downed a couple of pints of Murphy's while chatting to a few fellows. Nobody suspicious as they were obviously used to him dropping in. What I didn't expect him to do next made my job even easier. When you were looking for this hotel, you may have noticed a couple of casinos on the waterfront. Well, he went into one of them and I asked the doorman, politely of course, if he's a regular there. Likes to gamble, particularly roulette. I simply changed my appearance to suit and mingled with the crowd already in there, but stayed away from his line of sight. At the right moment, I just pickpocketed his phone, swapped the microcard over to mine, downloaded it, then replaced it back in his pocket."

"That easy eh?"

"Yup. That easy."

"How polite were you with the doorman?"

"A hundred Euros and he was ever so cooperative." Miles grinned. "I couldn't stop him talking once he started, and he told me that Donnelly regularly lost quite a bit of cash. That bit of info gave me the perfect opening, as I explained to the doorman that I was from an accountancy assessment association, a credit rating agency to you and me, and needed to evaluate Donnelly's credit worthiness.

"Huh. Cheap at half the price. I see you ate your sandwiches." She motioned to the wrappers still on the sideboard.

"Yes, thanks for that."

"So, all we need now, before we meet Donnelly, is to know who he's been speaking to on his mobile."

Miles glanced at his watch. "We need to leave here in under ninety minutes He didn't need to add that he hoped her 'somebody' would be able to crack the phone code.

"Let's assume that apart from this Mr. Huseyn that he's been in contact with, there's that pair you disposed of on the rig, and if not directly with them, through another intermediary. A third party who has contacts with that ilk of person. And like as not, we'll have that person's details on record. From there we can start to put together a picture of who else is involved."

Miles nodded in agreement, and added "But these people have a habit of staying under the radar."

"So do you and I."

"True."

"And we know our details are on file, so why not them as well?"

"Perhaps your somebody can tell us." He motioned at her laptop that had sprung to life again.

Patricia attended to the keyboard and within a few seconds, lists and depictions appeared on the screen.

"That was quick." He observed. "But is it what we want?" He went and stood behind her.

"Yup… hang on a mo while I save it." She tapped away. "Ok, let's see what he's been up to."

It became clear after a while that it wasn't an exact copy of Donnelly's phone, but more of a list of what was on it.

"Here, what do you reckon this might refer to?" Miles' finger hovered over the screen, and she reacted by initiating the link.

She stared at the semi-indecipherable letters. "I reckon that's in Gaelic."

"Yeah, I agree. So we need to download an Irish translating app which understands local dialect, but not the run-of-the-mill option that comes with phones. But what will pique our interest is who he's been speaking to, especially since our friends disappeared into the Irish Sea. Look, you can see here that he's in frequent communication with the same person in Baku; much as he suggested yesterday, and indeed he did make that call while we were there. The length and time corresponds, and I'm guessing he knew Mr. Huseyn was not going to answer."

"I wonder why he didn't use the office phone on his desk?" queried Patricia.

"Perhaps Mr. H might have answered that one, but that really is a guess."

"And do we know if that's his real name? What's he listed under and who else is there? Let's have a look." She went to attend to her laptop.

"Hold on a sec." Said Miles before she moved off

that page. He craned his body nearer and pointed at the screen. "Here. By the look of it, he made three other calls before he left last night; local as well."

"Well, they won't have been to one of his mates he met down the pub, sister, or even his girlfriend." Look at the length and times of those calls. One straight-after the other. They'd have been business calls in reaction to our visit, so he's definitely worried."

"Who would you call if you'd just been visited by the police?" Miles asked rhetorically.

She looked up at him. "I'd call my superior. Who would you call?"

"Me too, if anyone."

"And who else?"

Miles frowned in thought. "When we meet Donnelly, we'll only have the upper hand if we can put definite names to those numbers instead of pseudo names in gobbledygook Irish."

"Let me have a look at that a sec." Naturally starting with the letter A, she arrowed the screen down and as Miles had suggested There were names, addresses, numbers, and other random bits and pieces, mostly in Gaelic. The numbers were easy enough to read and one could marry them up to corresponding names, but as to the rest, it was all but impossible. She thought she recognised one particular number, but couldn't place it.

"That's got to be an Arabic name, surely." Commented Miles as she paused over one at random after skipping a page or so.

"But the next one's not. Even in Gaelic, Paddy is still Paddy." She retorted.

"How about texts?".

They scrutinised several; half of them in English, the other half in brogue Gaelic.

"We haven't the time now, so how about we concentrate on calls and texts made in the past forty-eight hours. Can you make some notes and let's see if it helps?"

She skipped back to the calls sent and received, and after twenty minutes, Miles' list correlated some of the names and numbers against the times.

"It's only five minutes' walk to Donnelly's office, but we'd better go if we want to be a little early. Have you paid the hotel bill?" Asked Miles.

"Settled last night." As she shut down her laptop.

"Do you reckon he'll be there?" Asked Miles as they left the comfort and warmth of the hotel and immediately faced a bracing westerly wind as it buffeted between the streets.

"Oh yes. He'll be there."

"How can you be so sure?"

"He has a defiant attitude, and that kind of person doesn't like to be upstaged by a blonde. Even if that blonde is a police inspector."

"Or even a black man come to that." Commented Miles.

"You might be right there. Defiance and bigotry tend to go hand-in-hand, so he'll not pass up the opportunity to stick two fingers up at us."

They knew they were a few minutes early; exactly as they wanted to be so that they could observe who was coming, or going. Without saying a word to each other, they took up station in a doorway down an adjacent alley, so that they could see Donnelly's office door. Nobody appeared. After climbing the single flight of stairs, they opened the door to Donnelly's office without knocking. It was hard not to show any emotion, but they were both taken aback by the number of people already seated around Donnelly's desk as though in conference.

With an obvious haughty expression on his face, he looked up. "Don't bother closing the door as you won't be staying long enough to waste energy closing it again."

Being the last in, Miles compliantly left the door wide open; both of them needing to take a moment to assess what was going-on.

With his supercilious smile looking defiantly at Patricia, Donnelly sat centre stage behind his desk, flanked by two suited gentlemen who she mentally designated Suit A and Suit B. Several thoughts went through her head in those first few seconds, but she quickly arrived at just one conclusion; that Donnelly had this well planned. "You will be helping us with our enquiries, won't you." It was a statement, but doubled-up as a question.

Donnelly stared at her and thoroughly relished the moment before responding. "Oh, I intend to co-operate fully."

She couldn't but help compress her lips as she realised that he had them over a barrel, and guessed what was coming next, but she had to ask if only to see if he really was going to cooperate. "So you'll be answering our questions then."

"Yes."

"Good. Let's start with the name of your direct superior, and was it he that employed you?"

Hardly had the words left her lips than Suit B on Donnelly's left responded "You don't have to answer that."

She retorted almost as quickly. "And who might you be?"

He was prepared, wordlessly handing her his business card. Her glance at it depicted what she suspected in that it bore the name of a firm of lawyers.

She only glanced at it before turning to Suit A. "You?"

He too handed her his card, which she initially didn't bother looking at. With Donnelly responding with just one letter words and the two Suits adding as little as possible, this interview was going to be akin to extracting blood from a stone. And just as pointless.

She looked a little more closely at the second card, then compared the two side by side; one in each hand. Two different firms which to her mind would mean two different briefs. Suit B was the corporate lawyer, and she assumed that Suit A was Donnelly's personal representative. She cast her eye over A and thought he looked more like a body builder than a lawyer. Donnelly spoke. "They're both here to help me with your enquiries and to make sure that I am being fully cooperative, so ask your questions." The contemptuous look on his face portrayed otherwise.

Patricia decided to have one more go with an easy one. "How long have you been employed by Blue Lizard?"

"You don't have to answer that." It was Suit B interjecting again.

"So exactly what questions do you think he can answer?" She adjusted her stance so that she was square-on to Suit B.

He looked up at her with a deadpan expression. "I think that's for you to determine, but under the current legislation, my client doesn't have to answer any questions whatsoever."

"Even though he's just said he'd be cooperating?"

"There's a difference between cooperation and obligation." He paused to let that sink in. "My client is required to fulfil his obligations and will cooperate fully with any aspect you care to raise under international maritime law. The Blue Lizard Oil Company is listed in Dubai and registered in Baku, Azerbaijan. The rig concerned is more than twelve miles from any shore which places it firmly in international waters, and furthermore, since the employees come from every corner of the world, only international legislation is applicable here."

Suit A on her left joined in the conversation. "Also, I must point out that my client is an Irish citizen which brings him under the auspices of the European Court of Justice and not the UK's supreme court. Clearly then, it is The United Nations Convention on the Law of the Sea that takes precedent here and not section ninety of the UK's 1984 PACE Act." He paused. "My client has already told me that you have questioned several employees abord the rig, but that you have failed to advise them under which legislative authority." Suit B added, then continued. "The four-point-one clause under section eighty-nine of the Act therefore doesn't apply, so before my client cooperates with your enquiries, please tell me by what authority you are intending to exercise."

To both Patricia and Miles, it felt like a well-rehearsed routine; patently designed to put them off. Miles wisely left it to Particia to provide an answer, but it took her a few seconds to conclude that even if she did manage to raise a question that Donnelly' lawyers didn't object to, the answer wouldn't be worth listening to.

The room felt like it was closing in on her, and not daring to speak her mind out loud, she inwardly swore. For just a moment, looking for inspiration, she stared at a picture of a tanker on the wall, but it was no help whatsoever. She knew it would be pointless complaining that they were being uncooperative, and it would only gratify their own egos if she started shouting and swearing at them, but she wanted to leave with at least some form of dignity. "In that case, we'll be reporting back to London."

Miles left the door open as he followed her out and caught up with her in the side street they had waited in earlier. "We walked into that one, didn't we."

Patricia was fuming, and Miles had the impression that if he'd been a midget, she'd have clobbered him; just to vent her feelings. "Those fuckers... bastards... they..."

Miles let her pace up and down the narrow street.

"They bloody ambushed us." She nibbled her lower lip and kicked at an errant empty pizza box which would have scuttled into the gutter, had there been one. "How could I have been so blind?" She turned and looked directly at Miles. "They did this on purpose, didn't they?" She turned again and carried on swearing, then turned back again. "I've never been so humiliated in my life."

Miles thought it time to bring some rationale into the equation; but delicately. "Not so much they, but Donnelly."

She stopped her sentry-like pacing, ceased her lip-nibbling, and thought about his comment for a moment. "Donnelly... poxy bloody Donnelly... I'll have his balls before this is over."

They stood and stared at each other until a wandering seagull's overhead cry penetrated their thoughts, but it was Miles who spoke first. "Then let's get back to London where we can find something to nail his balls to the wall with, because there's nothing more we can do here."

Patricia took one last look round the corner at Donnelly's office, then reached for her mobile to contact the helicopter pilot.

Chapter 10

Donnelly waited for their departure sounds to recede and took his time taking the few steps to his window which overlooked the street below. He watched them disappear down a side street, turned and smiled at the two men who were still seated. "Well done, lads. Perfect. They won't be back." The pair of suits stood up; Suit A spoke first after glancing down at his watch. "Oh, no problem at all. I've even enough time to drop in on Sheilagha's on my way to open up the gym." They all laughed at his suggestion that he would have time to enjoy himself in the local whorehouse.

"What? Not a quick one in Dag's first?" Asked Suit B.

"Don't need a livener with what I've got." Replied Suit A with a knowing grin on his face; they all laughed. "I'd have given her one though. She was pretty." He added.

"Only one?" Jibed Suit B.

"Oi. Don't you start that again."

"Come on, fellas." Interjected Donnelly. "Here's a hundred each. Now bugger off and let me get on with things."

As the pair sauntered out of his office, Donnelly shouted to shut the door behind them, waited a moment, listened, then walked over and locked it. He didn't want to be interrupted. He stared at the picture of the oil tanker for a moment, then reached out and unhinged it from the wall to reveal a flush combination lock safe behind it. Nobody but he knew it was there. He ignored the few sheafs of paper and the wads of elastic-banded cash, instead withdrawing a mobile phone which he proceeded to powerup. He waited for it to wake up before entering the security code.

Donnelly was a very careful man, but the visits from the two London coppers had him thinking that it was definitely time to cut and run. 'One more venture' he thought to himself... after the current operation... he'd have enough stashed away to disappear... not to Dubai because he was known there... ;Perhaps to French Guiana where he had a contact... and an understanding woman... .Not too far from oil-rich Venezuela.

He had not saved any phone numbers on that mobile but had to consult two seemingly random pieces of 'scrap' paper he kept in two separate drawers located under his desk in order to obtain the number he wanted. If anybody rifled-through his office, they would have to be a genius to connect the apparent haphazard numerical scribblings.

"Hello Michael."

"I wondered when I was going to hear from you." Replied a hollow voice at the other end. Donnelly expected nothing less than this sort of comment from Michael, who would be using his satellite phone somewhere in the Atlantic Ocean. It gave him assurance that all was as it should be.

"How far away are you?"

"As the seagull flies, about two, maybe three days. Weather's good enough at the moment but there's a lively front coming across from the States about the same time as we're due to reach the rig."

"Full cargo?" Donnelly and Michael had had similar conversations before, and both were circumspect as to what was said over the airwaves.

"Aye, nearly. But for some reason this bunch aren't quite as happy as the last, and I've had to keep an eye on them. Oh, not to worry, the Mate and I have got them under control, and the rest of the cargo's safe."

"Glad to hear it. Let me know when you're in the usual place and I'll confirm timing with the others." Neither of them said goodbye, but they both hung up. Donnelly consulted his scrap sheets again and made another call; this time local. He preferred to make calls as texting was more likely to leave a trail that could be traced.

"Yes?" Answered an anonymous voice.

"Donnelly. Two, three, possibly four days."

"Night time again?"

"Almost certainly."

"Right."

Their colloquial brogue accents would have sounded more like gibberish to anyone other than someone from that neck of the woods.

He turned his thoughts toward how to create a false trail for those four men who had disappeared from the rig. He frowned because he couldn't understand how it had all happened. Two of them he knew about, and he would be able to find another willing pair of heavies fairly easily, but he hadn't the first clue as to who the other two from the agency were. It really didn't matter, because he'd get on to his contact in the employment bureau to create false identities, just long enough to keep the authorities at bay for another few days.

He turned off his phone, stood up and placed it back in the hidden safe, making sure that the magnets that held the picture to the wall engaged with a click. Thoughtfully, he gazed at the photograph of the ocean-going oil tanker the Pan Maru, then, with a broad grin on his face, patted it affectionately. "You're going to make me a rich man.

Chapter 11

Even though the windy weather had relented a little, they were still buffeted during their trip back to London in the helicopter. Patricia had planned to spend the time on her laptop, but found it too difficult to focus on the jiggling screen. She gave up, closed her eyes and concentrated on their recent encounters withDonnelly and the two suits on the rig. She went over what had been said, implied or suggested.

It was abundantly clear that they had been given the brush-off, and her thoughts turned to why The Commander and Tates had really sent her out there. They must have suspected that she would have been given the runaround. She had hardly scratched the surface of where the missing oil was going, but at least she had seen the rig for herself and experienced some of the working conditions. By concentrating on the missing personnel, she acknowledged that she had been side-tracked, but felt she would be able to discover what was going on with more computer time.

She pressed the button on the Peltor headset lead to talk to Miles. "Do you reckon those two on the rig were being directed by Donnelly?"

He thought about her question before answering. "I'd be surprised if they weren't. Who else would they be getting their orders from? They're there to do a job, but there's more than one way to carry that out."

"How do you mean?" Their conversation was a bit limited due to the noise.

"If you were employed to do a job, you'd do it your own way. Within given parameters of course."

"There's got to be some pretty strict parameters on a rig."

The sonorous noise from the helicopter didn't make for easy thinking, or even guessing, but they managed a sporadic comment or two as they flew over the southern English counties towards Northolt.

She shut her eyes again and bent her mind as to what angle of attack she ought to take in trying to locate the missing oil. Once the Irish gobbledydook had been deciphered, she'd have to trawl through all those contacts on Donnelly's phone to find out who he'd been talking to, and then she'd start investigating them.

Hamilton! Her eyes opened wide. God, how she would love to nail his hide, but this time, she would make sure he wouldn't be able to wriggle out of it. She'd have to gather so much hard evidence first, but for the moment she would steer clear of him.

All too soon, the helicopter slowed and banked before settling on the ground.

"It's been nice working with you." Said Patricia as they walked away.

"You too. Shame it worked out the way it did."

"Oh, it's not over by a long chalk. I just need time to add two and two together, and then add some more twos." They entered the silence of the building and as they presented their passes to the armed security guard, she added with a smile "It's my job and it's how I work. Within the given parameters of course."

They stopped and looked at each other outside the terminal building. Patricia spoke first. "I won't ask where you're going, but I'm off home to do some serious digging."

Miles looked thoughtful for a moment. "I've a funny feeling we'll be seeing each other again soon."

* * * * *

Justin was out when she got home. Despite it being mid-afternoon, she decided to run a hot bath rather than have a shower. All too late, she remembered the length of the extraordinarily long bath and torpedoed under water until her feet bottomed out at the far end. She surfaced with a splutter, and gave a little laugh; it reminded her where she was.

Half-lying on the sofa in her dressing gown with a cup of coffee on the low table, she attended to her laptop and dug further into the history of Blue Lizard, cross-referencing against what was on the memory stick. She knew she was good at this type of investigation and hoped it wouldn't take too long before she came across something useful, but before she knew it, she had to get up and turn on the light. She needed a break as she felt she was going round in circles. She rubbed her eyes, stretched, then headed for the kitchen to make another coffee.

On the way, she turned the radio on and diverted via the toilet to help clear her mind. Her phone warbled in the background; it was Justin's text letting her know he'd be home late, and it was then that she realised she was hungry. Neither the cupboards nor the fridge revealed anything that didn't need effort or time, so she dialled the local takeaway, ordered a pizza for delivery, and went straight back to her laptop.

So far, Blue Lizard appeared to be whiter than white other than the fact that it was struggling to break even.She kept asking herself how one would disappear volumes of oil without being discovered. She'd read reports about the trick of tanker captains turning off their tracking systems so that they could evade sanctions, but this didn't appear to be the case with Blue Lizard. All their journeys and deliveries appeared to be logged, and they corresponded with the respective ports at the correct times. They had to be utilising some other undetectable system.

According to their records BLOP had had three tankers in their fleet; the Orbis Maru, the Trans Maru and the Pan Maru. She studied their itineraries starting with the Orbis, and discovered that there was over a decade of history. Every item was available online, from where it had visited, bunkered, discharged, been maintained, through to even who crewed it at various intervals. There was nothing that appeared to stand out from the ordinary when she compared itineraries with other oil tankers. She turned her attention to the Trans which showed a similar profile, only its history went back nearly eighteen years, and she was halfway ploughing through its schedules when her doorbell rang.

Despite knowing that time flies at double the speed when one is on the computer, she could hardly believe that was half an hour since she ordered. She gratefully set the pizza box down on the kitchen counter top and was just ferreting around in the drawers for the requisite cutter when her ears pricked up at the news on the radio. She caught the back end of a report on an oil tanker going missing somewhere in the Gulf of Aden and that The Royal Navy had dispatched one of its vessels already stationed in the area to co-ordinate the search.

She didn't believe much in coincidences, but surely this was just one such occasion. She attended to dividing up her slices with the pizza wheel like an automaton while her thoughts attempted to find some sort of similarity, or even any kind of associated sideline. She grabbed a can of Guinness from the fridge and sat in front of her laptop with the pizza box on the table; all the while conjecting how an entire tanker could go missing. She went through the possibilities: Hijacking, terrorism and malfunction were high on her list. She didn't consider a collision much of a possibility otherwise there would have to be another vessel involved, and surely someone from either ship would have reported as such.

She tapped into Reuters News Agency for more up to date information, and clicked on the story about the Glory Bee. She learned that it was a Panamanian registered oil tanker that had been en route from the Mina Abdulla oil refinery in Kuwait to Dar es Salaam in east Africa. There had been no distress calls and no answers from any crew members but the main mystery was that the ship's transponder had suddenly ceased sending out a signal. According to the captain of another vessel who was over the horizon but had her on his radar at the time, one minute she was there off the port quarter, and the next it had just vanished. The story thencentred around the search for survivors.

She exercised her tongue to catch an errant strand of cheese while simultaneously looking at the screen and clicking on other links, and decided it was better to pay more attention to her pizza since the same cheesy strand had elasticated onto her keyboard. It had interrupted her train of thought, so she returned to looking at the detail of the last Maru ship; the Pan Maru, and was startled to find that it was no longer listed. Not only that, but there wasn't the detail that went with the other two ships in the fleet.

There were no records of it having been renamed or sold; so where was it? Her surfing revealed that the renaming of tankers was not that uncommon, and one link cited the Onassis fleet where all the tankers had been named 'Olympic' something or other; either second hand or brand new. She turned to international shipping registers and shuddered at the enormity of choice, but persevered.

She thought she'd start with the letter A, as in America, but was diverted to Panama, as it registered the greatest number of vessels, apparently due to less rigorous maritime legislation. There were thousands of them, and even in the renaming or discharge sections there was no mention of any Pan Marus. Wondering where an oil company based in Baku might register a tanker, she looked up the Azerbaijani register, but drew another blank.

The task was just too enormous, and looking at the time on the bottom right of the screen, she decided that she would need some AI help in finding what had happened to the Pan MaruShe clicked onto Lloyds List. If the world's leading insurers didn't have anything, then she would call it -day. It was past one in the morning and her can of Guinness was empty.

Wearily, she followed link after link without success, but she perked up a little when she came across a report of an oil supertanker named SS Salem. What caught her interest was that it had been named SS South Sun at its launch, renamed and re-registered by new owners, and soon after, was lost at sea somewhere in The Atlantic Ocean, probably some distance off the West African coast. The wreck had never been found, hence the removal of its name from the shipping registers. It didn't take her long to discover that fraud and criminality was suspected at the time, albeit almost fifty years ago, so she shifted her buttocks on the sofa, and became engrossed in a most unusual story.

She started to read about oil embargos effected upon the apartheid regime in South Africa, and the desperate measures the government had been taking to obtain oil. This had included trading with some dubious administrations whose sympathies aligned with their own, and naturally came to the attention of some criminal elements.

The gist of the story was that the oil-laden SS Salem had disembarked from Saudi Arabia, and in the middle of the high seas the crew had painted a new name on the bows and stern so that there was no trace. They then called in at Durban in South Africa where she had illegally discharged her cargo of crude oil, filled her tanks with sea water so as to appear to have a full cargo when she sailed, then set off round the Cape of Good Hope and into the Atlantic. At some point off the West African coast, the crew opened the sea cocks before embarking into the life boats, thus leaving her to sink without trace into deep waters. They had plenty of time to consider their cover story that the engine had inexplicably exploded and caught fire, forcing them to abandon the ship at very short notice.

Those involved with this brazen plot were happy. The Saudis were happy as they had received payment for their oil. The tanker brokers were happy with their fee. The charterers had received their commission. The South African government were overjoyed with this lifeline of oil. The crew, including the master and officers, were rubbing their hands with glee as monies had been transferred directly into their Swiss bank accounts by the SA government.

Conversely, Shell Oil had to explain to their buyers in Genoa that the oil they had already purchased would not be arriving, and Lloyds of London, as insurers of both the cargo and the vessel, were most unhappy. The potential claim had been estimated at nearly sixty million US dollars, just about as big as it gets.

Patricia was so absorbed in this extraordinary conspiracy that she never heard Justin quietly open the front door and creep up on her. It frightened the life out of her when he put his hands over her eyes, and firmly pressed her head against the sofa.

"Good morning, gorgeous."

Her knee jerk and shrill exclamation attested to her surprise as she automatically grabbed his arms; but only for a second. "Bastard!"

"Nothing like a nice welcome home."

"You're still a bastard. Frightening women like that in their own homes. I suppose you've been enjoying yourself."

"If you must know, I've been indulging in the sport of kings at Newmarket." He teased her with his description of going to the horse races as he walked round and sat next to her on the sofa.

It took her a second or two to realign her thoughts away from high seas piracy to his wavelength. She looked at his smart sporting attire and caught a whiff of alcohol. "I suppose you've been rubbing shoulders with the high and mighty."

"You'll be glad to hear that we're richer by nearly one hundred pounds."

She looked suspiciously at him and waited for him to continue, since the inflection in his voice betrayed that there was more to it than that. "And?"

He smirked before replying. "Well, it was nearer a thousand, but I had to ply this chap with expensive champagne and brandies, mixed mind you, before he would open up."

"And did he?"

"Eventually." Justin was now grinning from ear to ear. "But it was the outsider 'Lucky Bamboo' that came in at twenty-to-one that might have helped. This chap I'd been put on to…"

"Oh, do stop boasting and tell me something worthwhile."

Justin mused for a moment. "Oh, definitely worthwhile, and I'll tell you all about it later. I've just one more person to interview before I hand the case over to our client. This'll cheer you up though... you'll never guess who I came across there."

The blank look on her face betrayed her ignorance, but Justin hadn't finished teasing her. "Ill give you a clue. One word. Three syllables. First syllable: It's something you put in a sandwich."

Her weary mind struggled to change tack again. This was not something she wanted to do right now, but the look on Justin's face begged her to play his game, so she forced herself. "Cheese".

"Nope."

She closed her eyes, imagining standing at the kitchen counter, and deciding what to put in her sandwich. She opened her eyes. "Beef."

"Nope."

"Pork."

"Nearly."

"Ham."

"Correct. Third syllable. Sounds like something that weighs a lot."

"Whale."

"Rhymes with the opposite of off."

"On." She huffed, tiring of the game.

"And the whole word spells the name of a town in Scotland."

She cringed as she scoured her mind for a

town beginning with Ham, and then it dawned on her. "Hamilton... Oh, no. Not Maurice bloody Hamilton again."

"The very same. But don't worry, I was very careful that he didn't see me. But as he was in the box next to us, I did manage to overhear a little of what he said now and again."

"I don't suppose he mentioned anything about oil tankers, because I'm pretty sure he's involved with some sort of scam off the Irish coast?"

"Nah. I reckon he was being treated to a day at the races by this Arabic horse owner, and as usual, he had a buxom filly tagging along with him."

"Listen. I'm really rather tired and I'm off to bed soon, but I think I might be on to something here and I want to follow this string while it's still fresh in my mind. Speaking of Hamilton, I don't suppose you ever heard about a supertanker called The Salem?" She gave him a chance to delve into his memory. "Fraud case back in the eighties."

"No. Before my time... and by the way, before yours as well. Want to tell me about it?"

She went to attend to her laptop, but before she had a chance, Justin got up. "Looks like you need another Guinness, and I think I'll join you. Thirsty work, all this travelling."

As he disappeared into the kitchen, she reflected that she had travelled a damn sight more miles than he had today; or yesterday. When he sat down again, she gave him a truncated version of her Irish escapade, pointed at her laptop and revealed the story behind The Salem. "I haven't finished reading all the relevant stuff yet, and it might not even be a precedent for what I'm looking into, but something tells me there's more than a coincidence here. I've just got to find a common denominator. Add two and two together. Look." She pointed at her screen. "It says here that criminal investigations were carried out by several agencies including Lloyds of London and Scotland Yard, and, hang on a mo." She read down a few lines, then started laughing. "I don't believe it."

Now it was Justin's turn to be teased, although it was unintentional. "Don't believe what?"

She scanned the text again. "The bloody idiots." She kept reading. "Due to the sudden explosion, the crew claim they didn't have time to send off an emergency SOS, but they did have enough time to pack their bags, and get this... " She was almost agog with disbelief. "When interviewed, The Master of the ship that rescued them commented that he was surprised to find that they had packed lunch boxes and crates of wine in their lifeboats." She turned to look at Justin. "They were pissed as parrots when he picked them up... celebrating. All the officers and crew must have been in on it."

Justin blinked, trying to fathom the crass stupidity. "What happened to the boat? Did they ever find it?"

She skipped a few lines. "Doesn't look like it. Remember that in those days they didn't have GPS, so it would have been a lot easier to disappear. Even an entire super tanker."

"So what's this got to do with your oil rig? They don't go very far."

"I don't know yet, but I'm tired and need to sleep

on it. Something will jell." She slurped the last of her can. "Bloody hell. It's half-past-two."

"Yeah, I could do with some shuteye as well."

Chapter 12

Jason Donnelly had been busy on his secure phone in his office, so much so that he had had to recharge it halfway through one conversation, then change arms to give the other a rest. He exhaled a sigh of relief, reclined and settled his head on the tall backrest, regretting that he had lost his two henchmen he had installed on the rig; but it gave him a chance to ruminate how his luck seemed to be changing for the better, as he now knew that this would be the last run of the Pan Maru, or whatever name her Captain chose to give her at any given juncture.

He casually looked up at the photograph hanging on the wall to his right. "Goodbye old girl. You've done me proud." He carefully folded the marine chart on his desk, rose and placed it in the safe behind the picture. That, along with other revealing documents, was something else he would have to burn. He also knew that within a few days he would disappear forever, away from all those local Garda busybodies and especially that pair of detectives from London; they had been particularly irksome.

He'd have to make sure he left absolutely no trace of his future whereabouts, because he was going to piss-off several powerful people when he double-crossed them. Thieving from the thieves, and that theft would not be easily forgotten by his Arabic partners in crime.

As for the Englishman... well... he'd be halfway across the world from him and well away from his jurisdiction.

He went over in his mind what he had spent the last couple of hours checking and rechecking. Confirming and reconfirming. Arrangements that he had started to put in place over several years, and could feel it all coming together very nicely, thank you. Up to now, it had mainly involved oil, and although it had been profitable, the icing on the cake would come from this last run. He'd have to disappear, otherwise he'd be a dead man.

Just one more call to make before visiting his favourite casino on his way home. Before dialling, he went over how he would manage to buy himself a few days before the inevitable questions were raised. He needed to give a believable reason why the Pan Maru was lagging behind schedule, and he had a favourite in mind. One of the propeller screws would supposedly hit some floating debris on its voyage en route to the rig, and would have to reduce speed significantly, thus causing a delay. Mr. Huseyn in Baku, together with other Middle Eastern gentlemen, would not be happy, but they would have no other choice than to accept the news at face value. After all, although rare, it was not that an uncommon an occurrence.

A couple of hours later, he exited Victoria's casino with a wad of Euros stuffed into his inside jacket pocket. He knew he was addicted to the hushed atmosphere that was interrupted by the clacking of the ball as it skipped from number to number on the roulette wheel, and he knew his luck had to change at some point, and tonight had been the night. Not only had he won enough to settle his account, but he was richer by something in the region of fifteen thousand Euros.

In the small hours and safely back in his rented apartment, he flicked through the elastic-banded sheaf of notes and nonchalantly tossed it onto his sideboard before pouring himself a small bedtime tumbler of Bushmills. He sat down in his one and only armchair, gazed into the golden liquid as he swirled it round in the glass, and mulled over what he had set in unstoppable motion.

Michael Windaw and he had first met each other by accident at a Sunday youth club, not far from the Harland & Wolff dockyard in Belfast, and had taken an instant liking to each other. In their mid-teens, they shared the football scene, the pool table, and all the other games that were organised by their elders who wished to see lads such as them kept off the streets, but it didn't take them long to discover that there was a sympathetic landlord at a backstreet pub who turned a blind eye to their age. In there, they shared the darts, the whiskey, the roll-ups, and sometimes the young girls that frequented that part of the city, and learned implicit trust in each other.

Most of all, they shared the desire to become wealthy, and what started out as a daft idea, spawned into a ragged plan to steal a ship-full of oil and flog it to the highest bidder. Desperately short of cash, they had no other option but to seek out employment. Through a charter company, and with a forged certificate, Windaw was offered a job as third mate on an oil tanker, while Donnelly's father found him employment on a North Sea oil rig; but they kept in touch, and fostered their dream.

Windaw hadn't wasted his time like he had done as a juvenile, but instead swotted and passed all the necessary exams to enable him to be promoted all the way up to first mate, and it was while he was in that position that he finally gained his Masters' Certificate. It could take months or years before he was offered the captaincy of a suitable vessel, and as he didn't want to wait that long he hatched a plan to expedite his elevation.

A suitable opportunity came out of the blue whilst they were bunkering in the Ghanan port of Accra. While docked overnight, he persuaded the captain to join him in one of the backstreet bars, and it was there that he spiked him with the local Raki, while staying completely sober himself. The dock authorities, persuaded by a few dollars, found that the captain was unfit to command a vessel and was duly arrested. He feigned regret when he reported to the owners that his captain had been found drunk while about to go on duty.

With the ship due to sail in a few hours, the owners had little choice but to appoint him captain; albeit on an initial trial basis. He duly contacted Donnelly with a gleeful report that the first part of their scheme was dropping into place. As master of a vessel, his word on board was law. Although it was the ship's owners who arranged the employment of the other officers and crew, over a period of time, he wheedled-out the naysayers and replaced them with a more compliant crew. Compliant to what he eventually had in mind, and what he and Donnelly had cooked up.

His travels took him halfway across the globe, sometimes on regular routes, sometimes to out of the way destinations, and it took him some years to seek out those with whom he could trade on the black market. He had found his ideal customers in the ex-Portuguese colony of Goa on the Indian continent; ones who were willing to swap gold for oil.

The plan was really quite straightforward. Donnelly provided the oil from the rig which was pumped into the hold, Windaw would sail the Pan Maru round the Cape of Good Hope with the satellite tracking system turned off, dock at Goa and exchange oil for gold, then return. Meanwhile, Donnelly had lined up a cash buyer for the precious metal. The officers and crew were paid off handsomely once the cash from the gold was transferred, and although it would never guarantee their silence, they would be hard-pressed to explain how they had come by such relatively large amounts of cash.

After several years of the Pan Maru toing and froing, both Donnelly and Windaw were savvy enough to recognise that such a lucrative trade couldn't go undetected forever and had had the foresight to make provision for their own disappearance, along with the vessel.

Ensconced in his cabin, and having just had a lengthy conversation, Windaw pressed the red button on his satellite phone, terminating the call. He reinspected the familiar chart in front of him, recognising The Golden Spur which was a slight rise in the east-of-middle Atlantic seabed; often referred to as the Celtic Sea. The co-ordinates he had been given were some distance to the northeast of it. It was certainly well away from the normal shipping lanes, and unlikely to be seen by any other vessel.

Donnelly had given him the waypoint en route to the rig, and it was there that he would discharge his human cargo of over two hundred and fifty migrants. They had been picked-up in Liberia, all of them seeking the easy fleshpots of the British, and safety from persecution by the local warlords in that part of the world. Over the years, those migrants had somehow managed to scrape enough cash together, and collectively it totalled over one million dollars. Very profitable.

The changeover would happen during the hours of darkness, onto a trawler out of Milford Haven, and Windaw was wise enough not to question where they would go from there. He had his suspicions that they would melt away into society, but if caught and questioned none of them would be able to correctly name the vessel they had transited in. Windaw had had his crew repaint a made-up name on the bows and stern before arriving in Liberia, and that name too would be changed soon after the migrants had been transferred and were out of sight.

It was a relatively easy task to change the painted names, and he alternated between 'Spanamar', 'PaniMari', 'Aspanamar', and 'Pa Manus'. The quickest method of repainting the name was to blank out just one or two letters and use a template to paint on just another couple of letters. Simultaneously, he would alter the settings on the GPS tracker to reflect a totally different vessel to one that either didn't exist or was on the opposite side of the globe.

From his drop-off point, he would sail the Pan Maru to the rig, arriving soon after dusk, and it was there that he would meet up with Donnelly. Stowed safely away in a large locked chest in his cabin were bags of Krugerrands, a bag of gems, wads of cash in varying currencies, and twelve full-sized ingots of 22 karat gold, each weighing around twelve kilograms and each worth in excess of $800,000. This was the culmination of years of smuggling. None of the officers or crew knew that he had secreted them there several weeks ago, two-by-two in briefcases, before sailing from Goa. They assumed their pay-off was coming from the illicit sale of the oil, and the migrants; not gold.

The next stage of their plan meant that once docked at the rig, Windaw would empty the seawater from the hold and replace it with crude oil. Donnelly had already arranged for it to be delivered to Reykjavik in Iceland, and payment was already held by agents to the oil brokers, pending delivery of that oil.

They were raking it in from all angles: From the free oil that was extracted by the rig, from the sale of the gold to a nefarious character from the criminal underworld, from the transport of migrants, and from the sale of yet more free oil. The circle of profit was constant. Only one of the Middle Eastern syndicate that owned the rig and the Pan Maru was partially aware, and indeed, complicit, in what Messrs. Donnelly and Windaw were up to; the others were oblivious to what was really going on and certainly ignorant of what was about to befall them.

Deep in thought, and with elbows resting on the maritime chart, Windaw rubbed his hand over his chin and decided that the beard he had started growing a couple of weeks ago just about matched the photograph on the false passport he had picked up in Liberia. He cast his eyes sideways and down at the padlock on his chest and satisfied himself that nobody had interfered with it. It would remain locked until Donnelly came on board, then together they would carry the contents down to the motor cruiser that he would be arriving on. The C-4 explosive would stay in there until needed.

Chapter 13

Inspector Patricia Eyethorne fell back on the skills she had learned as a detective inspector while stationed at Maidenhead police station. Only a certain amount of information could be gathered from the computer, but face to face interviews tended to embellish her knowledge of a given subject. In this case, she wanted to get the reaction of one of the Lloyds syndicate underwriters who had insured 'The Salem'.

She had never been to Lloyds before, and was very impressed with the modern building at No 1, Lime Street, in the heart of the City of London. Several nearby offices overshadowed the modern building, but its contemporary design made it instantly recognisable as one of London's landmarks, and she had no trouble finding it.

A smartly-dressed Guy Simpson had a natural gleam in his eye as he greeted her at reception on the ground floor, and once through the stringent security system, whisked her to the glass lift which took them quickly to one of the top floors. Considering that the Salem case was getting on for fifty years old, she was surprised at his relative youthfulness, but it all became clear once the initial pleasantries were dispensed with on the way up in the lift.

"Oh, you thought you'd be meeting with my father,

but I'm afraid you're several years too late. He fronted one of the syndicates that was involved with insuring The Salem, and his name was also Guy, but I'm now one of the senior members. It's becoming a bit of a family tradition as I'm the third generation in the same Lloyds syndicate, and my son is heading in the right direction; if you know what I mean. Here. Come and look at this."

He led her to a room that he obviously shared with three others, and beckoned her to stand next to him against the full length window that revealed a panoramic vista. "You can just about see the top of the Tower of London, just to the left of the walkie-talkie building, and behind and to the right of it, Monument. That was erected to mark the spot where the fire of London started in 1666." While she took in the glorious view, he looked in admiration at her shapely figure and with a touch of levity added "Just as well we weren't in business then, as the fire wiped out most of London."

His attitude exuded nonchalance and put her at ease, but she knew that he wouldn't have risen to the position he was in now without having some backbone. She recalled last years' experience, when she not only stayed at the Tower Hotel with a direct view of The Thames, but her near-fatal ordeal on top of the roof of Tower Bridge. At that point, she really hadn't had time to enjoy the scenery. She gave a brief shudder at her recollection, and wondered if she'd ever manage not to recoil at the memory of such a terrifying moment.

"Coffee or tea?" Guy asked as he turned and ushered her towards the chair opposite his desk.

"Neither, thanks." Time to get down to business.

"It seems as though I've wasted my time if it was your father who knew about The Salem." She sat anyway.

"Not at all. Anyone worth their salt around here has heard about The Salem. After all, the size of the claim was potentially a syndicate breaker. Back then, a call upon the syndicates' members for over fifty million pounds would have bankrupt half of them, and there's a standing joke that went with it, which went along the lines of it still being cheaper than a divorce. But it was really the other way round."

"You know about it then?"

"Ha. I was still at school then, but I remember Dad coming home one day and telling us how worrying it was. It was probably that story that got me interested in marine insurance. I don't know how much you know about how Lloyds works, but back then, it was the individuals of the syndicates who insured whatever needed insuring, and those syndicates were made up mainly of wealthy families. It was they who guaranteed that cash was available for settling claims, and I remember Dad saying that we may have to sell the house. You see, each individual puts his entire wealth on the line, and should there be such a large claim, he would have to sell some or all of his assets to cover the call. Nowadays, there are fewer individuals, as corporations are getting in on the act. Even foreign governments."

"Tell me more about The Salem."

"Oh, it was pretty obvious almost from the outset that it was fraud on a massive scale." He continued to relate the story very much as Patricia had learned about on the net, but embroidered it with a few second-hand rumours. "Once the officers and crew had disembarked to shore in Liberia, interviews were carried out, and what initially raised suspicions was that the description of the engine catching fire given by the crew didn't match.. Apparently, some said there was so much smoke they couldn't see, but others denied that there was any smoke at all. It all snowballed from there, and contradictions abounded from what actually happened."

"And what did actually happen?" She had read about it but wanted to hear it for herself.

"I can tell you the long version over lunch if you like, or the short version now." He was thinking what a pleasure it would be to take this gorgeous woman to one of the classy restaurants in The City; and to be seen by his contemporaries with her.

"Better make it the short version."

He continued without betraying his chagrin. "The sneaky so-and-sos swapped their cargo of oil with seawater in South Africa so as to still look full when she departed, then sailed her mid-Atlantic, opened the sea cocks, took to the lifeboats, and waited for an insurance payout. Dad told me that he'd only ever heard The Bell rung twice before."

"The Bell?" Queried Patricia.

"Um, the Lutine Bell. A historical remnant from the Napoleonic wars, rescued from an old French frigate, that has hung in the main hall ever since. It was usually rung when the old sail ships returning from the Far East became overdue, or a ship sank in some storm or other and was declared a total loss. Gave the underwriters a chance to steel themselves... or to go down the local coffee shop. Personally, I'd go down the pub for a stiff drink or two."

"So you've never heard The Bell rung then?"

"Never. And I hope I never do. You see, at the time it was a shock on such a large scale that it shook all of the syndicates in Lloyds, and before the fraud was reported, it was rumoured that one chap had committed suicide."

"But it wasn't just the crew's versions of events that gave them away, was it?"

"Oh no. They were up to all kinds of skullduggery. By the time the investigators had finished with them, they found an entire assortment of other crimes, and they all went to jail. It wouldn't surprise me to learn that some of them are still there. Needless to say, there was no pay out. But it was the biggest thing back then by a long chalk."

A short silence between them was interrupted only by gentle background noise from the other occupants in the room. She felt it time to mention her own particular dilemma. "What is the best way of finding out more about a certain ship?"

"Simple. Just ask me." He gave a generous smile. "And I'll see what comes up on our system. Failing that, Lloyds Register ought to have some records. What ship have you got in mind?"

"I was wondering what happened to the Pan Maru, because it seems to have disappeared off the records."

Guy sat forward and attended to his desktop computer. After only a few seconds, he repeated the ship's name. "Pan Maru... Pan Maru.. Let's see. Ah. Here we are." He tapped a few more keys and moused the screen. "It says here that it was sold to a scrapyard in Chile over ten years ago, but it seems to have reappeared again three years ago." He looked up at her. "It's not unusual for aging ships to be renovated or converted and then re-enter the marketplace, usually under a different name, but they certainly took their time in doing so in this instance. Daa, di daa, di, daa..." He speed-read the semi-irrelevant parts. "Eh? Someone's not keeping their records up to date." More speed-reading. "Here it is in one port... no transition records or voyage data... and then it re-appears in another port. Daa, di daa, di, daa... same again here... but hang on... it's still officially listed as being scrapped; In Chile." He frowned as he perused his screen. "No, I tell a lie... it was reinstated in Georgetown, Guyana, three years ago.

He briefly diverted his eyes away from his screen. "Each commercial vessel has a GPS tracker which locates and tracks various ships, and running in tandem to that, there's such a system as AIS, which stands for Automatic Identification System, but that only has a range of, say, twenty miles from the coast. Line of sight only. The website Marinetraffic is a useful source of information when trying to find a certain ship, the itinerary of where it's been and where it's going etcetera, but your Pan Maru seems to have quite some gaps in its history. Er... hang on a sec; I'm just looking. It seems she was docked in Muscat nearly a month ago, chartered by Heurraflax Costal Shipping and carrying a hundred and fifty thousand tons of crude... that's funny... there's no destination logged." His frown deepened. "But soon after leaving port, her GPS tracker ceased to function." He looked her straight in the face. "God knows where she is now."

Patricia started to get an uneasy feeling that she was on the right track, and she felt she had to ask the question that had been brewing, "Could a scam such as the Salem happen again?"

She was expecting some sort of shock reaction from Guy, but it didn't materialise, and he gave a half-laugh before responding. "I suppose it could, but it'd be mighty difficult. You see, everything is digitally logged these days, and everybody knows in advance what's going where. Who the buyers and sellers are, where they've come from and are going to, and even where they're off to next. And then there's the financial sanctions aspect, as no monies can change hands unless it's been approved by IMF, that's the UN's International Monetary Fund. But we occasionally hear about black market deals, more so nowadays, as the Russians seem to be able to operate with impunity when it comes to supplying their comrades in the Middle East. In the main, we know what vessels they are operating, but insurers in the free western world don't touch them with a barge pole."

Patricia thought about his comments for a moment. "So, what you're telling me is that as long as it's sanctioned and you know about it, you can trace it, but you don't really know what's going on behind your backs?"

It was guy's turn to think. "Er... in a nutshell, yes."

"A perfect example is the Pan Maru then, because even though you say it's been registered visiting various ports, you also say there's sporadic history, but you're not a hundred percent sure if it's been scrapped, and you don't know where it is right now, nor where it's heading."

Guy shifted in his seat and gave another half-laugh. "You could say that. Perhaps if you gave me a bit more of what you know, I might be able to help with whatever you're looking for. I might even be able to trace her and let you know when she turns up."

She quickly weighed-up the risk of revealing what her investigation was all about, but decided that if word of that reached the likes of Donnelly or Hamilton it would forewarn them. Donnelly would scarper, and Hamilton would pre-empt anything likely to affect him with some fictitious yarn. "I really appreciate your kind offer, and I'm sorry I can't tell you what this is about yet, but I'll see if I can warn you in case there's an impending claim. Down the coffee shop perhaps?"

Guy recognised that their discussion had come to a useful end, and stood up. "I'll look forward to it, but the coffee'll be on me. Ok?" He admired her shapely figure again as she turned to go, and strode to open the door ahead of her. As he did so, he added. "Unless my memory is fading, aren't you the woman who's been in the press recently? You rescued someone from on top of Tower Bridge didn't you?"

She smiled politely at him. "Almost right, but it was me who was rescued."

"I stand corrected, so any time you need rescuing again… "

A mixture of towering skyscrapers and elegant Victorian buildings were ignored as she wended her way towards Cannon Street underground. What she needed most was quiet thinking time to start knitting together loose strings of information, and she was now so deep in thought that several minutes later she woke up to find herself sitting on a utility bench next to the ticket office.

The rat she had smelled before was starting to reek.

Chapter 14

The meeting in the cabinet office at number 10 Downing Street adjourned when several ministers repaired to an adjacent room to continue their discussion, as directed by the Prime Minister. Even though the conversations had not centred around his portfolio, as Secretary of State for Northern Ireland, and prominent member of the inner cabinet, Hamilton had been obliged to attend. He had contributed little, but as per normal, he took the opportunity to belittle one of his rivals in front of the others. One of the 'wets' as the press had described her, and as far as he was concerned, an easy target, who became riled far too easily. She scowled at him as they made their way out of the narrow room, but then again, she tended to scowl at most people, but the 'put down' hadn't gone unnoticed by their colleagues.

"Just a minute, Maurice." Called the PM as Hamilton was just about to reach the doorway. The cabinet secretary and minute keeper were dismissed, leaving just himself and Hamilton in the long room; he decided to sit more or less opposite as papers were tidied away.

Andrew Barrows had led his party and the country for nearly four years and suspected he would probably be asked to step- own after the next general election, but in the meantime, he would do his utmost to maintain cohesion within the increasingly diametric opinions of his cabinet. Fortunately for him, he and Hamilton were like-minded on most topics, and he didn't want to lose a valuable supporter; which is why he needed a quiet word.

"You upset Sheila again." Andrew was direct with his close colleagues.

"She deserved it."

"She might have deserved it, but if you keep sniping at her like that, sooner or later she's going to fight back, and if she digs deep enough, she might actually find something worthwhile."

Hamilton detected there was something more to it than just 'worthwhile' and his self-preservation mode kicked in. "In what sense?"

"I think we both know what I mean… " Barrows purposely left the sentence unfinished, but as Hamilton showed no sign of responding, he continued. "It's no longer a case of there being rumours about your philandering lifestyle, but more of a fact really. At the moment, I've only had a verbal report on your goings-on, but if you continue to flaunt your virility with some luminary or other, then it's likely Sheila will get to hear of it, and she could make life rather awkward for you… and me, I might add."

The suggestion that Hamilton was becoming less discreet was clear, and he recognised it as a warning from a friend, more than from a PM; otherwise why would there be just the two of them having this conversation? After all, when Barrows did eventually step down as PM, he would be a likely candidate for his replacement. But the PM was right… if the rumours became widespread, it wouldn't do his election chances any good at all; either with the party or the general public. He didn't want to justify his actions to anybody, but felt that he needed to mollify his superior; at least for the time being. "I take it that word has come through to you from The Diplomatic Protection Squad?"

"Dammit, Maurice. The bill for your security detail is as big as mine."

"Only because of those Fenian bastards in Ireland."

"Not just them, but also the way you,… shall we say… entertain members of the opposite sex on a daily basis. Good God man, I've heard that you have as many as three women at the same time in your apartment across the river. Is that true?" Barrows inflected the question in such a way that it sounded on the complimentary side.

The way the question was put was not lost on Hamilton, who smugly admitted as much with a smile and a "Might be."

"Look." Said Barrows resignedly. "Personally, I don't care how many children you might inadvertently sire, but Special Branch, who supply the Diplomatic Protection Squad with information, tell me that there are some vengeful women out there who have made certain enquiries about you. Apparently there's an increasing threat of blackmail." He let that comment hang for a moment, before continuing. "As PM, and for the sake of the party, I'm telling you to behave as a minister of the Crown should; but as a friend, I'm suggesting you be a little less conspicuous."

Hamilton resisted the urge to look at his watch, as he had an appointment with a lady from the Portuguese embassy coming up, and he wanted to be away, but before he left he decided that he needed to placate Barrows. "I'll see what I can do."

"Well, whatever you do, do it out of sight of the public eye."

* * * * *

A couple of hours later, Hamilton dealt with various documents from his briefcase in the back of the government supplied limousine as it was driven up the M40 towards his family home in Worcestershire. The nondescript car that closely followed behind contained a pair of officers from the Diplomatic Protection Squad, and it would be they who would take-up positions around Hamilton's grounds that evening. A bump over one of the village speed humps reminded him that he was nearly home, so he put his paperwork away and looked around at the leafy English countryside leading up to the twin brick pillars that marked the entrance to his small estate.

The driveway up to his house wasn't that long, but he still appreciated that the grass on each side had been neatly mown in a stripy pattern, and that the shrubberies looked to be in trim order. It prompted his memory that his wife Caroline had employed a pair of groundsmen recently, and he spotted them round the side of the house attending to something or other in the area of the tennis court. He frowned lightly as their gait agitated his memory, but the recollection was ever so brief as the car neared his front door and they were lost to sight round the edge of the building.

He turned left off the hallway and went straight into his study with one thought in mind; to see if a further quarter-of-a-million had been paid into his account. He rubbed his hands with glee, and as he waited for the screen to confirm that he had correctly inputted the lengthy security keystrokes, he toyed with his gold pen that rested on the green sculpted marble stone on his desk. Had he been looking in a mirror, he would have seen a look of disappointment spread across his face as he realised that no further funds had been deposited in his 'off shore' account.

He reached for his phone and messaged Donnelly via Whatsapp, enquiring as to the delay, but he didn't expect an immediate response from him, as it quite often took a few hours, or on one occasion over a day, before he usually replied. With a look of languor, he stared at the pile of mail on his desk for a moment before deciding reluctantly to make his presence known to his wife and family. He came across the aging housekeeper-cum-cleaner dusting the windows in the billiards room, and was told that Mrs. Hamilton had left the previous day.

"She left in an awful temper in her car yesterday morning, and nearly knocked one of the gardeners over as she left. She didn't give a reason, but she was cussing and swearing as she went round the house. That was just before she left."

Hamilton frowned, as this was definitely out of her character. "Did she say why she'd left in a such hurry?"

"No sir, she didn't speak to me at all. I haven't heard that kind of language from her before, but it must have been something upsetting. Perhaps it was some bad news that the postman had bought, because it was soon after he left that she started stomping up and down the stairs."

He left her to her duties and sauntered outside, wondering what had made Caroline leave at such short notice, but concluded that because she hadn't phoned him, whatever it was couldn't have been that serious.

He headed for the tennis court; even though it brought back memories of an almost fatal encounter with their dog the previous year. He pictured the damn animal chewing a cyanide-laden Rubick's Cube while he attempted to get away from the bloody animal. He still kidded himself that he had escaped all by himself, and ignored the fact that his life had been saved by some pesky security busybody; including that damn Eyethorne woman and her partner, whose name he had forgotten.

He shrugged off the recollection as he approached the two labouring gardeners, and as he neared, they ceased their weedkilling exercise, stood up and acknowledged his approach. Only then did he remember that they were twins.

"Sir." Almost in unison.

"And what are you chaps up to today?"

"Clearing the weeds growing through the wire mesh at the base." Replied the one on the left.

"By spraying them with Grazon." Said the other.

"Then once they've died back, we'll strim off the dead stalks and leaves."

He hadn't a clue what Grazon was, but concluded that it killed weeds, and therefore must be the right thing for the job. "Right then. Carry on." He spun round and returned to the house via the front door, noting that his security detail was sitting in their car by the entrance, while another was casually walking round the side of the outbuildings. He resolved to go through his inbox in his study.

Once he was out of sight, Eric turned to Ernie and rhetorically asked "He really hasn't the faintest idea of who we are, does he?"

"Just as well with what we've got in mind for him, but it'll come to him; eventually."

"He might have forgotten what he did to us on our wedding day, but we certainly haven't."

"And just as well his wife's left him. I'd have hated to have upset her."

"I know what you mean. She was a sweet lady."

"Even though she nearly ran your boots over yesterday?"

"Get away. I was at least a foot clear of her car. Got showered with gravel mind you." He half-laughed.

"Left or right?"

Ernie looked down at his feet. "Don't rightly know. It all happened so fast, but there's no tyre tracks on either of my boots."

They both chuckled.

"How long do you reckon it'll be before he realises that she's left him?"

"Um... he's not that smart, so probably not until tomorrow morning when he wakes up to find the other half of his bed empty."

"She must have found out that he was two-timing her."

"Rumour has it that he was ten-timing her."

"Well in that case, we'd better get on and do what we've always wanted to do."

"Yeah, but let's finish up here first, then we can get our revenge."

* * * * *

One of Hamilton's most prized possessions caught his eye as he opened the door to his study, and he purposefully strode up to his gold-plated Bentley that was at eye-level on one of the wall-mounted shelves. He stroked the palm of his hand over its smooth lines, relishing the tactile sensation of real gold. Not that he realised it, but he was smiling; one of the rare occasions when he did so, but the moment soon passed.

Sitting in his leather chair, he eyed up the two foot high pile of various files and envelopes that were stacked on the corner of his desk, reached out and retrieved an A4 brown envelope from the top. He was reaching for his letter opener with one hand while he turned the envelope with the other, and was surprised to find that there was no name or address on the back or the front; further, the flap was unsealed, and did not require the sharp edge of an opener. He pulled out the sheets of paper and was immediately stunned at what he read. It was written by his wife in untidy red felttip capital letters, almost diagonally across the page.

YOU'VE GONE TOO FAR THIS TIME SO I'M LEAVING YOU. SEE YOU IN THE DIVORCE COURT YOU INSUFFERABLE BASTARD.

Initially, he was stunned. He leaned back and placed

the page back down on his desk as though it might help, but it didn't, and it took him a bit more than a moment to get over the shock. Why now? he asked himself. Didn't she remember that they had an arrangement allowing him to have a mistress while he was away in London? Certainly that was some time ago, but surely she couldn't have forgotten? Could she?

They'd discussed it a few years ago, and under pressure from her, he'd admitted that he had needs while he was away, but in return for his occasional infidelity, she would be able to fulfil her own needs; only while he was otherwise engaged on government business. She had declined his offer to satisfy herself locally, stating that she would remain faithful to him; as well as her family.

As he was pondering what had bought on this sudden rebuff, he reached out for the second page underneath the first, and then it all became clear. The colour sheet of twenty something thumbnail photographs showed him in various poses, on or about a sofa, with a different woman in each shot. In some, he was less than half-dressed, and others totally naked; as were many of the females. There was one particular explicit shot with him lying on his back on the floor with a buxom woman sitting on him; it clearly showed the features of his face in ecstasy.

He instantly recalled some of the individual women and the joy they had given him, and even remembered one or two of their names, but as he scanned further down the page, he noticed that all the photographs had been taken from the same angle. Then he realised that it was his sofa in the living room of his apartment that overlooked The

Thames; almost opposite the Houses of Parliament.

His thoughts then turned to how all these shots had been taken without his knowledge. He didn't have any CCTV, although he had thought about having one installed for personal gratification, and he knew that the window wasn't overlooked by any other building. Besides, all these shots had been taken from a high angle, and showed just his sofa and carpet without any walls in the background. Whoever had taken them had to have had their camera high up on the wall or even mounted on the ceiling.

He looked up at the study ceiling and back down at the photographs to see if that might create a similar angle, and then imagined himself in his apartment and where the camera could be located. The window. Of course it was the window. But who? And how? He pictured the Georgian-styled windows, interspersed with thick limestone columns that ran the length of his living room which provided a magnificent view of Westminster Bridge and the Palace of Westminster beyond. In the other direction the only notable feature that could possibly overlook him was the giant Ferris wheel of the London Eye, but as that was constantly moving he discarded it as irrelevant.

A worrying thought crossed his mind. Whoever had taken those photographs knew what they were doing. They would have planned access to the outside without anyone else's knowledge and somehow secured themselves to the roof and strap themselves on to prevent them falling the fifty-foot drop to the very solid paved river path below; and all that before surreptitiously taking a snap shot. From the number of shots taken, they had been doing this on a regular basis, and over a period of time, but above all else, they would not want to be seen doing so.

He asked himself who could get away with such a frequent act. He tried to remember if he had seen any window cleaners, but couldn't recall ever seeing one, and racking his brains his logic turned to the security services. His thoughts started to go round in circles when he realised that he had not included his wife in the equation. Maybe she had employed a private photographer, and with all other options discarded, he concluded that she might well be responsible. Scowling, he considered forms of retribution on her and her bloody photographer, but one thing was certain; he would have to be ever so careful as to whom he approached to find out if his theory was correct. It really wouldn't do to be self-incriminating.

He thought that tracking down the photographer would be the first step, but he didn't know anybody who would be reliable or discreet enough to be taken into his confidence. Should the photographs somehow reach those who wished him ill, and he could think of several off the top of his head, it would be the end of his social and political prospects. He definitely didn't want to involve Mr. Postles, the head of security at the Houses of Parliament, as that would probably lead to his arm being twisted somewhere down the line. Nor did he want to approach Special Branch as he didn't trust them to keep a secret. Skeletons in the cupboard tended to emerge at the most awkward of moments, and he really didn't relish that prospect. If the powers that be couldn't help, then he would turn to those of a more nefarious nature, and his thoughts turned again to Donnelly. He would know someone, but he'd have to threaten them with a fate worse than death to maintain his secret.

He reached for his mobile again to contact Donnelly, but as he did so, an unnerving thought entered his mind. What if that bloody Eyethorne woman had been complicit in the taking of those photographs? His hand hovered over his phone as he conjected that this was exactly the sort of thing that she would do to get back at him. She would want her own revenge for his meddling in her affairs last year. Her and her sidekick Justin Crawford. Nobody else he had heard of would be audacious enough to take him on in such a manner. Yes... that was it. His wife must have contacted Eyethorne, perhaps even through Mr. Postles, then arranged for divorce photographs to be taken, and as a bonus, ruin his life and political ambitions.

He realised now what a cold fish he had been married to all these years, but had to admit that she was doing the same to him as he would have done to her. Well, she wasn't going to get away with it. He'd start by discrediting her, via chosen cabinet colleagues, that over the years she had secretly been educating girls in the art of womanhood and male manipulation. Those girls would have been far too young to know better. This would be a credible rumour as in the past, she was heavily involved with The Girl Guides.

Then, he would make contact with someone he knew who worked freelance for one of the left-wing newspapers, and embellish the story with some juicy suggestions; then leave it up to him to print what he thought he might have heard. At the same time, he would arrange to be invited on to a TV program where he would answer the interviewer's questions with suitable responses, all the while strongly rebutting any suggestions of impropriety. Indignant denials tended to make people think that there really was something amiss. No smoke without fire and all that. He imagined that by the time it came to divorce proceedings, he would be seen as the plaintiff, while she would be portrayed as an evil woman.

Meantime, he would deal with Eyethorne, and for that he needed Donnelly. It was high time she was removed from his life permanently, and he knew that his Irish confederate had links with the those who dealt in that line of work. His mobile rang before he managed to start reaching for it; the screen displaying that it was Donnelly.

"Hamilton."

"You rang." They kept their phone conversation brief for fear of eavesdroppers.

"There's a couple of important matters I need to discuss with you... face to face."

"Are they urgent?"

"Very much so. One's a bit delicate." He paused wondering how much to tell Donnelly over the airwaves. "My wife is about to become indiscreet."

The phones went quiet as Donnelly thought about his request for a long moment. "I'm a bit tied up right now but can you come out to the rig tomorrow? After ten o'clock?"

"I'll arrange a helicopter for the morning."

Hamilton heard the change to complete silence on his phone and likewise pressed the red button. He noticed he had a text from his wife, and opening it, saw the same divorce message. He sat back in his chair and reflected that he was taking the right course of action. His wife would be in an indefensible position, Eyethorne and Crawford would finally be consigned to little more than a bad memory, and he would hopefully be another quarter-of-a-million quid better off.

He had just finished contacting one of his secretaries to arrange to be collected early in the morning, when one the security team knocked on his door and half-entered.

"Excuse me minister, but there's a transporter at the entrance. They say they have a car for delivery."

It took him a second to redirect his thoughts away from skullduggery, and to the reason why he had left Westminster; his new car. He stood up quickly and retorted with glee. "Send 'em in, send 'em in." He went to follow the security chap, but the mobile that he had left on his desk rang. With a silent cuss, he turned back and answered it, replying tersely with one syllable at a time while looking out of the window at the lorry which was coming to a halt almost outside his front door.

It was just as well that there was a spacious parking area at the front of the house, otherwise the covered lorry would have had to churn up the manicured lawn in its efforts to turn around. Exiting through the front doors, he watched two blue-coated men step down from the cab and proceed to attend to the cargo straps at the rear. Annoyingly, his security chap entered his line of sight. "There's another gentleman at the gate wanting to come in as well... says he's from Haywoods and has a Bentley to hand over."

Hamilton cast his eye into the distance where the gates were, and saw a nondescript dark blue saloon waiting. "Yes, yes, let him in." He said irritably, and strode off in the direction of the lorry, while the security man spoke to his counterpart at the gate through his radio.

The blue coats disappeared into the back of the lorry while the blue saloon sedately drew up and parked not far from Hamilton. A smartly suited and booted middle-aged man got out and approached him. "Mr. Hamilton." It wasn't a question but a statement. "I'm Dominic Tindall from Haywoods and I'm pleased to be able to show you over your new Bentley." His diction and manner betrayed his expensive upbringing, which was exactly what was expected of him when addressing the well-heeled of society. "I must say, this is the first Continental we have ever ordered with your particular requirements, and I am rather proud to be the person to be delivering it to you. Once the chaps have unloaded it, may we park it over there to enable me to show you its refinements, and then afterwards, if you like, I can accompany you on a road trip?"

Once the pair of ramps had been fixed to the back of the lorry, it seemed to take an age before the engine came to life. This only encouraged Hamilton to edge closer to catch a glimpse of it, but he was ushered to one side by Tindall as the car slowly emerged into daylight, down the ramps, and onto the gravel.

The parking spot had been chosen well. The full

sunlight didn't just reflect off the highly-polished paintwork, it sent photonic shards darting in all directions, even reflecting onto the front façade of the house. And so it should, because the very expensive metallic gold paint, ordered by Hamilton, made it look like a million dollars. The two-tone gold, separated by a pair of silver coachlines that ran the length of each side, complimented and accentuated the two different auric shades. Had it been parked in a line of other cars, it would have immediately come to anyone's attention; even a blind man's.

Hamilton hadn't been so affected by this kind of emotion before, and with uncertain reverence, slowly walked over to it, eventually reaching out to touch it; just to make sure it was real. As his fingers made first contact, he felt a tremor run through his body as though he had touched a live wire. This is what he had dreamed of. This was what he had worked hard for all his life. This was utopia. He was so caught up with his inner feelings that he didn't take in Tindall's initial off-by-heart recital of the excellence of the Bentley Continental GTS. He followed the salesman round in a virtual trance, occasionally running his fingertips and hands along its moulded lines.

Returning to where they first started, he realised that the driver's door was being held open for him, and automaton-like, he sat himself into the luxurious seat, put his hands on the steering wheel and gently gripped it. He hardly noticed that his sense of smell was taking in the pervading aroma of the hand-stitched leather as he cast his eyes along the glossy walnut dashboard. The mixture of analogue and digital dials complimented each other, the cushioned armrest, the perfectly-sited controls, and even the seat was perfectly positioned for him.... and all the while, Tindall continued with his unheard monologue.

"How does it start?"

Tindall was standing next to the open driver's door. "Ah, well sir, there's more than one way to start it, and if you've got a... "

"Just show me how it starts." He said tersely.

Instead of leaning over and pressing a button, Tindall pressed a button on one of the remote devices he had in his hand.

Hamilton beamed, not just at the sound, but also at the slightest sensation of vibration that surrounded him. He closed his eyes and played with the throttle pedal, taking in as much as he could.

Before Tindall could stop him, Hamilton slammed the door shut, found a knob that engaged the drive system, and pushed the pedal halfway down. The inevitable happened. With over five hundred brake horsepower available, the Bentley's wheels spat gravel, found traction, and leapt forwards and onto the grass, where it spun round until Hamilton wisely took his foot off the pedal. Rarely did he smile, but he was in a state of nirvana. This was all he had imagined it to be. He gave another hefty boot of the pedal and pirouetted a couple more times.

The two blue coats stood beside Tindall, watching the antics of a frenzied driver. "Who does he remind you of?" Questioned one.

"Not the Formula One driver, that's for sure."

"I was thinking more of someone like Toad of Toad Hall."

Up to that point, Eric and Ernie had kept a discreet watch on the goings-on by standing in the shadows at the side of the house, but couldn't resist joining the trio of spectators.

"He's more used to driving military APCs and Land Rovers." Commented Ernie.

"That's if he's not being driven by his chauffeur." Added Eric sarcastically.

Tindall just stood there with a tight lip, as his primary job was to keep the customer satisfied.

"Here we go again." Said one blue coat as Hamilton failed miserably in attempting what might have been a figure of eight across the slippery grass. "And I pity the poor gardener who has to flatten out those bloody great divots. Look at the mud he's churning up."

"That'll be us." Eric was already remembering how much was left of the pile of top soil they had left.

They all took steps in differing directions as Hamilton aimed the Bentley towards them, but it managed to stop short by a few feet on the grippier gravel. Tindall showed no signs of his disapproval in front of his client, but noted the mud splats down the side of the vehicle. That reminded him that he would need to carefully advise how to apply the cleaners contained in the kit that came in the matching leather bag.

Waiting for Hamilton to get out, they all congregated around the driver's door, and as it opened, they heard his comment in an ebullient voice. "Now that's what I call a proper car." Despite his middle-aged frame, he leaped out, stood up and surveyed the throng. "As lively as a young filly before breakfast." He said at nobody in particular, but then turned to Tindall. "That'll do nicely, thank you."

"But sir, I haven't yet... "

"Don't worry about the details. She's perfect. I'll take it from here."

A flustered Tindall didn't hesitate, as he realised that all Hamilton wanted to do was keep the car. "But I need your signature on the delivery document, sir."

Hamilton had already started to turn, and in response, nonchalantly waved his hand over his shoulder. "Fine, fine. Whatever."

While Tindall rushed over to his car to retrieve the paperwork, with hand on hips, Hamilton stood back and admired his latest acquisition, then strolled round it once again. He approached the bonnet square-on and caressed the mounted Bentley emblem. "Oh, you beauty." Not even when he had met his wife had he expressed, or even felt, such emotion, and his children certainly didn't match this level of affection.

Tindall hovered to one side with pen and papers in hand, and eventually, catching his eye, he took the bold few paces to come between Hamilton and the Bentley. He was met with a brief scowl when he offered up the clip board, and retreated hastily once he had obtained what he needed. Ideally, he should have had his client sign several papers, but just one on the Bentley's log book would have to suffice on this occasion. He made sure Hamilton was not watching him as he opened the driver's door, and placed a matching, leatherbound voluminous file and associated bits 'n' pieces next to it on the seat.

The two blue coats finished packing and gingerly

drove their lorry away, closely followed by Tindall, leaving Hamilton to croon over his golden baby in the bright sunlight.

Eric and Ernie retreated well out of the way and returned to their gardening duties, which now entailed assessing if the heap of top soil located on the edge of the treeline was going to be enough. Hamilton spotted them and marched the hundred yards or so over and addressed them in his usual terse manner. "Right, men. Whatever you two are doing right now can wait. I want you to make sure there's plenty of room in the garage for my new Bentley, move whatever's in there well out of the way, sweep the floor clean and make sure nothing's going to fall against it. And when you've done that, I want you to wash it thoroughly. I don't want to see a speck of dirt anywhere. Then polish it, and polish it again. Clear?"

"Yes sir." In unison. They watched him jaunt over the lawn and gravel towards his house and waited for him to disappear back inside. "When are we going to mention that we haven't been paid?" Piped-up Eric.

"I was thinking just the same thing. No good asking him now, he's either too busy gloating over his car or shafting someone on the phone."

"Now that his wife's left him, we've got to ask him at some point."

"I think she paid the housekeeper directly."

"How about leaving a note with his secretary? She comes and goes occasionally."

"Good idea. Come on, let's go and see to his new car."

Chapter 15

Nearly five hundred miles away in his Cork office, Donnelly sat back in his chair. He pondered over what Hamilton wanted to say to him and suspected it might be to do with the £250,000 that he was obviously expecting. He knew it was sitting in his own bank account, but in view of the other operations he had set in motion with the Pan Maru, if he could hold-off Hamilton for another few days with some cock-and-bull story, he wouldn't have to hand it over to him. It would be his, and there would be nothing that Hamilton could do about it. He would have to wait and see what the other matter Hamilton had mentioned was all about, but he felt confident he would be able to handle that as well. The more he thought about it, the better it became. With Hamilton on his own rig, all manner of accidents could befall him. He closed his eyes for a full five minutes, and plotted his next move in response to Hamilton's unexpected arrival.

He made another phone call and arranged to be taken out to the rig on the morrow, this time by boat. Eamon enjoyed his fast, ocean-going speed boat that he charged tourists for by the hour, and he was very happy to take Donnelly's cash on the odd occasion. Donnelly preferred chartering a helicopter, but he didn't want any records of an itinerary being logged, especially on this run.

* * * * *

The alarm clock Patricia Eyethorne's bedside cabinet was silenced before the third buzz by the thump of her outstretched arm, and accompanied by a curse. She didn't feel as though she'd been asleep for more than a few minutes, and knew that if she didn't get up and shower straightaway, she'd likely drift back into slumber again. She'd fallen asleep thinking about tankers, Donnelly and rigs, and vaguely remembered dreaming about pirates; which didn't really help.

It was halfway through her shower that the little cogs in her brain that had been turning while she slept started to produce results. Her 'what ifs' started to turn into realistic scenarios, and the more she soaped herself, the more she found she could discard the irrelevant options. Her hair was laden with shampoo when she stopped lathering and hypothesised that Donnelly was about to carry out another 'Salem'. But, sinking a vessel would mean interference from the authorities, which he clearly wouldn't want, so he had to have another angle. In any case, he would want to off load the oil in her hold first, and the question was where. No, not where, because that was irrelevant and she didn't have time to work that out.

Her thoughts turned to the three vessels in the fleet, and as she played the drier over her hair, it dawned on her that it would be the Pan Maru. It had to be that ship, because the other two were accounted for, and the Pan was quasi-missing. She asked herself who would worry about a ship that had gone missing ten years ago.

Hadn't Guy Simpson told her that it had a chequered history of being scrapped and then reinstated?

Sitting on the side of her bed, she went over what she suspected to see if it would fit with what few facts she had.

Blue Lizard was losing money when it ought to have been raking it in. It was on Blue Lizard's rig that Miles had dispatched a pair of killers. Donnelly was in charge of the rig and had been covert when questioned. Donnelly was obviously the king pin.

Rather than stay sitting naked on her bed, she got dressed, wandered through to the kitchen where she found Justin brewing up a pot of tea, and after perfunctory good mornings, sat in front of her computer, but didn't turn it on. This was not the time for more discovery, so she leaned over and retrieved her A4 notepad and biro from the table. This was a time for separating facts from suspicion, conjecture from reality, and possibly a flow chart. She scribbled, and once the first page was full, tore it off and started on another. This one was centred around conjectures, the next around unrelated items. She gently nibbled her lower lip, then as a thought crossed her mind, winced as she nibbled a bit too hard when she asked herself what Hamilton's role was in all this. He wouldn't debase himself with the day-to-day running, but would be more like a silent partner, hiding somewhere in the background.

The last page consisted of a list of what she needed to know, such as had everything been retrieved from the memory stick that Miles had rescued, and what was on Donnelly's phone. What had the local Guarda made of two employees disappearing, and what had the health and safety executives found out.

Another page set out what she knew of the Blue Lizard set up, and a big question mark covered half the page when it came to who was at the top of the food chain. Who was above Mr. Huseyn in the Baku office, and where was he based? She noted him down as Mr. X and wondered if he and Hamilton conversed. Maybe there were several Mr. Xs. These were questions she would address on her secure laptop. She glanced at the time and remembered that protocol demanded she attend to it before much longer, but right now, she wanted to return to Donnelly and work out what he was up to.

"Need any help?" Asked Justin on the off-chance as he sat himself down on the sofa next to her; mug of tea in hand. After half-a-minute without a reaction from her, he was about to rephrase his question when she stopped twiddling the biro.

"Let me give you an analogy. What if you had an old car that was worth bugger all and needed to scrap it, but it had a full tank of petrol worth ten times the car's value? What would you do?

"That's easy. I'd syphon off the petrol into containers, then get what I could for the old banger down the scrap yard."

"OK. So what would you do with those containers? Say there's a lot of them and they're not easy to move about?"

"Well, I'd find somebody who could come and collect them, but that would be at a knock-down price."

"And how would you go about finding that somebody?"

"Ah. That's a bit more awkward, but not too difficult. I'd probably start by going down the local car boot sale on a Sunday, and sniff around for an interested party. If that failed, I might visit a camping centre, and if I became desperate, I'd visit the local pikey camp."

She'd half-expected such an answer, and was ready with a retort. "In other words, you'd find a black market buyer." She let that sink in. "That's what I think we have here, but with twists. Look at this." She produced a blank page and drew five small circles near the edges, and designated them A,B,C,D & E. "You start at A with an empty tanker and go to B where it is filled with crude oil. Then you sail it to C where the oil's sold, go back to A again for a fill-up and repeat the journey time and time again. Then you learn that D is offering you a much better price than C, so you offload there on you next trip instead. Simple economics so far. Yes?"

Justin nodded with a quiet grunt.

"E then offers you a tanker load of oil for 'free'." She used her fingers to indicate that free was not exactly that; then continued. "Because he wants in on your operation, and since he doesn't have any tankers, he's figured out that by owning his own fleet, he can increase his profits. A much better return. So you go to him rather than A for your fill-up, then you continue to supply D. More profitable, but just when you thought you had a foreseeable regular operation, there's a worldwide embargo on trading with D, so you have to go back to trading with C again."

"School boy stuff."

"Here's where the first twist comes in. You offload

at C as normal , and leave with an empty hold. It is plain for all to see that you are empty because you're riding high in the water, with your plimsoll line clearly visible. You then nip over to E for a free refill, but then offload at embargoed D where the price of crude had doubled. Even more profit, with say half of it going to E. Nobody would blink an eye if you're seen filling up at E because that's what is expected. D welcomes you with open arms because you are breaking the embargo, and they pay handsomely for it. Somewhere in the middle of the ocean en route to D, you turn off your transponder, and nobody knows where you are, and nobody's going to notice one missing blip on their screens. Even if they did bother to look, there's hundreds of thousands of ships coming and going twenty-four seven all over the world, so it's a pretty safe bet you'll get away with it."

Justin tried to find a flaw in her logic, and had one question. "Why would E want to involve itself in a dodgy operation?"

"Simples." She quoted the Meerkat advert. "Money."

"But they ought to be making money anyway. Aren't they?

"They would if they were honest, but this way they avoid paying shed loads of tax, and some of the cash generated probably goes into crypto currency which is hard to scrutinise, but it could include diamonds, gold, or even drugs. Again, no tax."

"Sooner or later, someone's bound to notice that Es figures don't add up."

Patricia was pleased with herself that she had explained

the conundrum in such a way that was understandable. "Exactly, and that is what my brief is. To find out why E is not producing as much crude as it ought."

"You mentioned twists, but only one so far."

"Up to now, I've kept it really simple because there's a lot more going on here than I've just told you, and I didn't want to muddy the waters by giving you too much information. I'm so glad we agree on that front, because I can now put that to one side and concentrate on the other parts of this business."

"Now hold on a minute." Said Justin in a tone that betrayed scepticism. "I only arrived at that conclusion because of the way you put it to me. There may be other factors here that I don't know about, and might lead me to a different conclusion. Ideally one would want to double-blind the facts."

"I know, but you did ask me if I wanted your help, and that was the simplest way of explaining it to you. If I told you about all the peripheral stuff, we'd still be here scratching our heads at sunset."

"Fair enough. By the sounds of it, you've got a good platform from which to hypothesise further from."

"One has to start somewhere."

"Right then. Tell me who the A to Es are."

She pointed the wrong end of her biro at the page. "A is our starting point with a tanker called the Pan Maru. B will be somewhere in the Middle East because that where most of the oil fields are. Forget the Americas for the moment. Your C destination could be almost anywhere in Europe. Say Rotterdam or Portugal, but it could include any country off The Mediterranean, or even the UK. E is the Blue Lizard rig off the Irish coast and run by unscrupulous people who have contacts with D, which could be South Africa, or one of the West African nations that have fallen into disfavour with the United Nations. Hence the embargo at D. Somewhere along the line, Blue Lizard E acquired Tanker A and controls where it loads and unloads; sometimes legitimately to maintain a façade, sometimes not."

She looked at him while he mulled this over. He spoke after a sip from his lukewarm mug. "It seems to me that there would need to be a lot of people involved, because you can't just sail a tanker single-handed, so let's look at that part of the operation. Apart from the Captain of the... whatsit Maru, the entire crew must be in on it, because it's not rocket science for them to work out what's going on. The... "

"Hold it there a minute, because that's exactly what happened to The Salem a few decades ago. Remember I mentioned it a couple of days ago? Big insurance fraud, so let's discard that as being impossible. It has happened before and can do so again."

"Alright, I'll go along with that for the moment. How about those on the rig? They must realise that there's something underhand going on."

"Not necessarily, because tankers will draw up from time to time to fill up. As far as the rig crew are concerned, the Pan Maru is just another tanker. But you're right up to a point, because those in control of the rig must have had orders to release the crude oil to one tanker or another at certain pre-determined times and dates. It's not like a filling station where one can stop off if you're running low on petrol. The tanker itineraries are arranged weeks and months in advance, usually through brokers, but if you've got your own tanker, you don't need to tell anyone outside of the operation."

Justin pondered. "Ok. What about the embargoed countries? Someone would have had to have made high level contacts, possibly at ministerial level, for this to happen. I know nothing about how the oil brokering system works, but I'm pretty sure you cannot just rock-up at a port in a tanker and say you've got half-a-million gallons you want to sell. It would need to be someone senior in the organisation who has met with those concerned. Say it was Ethiopia that had sanctions against them, one would need letters of credit and accreditation to meet the appropriate government official. That all takes time."

"Again, not necessarily. If you've already got the name of that government official, or officials, all you would need to give them is a date when their oil will be delivered, and then you walk away with whatever form of payment you already agreed."

Justin went to take another sip, but decided against drinking cold tea. "What else can you tell me?"

Patricia retrieved one of her pieces of paper. "I'm trying to find out where the initial investment money for the Blue Lizard Oil Company came from, but so far, I've only got as far as Baku and possibly a gentleman in Riyadh in Saudi Arabia. Companies House doesn't hold in depth information, and it wasn't a help that the initial incorporation took place in Eire. But I've yet to have the analysed information from what was found on the rig's computer, and I'm hoping that Donnelly's phone has been decrypted. It's what I'm about to do next." She motioned towards her laptop on the table.

"So you're trying to find the man at the top who you presume is giving the orders?"

"Not quite yet, and if he is our Saudi gentleman, then he's most likely to be diplomatically protected, and anyway, he's probably unaware of what's going on. No, the man I'm now convinced who's making the day-to-day running is Donnelly, and I think there's an intermediary, possibly in Baku, between him and our Saudi gent. I have also considered that there'll be a syndicate of owners at Blue Lizard, rather than just one man, but I don't know who they are. That's not high on my priority list, because Donnelly wouldn't want most of them knowing what he's up to, so they'd be ignorant and useless to my investigation. Oh, and by the way, I reckon that Hamilton has his sticky fingers in this pie somewhere along the line, so if there's any chance, we can nail him at the same time."

Justin groaned and rolled his eyes. "Not again."

"Yep, but that's peripheral at the moment, so we can come to him later."

"Well, Donnelly must have someone else in his confidence, because he couldn't pull this off from his arm chair." Justin looked at his near-empty mug as if searching for an answer; then had an inspiration. "The captain of the Maru must be well tied up in all of this." They both thought about that for a moment. "He'd be the chap who's travelling worldwide with their precious cargo. He's the one who's taking the lion's share of the risks, and he'd have to have his entire crew in on it as well,"

Patricia picked up on his train of thought. "That rig hasn't been producing nearly enough oil for years, so in all that time, the captain would have had numerous chances to meet the right sort of people to deal with; all over the world. You're right. He's a major part of the equation." She made a note on her page of facts.

"But not the Baku man." Justin added.

"No, not him. He'd be another armchair chap."

"Then it seems one must find out all one can of the current whereabouts of the Pan Maru, where it's been, where's it's going and who it's captain is."

"Unless he's got his transponder turned off, but I'll see if our computer Doris can help." She reached for her laptop, plugged in her security dongle and went through the rigid security protocols. Once it had connected her to the main frame, she typed in a series of questions.

"Want a cuppa?" Asked Justin on his way to the kitchen. Five minutes later he handed her a mug.

She tasted it and nearly spat it out. "Ugh. What's this?"

"Hot chocolate."

"Hot chocolate." She repeated scornfully.

"Oh, I forgot to tell you… I had the last tea bag, so I thought I'd see if your sense of taste was still working." He grinned at her, half expecting a playful smack round the head; but it never came. Instead she just shook her head in exasperation at his childish prank.

"What does Doris say?"

"It's coming through now." They didn't have long to wait before Doris supplied answers. "Looks like the captain's name is Michael Windaw from Ireland and he's been the skipper of the Pan Maru for some ten years. He'd have had all the time in the world to pick a willing crew with few scruples, and come to that, from any port worldwide. That timeframe fits in with Blue Lizard's."

"How long did you say Blue Lizard's been operating? Asked Justin.

Before she could answer on her own, they both said it at the same time while looking at each other. "About ten years."

"Right then, let's see if Doris knows what the Pan Maru's been up to." She scrolled down the page a bit further and hovered the mouse indicator over an extensive itinerary covering the last five years. Sitting side by side on the sofa, it wasn't easy to pick out the dates, ports, cargo manifests which invariably consisted of crude oil, bunkering, lists of crew members and their nationalities, bills of lading, who had brokered which deal, buyers and sellers, insurers, docking fees… the list continued and was extensive.

"Bloody hell." Remarked Justin. If this is a sample of only one vessel over the past five years, just think of the amount of information someone's got to sift through if they're looking for something."

"The important thing is that this information is available, and we need to sift through it to find what it's been up to."

Justin looked at his watch. "Listen, you start trawling. I've a phone call to make. Won't be too long; I hope."

Patricia was faced with the problem of where

to start, and chose the first of January three years previously. On second thoughts, she got up and picked a small atlas on the bookshelf and set it beside her on the sofa. She'd never heard of some of the places it had called at, and she soon realised it would be quicker to open a map of the world on her laptop.

On her notepad, she listed the name places and put a tick next to each one every time the Pan Maru had been there. She soon got a picture of its regular trips. It would usually collect the crude oil in the Arabian Gulf, and deliver it to mainly European destinations, sometimes through the Suez Canal, sometimes via Liberia, sometimes via Portugal, and often via Capetown in South Africa. On the odd occasion, it would visit Goa in India, and on one occasion it went as far north as Reykjavik in Iceland.

The modern Whan shipyard in South Korea specialised in building oil and LPG tankers to their customers' specific requirements and had a healthy order book covering the next five years. Blqutab Star Offshore Marine Services based in Baniyas, Syria, ordered one such Aframax class oil tanker late in 1989. Typical of that class of tanker, it only needed na crew of twenty-one to operate despite it having a deadweight of some 115,000 tonnes, and being 232 metres long. It was unfortunate that it was the last of that class to be powered by relatively inefficient MAN diesels, and was rather uneconomical to run; at least by today's standards.

Soon after it was launched and commissioned in mid-1990, it was bareboat-chartered to The Super Petroleum Company, registered and operating from Accra in

Ghana on the west African coast. Almost immediately, The Super Petroleum Company went bankrupt, and the tanker was left marooned in an estuary, off the oil terminal in Banjul in The Gambia. After four years of legal haggling by various parties as to who owed what to whom, it was sold to a newly-formed French consortium whose offices were in Abidjan in The Ivory Coast.

At first, trading went smoothly, but the years of languishing and neglect in the unrelenting heat of The Gambia soon started to take its toll on the aging engines as well as the other mechanical workings; and she had developed a leak through her propeller shaft. The new owners, realising their mistake, sold it on at the first opportunity, and over the next few years it chugged inefficiently up and down the West African coast under different, sometimes dubious, operators.

It seemed as though she was destined for the breakers yard when it came to the attention of Windaw. Donnelly raised the funds and at a knockdown price, she was rescued, waterproofed, given a lick of paint here and there, and the leak repaired without changing the engines. All through her history, with changes of ownership came changes of names, but the Pan Maru was now on her final voyage; if Windaw and Donnelly had anything to do with it.

She soon realised that this obfuscation of beneficial ownership was one way to avoid scrutiny by global authorities, and she could now see why it suited Blue Lizard's brief.

She vaguely registered that the front door slammed in the wind and heard Justin go into the kitchen as she concentrated on the amounts of crude it was taking on board. That task was relatively easy, since it was just about the same volume of about 90,000 barrels on each occasion.

Next, with the aim of seeing if it had stopped off somewhere unknown, she started to put dates to those ports and tried to work out how long a journey from one to the next took. It was almost an impossible task as it never took the same length of time on those regular routes. Two weeks was an average on one route, nearly two months on another. Probably dependent upon the weather, she thought to herself.

Justin came and sat down next to her and asked the inevitable question. "How's it going?"

"Not too bad, but I could do with some help on these dates."

"Ok. What have you got?"

She showed him her pad of paper. "I'm hoping to come across a gap between two ports to see if it deviated anywhere, but it's so weather dependant, I'm not sure we can rely on what we find; if anything."

She started by reading off ports and dates which Justin dutifully noted down. They were still at it two hours later, and she'd nearly had enough. She leaned back on the sofa, shut her eyes, and let her mind wander, and rather think about the Pan Maru, her mind wandered in the direction of the rig. At least that didn't move anywhere. Then, out of nowhere, she remembered that she hadn't properly looked over the oil production figures. Someone had been killed trying to extract that information, so it must have significant relevance, perhaps even the key, to what was happening.

She left Justin working out itineraries etcetera, and instead sought Doris's opinion. Yet again, there were enough figures to fill a bath with, but one of the backroom boys had written his summary at the end. It concluded that while production figures didn't match the output figures, or any other figures, this was down to algorithms on the rig's computer that had been designed to produce false results.

Proof at last perhaps, but she kicked herself for not picking up on the subject sooner.

*****

Had Windaw known that he and the Pan Maru were being scrutinised to such an extent from thousands of miles away, he might have considered turning it around, and sailing across the Atlantic to some out of the way destination. However, he wouldn't have considered it for long, as he knew that this was to be the Pan Maru's final voyage, with a very healthy pay off at the end of the rainbow.

It would be more than inconvenient if the arrangements that he and Donnelly had set up over the past few years had to be changed at the last minute. It might take them half a lifetime to come up with another lucrative scheme. Short of being boarded by pirates, or worse still, accosted by the Royal Navy, nothing was going to stop his rendezvous with Donnelly at the rig. Perhaps that storm that had emanated somewhere in The Caribbean and was heading across The Atlantic in an easterly direction might slow him down a little, but he wasn't overly concerned. They'd all felt the lash of heavy rain and the swell of the sea as the leading edge of the weather front passed over them; even on a tanker as large as the Pan Maru. He'd endured worse in the South China Seas.

Playing on his mind was his human cargo of so called refugees he'd collected off the Liberian coast a few days earlier. They weren't quite like the usual docile bunch he'd transported before, and he blamed that on one individual in particular. Ever since their ringleader had embarked, he'd been trouble. For a start, there were more of them on this trip than he had agreed, and he didn't have quite enough provisions for nearly three hundred of them, so had had to cut down on their daily rations. They'd even managed to smuggle a couple of baby goats on board, and he thought he could almost smell them from his cabin. He instinctively sniffed at his clothing again.

He was looking at the weather chart on his repeater, when there was a familiar knock on his door. "Come in Tenmil." His first mate had always had the same offbeat rat-a-tat for as long as they had known each other; not so much as a secret code, but more of a natural way of announcing oneself.

The unusually tall Indian ducked just a little as he entered the captain's cabin. He hadn't needed to duck, but years of going through doorways had taught him to be circumspect; despite the number of times he had visited Windaw in his cabin. His height was the reason why they had first met. Windaw had finished concluding his business with a nefarious character behind the fish market in Goa just as Tenmil was passing.

Out of nowhere came a man on a bicycle, carrying a bundle of long thick poles over his shoulder, and as he turned a corner, the back end of them caught Tenmil on the head, knocking him to the ground, right at Windaw's feet. He immediately looked round to see if this was part of a scam, but nobody nearby was threatening. It was clearly a genuine accident, partially due to Tenmil's height. If he hadn't been so tall, the poles would have sailed over his head.

Nobody seemed to be paying any attention, but he couldn't just ignore the fact that there was a man sprawled over his feet, preventing immediate escape from the situation. He bent down and cupped Tenmil's head in his hands, and saw the chap's eyes begin to refocus. No real harm done then he thought, and he was about to leave the man to recover in his own way when an arm snaked out and grasped his. Windaw's natural reaction was to withdraw, but the grip on his forearm was such that the fallen man used it to haul himself up off the ground. They stood facing each other momentarily, before Tenmil changed his grip to shake Windaw's hand.

"Thank you for that." Tenmil's English was clear with a neutral accent, and with a brief shake of his head he asked. "How can I repay you?"

"You can let go of my hand for a start." Windaw retorted tersely.

Tenmil did as he was told. "It's not every day that one meets someone who helps another round here." He motioned with his head off to his right. "Those people over there would more than likely have robbed me if you'd left me on the ground."

Windaw cast his gaze in the direction of a gang of layabouts idling around an old oil drum, then turned back to examine the man in front of him. He was a good head taller, dressed in a clean white smock-like garment, but what impressed him was that he didn't smell; especially of fish. It might have seemed strange to others, but Windaw really didn't like the smell of fish; particularly wet fish. The man's clear bluish eyes didn't waver or look away when met by his gaze, which he found reassuring. In his experience, he found that those whose eyes darted to and fro tended to be untrustworthy.

"Well, you can give me your name which I might or might not remember."

"Tenmil Brajan, and I must thank you properly."

Windaw was in no hurry to return to his ship, as he didn't want others to see the Pan Maru depart during daylight hours, and he therefore had nothing to lose by accepting a gift from a stranger. "All right then. You can buy me a drink."

"I know just the place. Follow me."

He followed Tenmil down one alley, then another narrower one, until they entered a decrepit, colonial-built building not more than a couple of hundred yards from where they had started. It was a haunt obviously known to Tenmil, since the man behind the counter at the far end acknowledged their presence with a wave of his hand.

Windaw introduced himself as a mere officer of a ship, without mentioning which one, just as two beers arrived at their table. He then endured Tenmil's story about how his second cousin's uncle's father or whatever, had once been one of the local Rajas many years ago, andow his well-off father had sent him to England for his education. At one point, he had been tutored by a Mrs. Roberts who had rapped his knuckles with a ruler every time he mispronounced a word incorrectly. His father had been a well-connected but terrible businessman, but before the family money ran out he'd completed his degree in cartography.

Through his father's links, he'd picked up a job with the Goan government surveying underwater reefs and wrecks, and was responsible for producing legible charts for the tourist industry. He was fired from his job when their boat hit one of those reefs that he was supposed to know about, and was instead given a desk job in the finance department where his employers thought he couldn't sink any more boats. Surrounded by dullards who pushed paper around, he found he had a superb acumen for figures, and was soon advising senior officials on how best to control available funds to their advantage; particularly on the gold exchange. At weekends, and as a bit of variety, he would go out with the local fishermen and point out where the wrecks were, as this was where there were certain sought-after types of fish. It also helped to make ends meet.

It was only towards the end of his monologue that Windaw picked up on what he had been saying, particularly at the mention of gold, because that was the reason he had come to Goa in the first place. His thoughts centred around Tenmil's connections and who he could name if there was a better deal to be had. He knew there were corrupt officials, attested to by his latest transaction, but it would undoubtedly be more profitable if one could cut out one of the middle men.

He applied his shrewd mind on how he could best utilise the young man, and came up with a plan.

Six weeks later his plan was going tits-up, and he blamed Tenmil even though it hadn't been the lad's fault. As darkness fell, he gave orders to cast-off even though his navigator was still ashore. He wanted away from Goa because someone had got wind of his new deal and had alerted the authorities. The last thing he wanted to do was to be held for questioning, and if they searched his ship, they might even find the gold he had stashed away, hence his hurry to cast-off from the jetty quickly.

From the wing of his bridge, he oversaw the last of the gangway lashings being removed, and then from across the oil terminal he saw Tenmil running towards him. He didn't have time to argue with the lad, or countermand his own orders, and watched the lad jump the last few feet onto his ship.

After the inevitable row between them, he told Tenmil that as he no longer had a navigation officer, he would be it until he could find a replacement at their next port. That was nearly ten years ago.

"What's up mate?" He asked as Tenmil closed the door behind him.

"We may have trouble."

"When haven't we had trouble?"

"Their ringleader says he wants us to take them to Dover, not Ireland."

It took about three seconds before Windaw burst out laughing, and more than twice as long before he stopped. "Why the fuck would anyone want to go to Dover? It's a shithole. And anyway, there aren't any facilities for a tanker of this size to dock there." He spoke as though the matter was now closed.

"No. This is more serious....."

"How can it be more serious? We're going to the rig and you can tell them that's final."

"They have guns." Tenmil added with an inflection that carried a warning.

Windaw considered this for a moment. "I'm not going to ask how they got them, because if they can smuggle goats on board, they can smuggle guns. They're easier to hide. How many have they got?"

"At least two. I saw one pistol and maybe a larger automatic of some kind."

"Well, we've got guns too, but I don't want to break them out unless we have to, because that'll unsettle the crew. What's their leader's name and where are they now?"

"The ringleader's name is Omar and he has the pistol. What looks like being his son has the other weapon, and they're waiting for us in the dining area."

Windaw mulled this over for a moment. "Right. Go and fetch Haggis here and tell him to bring his blade with him, but to hide it."

Haggis's real name was Hamish and he was a massive six-and-a-half footer from Glasgow in Scotland. Windaw had seen him fight in a bar a few years ago, and had immediately recognised that if push came to shove, Haggis was a handy person to have your back. Which was why he was one of the crew.

It only took ten minutes for the familiar rat-a-tat, but this time, Tenmil didn't wait to be asked to enter; Haggis had to duck down further.

Windaw had wisely used those ten minutes to consider the best plan of action without recourse to guns. Those sorts of weapons were strictly forbidden on vessels, and there were very severe consequences if just one was discovered by the authorities; this applied the world over. Only Windaw and Tenmil knew where theirs were hidden. "Right, it's not often I like being diplomatic, but diplomacy is called for on this occasion, so this is what I want you to do." He explained until he was satisfied they understood.

An hour or so later, he and Tenmil returned to his cabin and dropped the two weapons on the sideboard; Haggis had resumed his duties in the engine room.

"That went rather well." Remarked Tenmil.

"Give the buggers an inch and they think they can take a mile. Bloody liberty takers." They both swayed a little as the ship ploughed into another deep trough. "I tell you, never trust a nomad." Windaw referred to all black men as nomads.

"You trust Haggis."

"Yeah well, he's different isn't he." He conceded. Although Haggis was born and bred Scottish, and had the abrasive Glaswegian accent, his skin was even darker than those they were transporting.

"That was a master stroke, you introducing him halfway through. What gave you that idea?"

Windaw reflected over how he had handled the tricky incident. Once Omar and his delegation of refugees had explained that they had heard that Dover was the best place to land in England, he'd asked them where they had got this information from. Omar had said that his brother was already in England and was being treated far better than back in Liberia. Apparently, it was the World War II song about the white cliffs of Dover that had convinced him when they had set off from France in an inflatable dingy.

He'd turned to Haggis who had been standing next to him, and asked him to explain to them that the refugee camp at Dover was just temporary, and that they would be transported elsewhere after a while. This, coming from a man of similar skin colour hadn't convinced them enough, but once Windaw pointed out that the port of Dover was a small ferry port and that it was impossible for them to dock, their attitude changed. Fine for inflatables, but no good for tankers, he'd added. The clincher was when he told them how the Royal Navy would come aboard, and if they found those guns, then the whole lot of them would be arrested and sent back to Liberia.

"I don't think Omar even knows where Dover is, and did you notice that he was looking a bit sea sick?"

"I think all of them were. Serves them bloody right."

The ship lurched a little too much for comfort. "I think we'd better go and check on the bridge. Who's on watch?" Asked Windaw.

"Jerry and Roger."

"Probably Ok then, but I'd be happier just checking that there's nothing amiss. Come on."

Nothing appeared to be amiss, but the storm was

certainly battering the tanker. "In view of this nasty little storm and the swell, we'll delay our docking with the rig until the following morning, and not at night as arranged, but keep her speed up to maintain steerage." Windaw received an acknowledgement from Jerry, and returned to his cabin to make a phone call. When he got there, he checked again that his oversized sea chest, hidden behind a curtain, hadn't been tampered with. It hadn't.

* * * * *

"We're getting nowhere with this." Declared Patricia as she stood up and stretched her arms and legs. "Back in a mo."

She returned a few minutes later with a glass of water. "We've not found anything out of the ordinary, so let's look at it from a different angle. How about I check the transponder tracks with Doris?"

"Good idea. I'm just about done with the loading and offloading figures."

They sat in silence, each pursuing their own lines.

"Ok. I might have something here." Patricia's comment was hesitant.

"What's that?" Justin didn't look up.

She carried on scrolling for a bit before continuing. "Let me go back a bit further."

Justin came to the end of his calculations, waited another minute, and looked over at her. "Well?"

She carriedon with her scrutiny. "Over the past six years, the Pan Maru's transponder has either been broken, disabled or deliberately turned off in various places."

"Which places and is there a pattern?"

"I'm just working on that now... here we go. Look."

Displayed on a flat picture of the globe were yellow lines depicting the Pan Maru's course. Those lines multiplied with each chronological journey going back six years, thickening where the tanker's route had criss-crossed its own track. As she focussed in on The Arabian Gulf, the lines separated a little more with each incremental zoom. She traced the routes that all started off from the oil terminals and went in a southerly direction; this was due to the geographical constraints of The Gulf. From there, nearly all lines continued down the East African coast and round The Cape of Good Hope before turning north up the West African coast and beyond. The Suez Canal was seldom used, but occasionally the yellow lines went east towards India.

" certainly gets about, doesn't he?" Remarked Justin.

"Yes, but look at this one." She zoomed-in on an area off The Horn of Africa where a yellow line stopped in the middle of nowhere.

Justin leaned forwards a little more. "I think that's where the Houthi pirates operate isn't it?"

"Maybe he turned it off to avoid detection?" She hypothesised. "But let's have a look elsewhere, away from The Gulf." She moused the cursor across the screen to the west side of Africa. "Look, here's another."

"And another there." Pointed Justin. "What's that further down?"

A yellow line stopped and started again off Cape Town.

They both came to the same conclusion simultaneously; that Captain Windaw was being a naughty boy by turning the transponder on and off.

"The sneaky bugger's up to something he shouldn't be, and my guess is that he's smuggling oil into embargoed countries."

"Or anywhere else where it's profitable." Added Justin.

"Hang on a mo. Let's have a look at the area around Blue Lizard's rig." Once the cursor hovered over the area, there was a dearth of yellow lines; until she zoomed-out and saw several of them truncating in the mid-Atlantic, well outside of the normal shipping routes. "That's what he's doing. He's disappearing out of sight of other ships when he nears Blue Lizard, so that nobody can see he's been there. He'll pick up oil and sell it wherever he likes."

"Off the grid, when it suits him. Looks like he turns it on again when he's rejoins the shipping lanes, and becomes just another blip on a screen, among thousands of others. Who's going to notice that?"

They both sat back. "Cracked it." Commented a satisfied Patricia.

"Not yet we haven't, because if challenged, he can just turn around and say that it's a faulty transponder, or even a temporary one while the other is being repaired. Anything but the truth. Where is he now?"

Overlooked by Justin, she leaned forward again and played the screen. "Oh shit. He must have it turned off again. Look. The line stops soon after he left Cape Town, and that was over a week ago."

After a moment, Justin rhetorically volunteered what Patricia was beginning to think. "He's on his way to Blue Lizard, isn't he? Ok then. Let's try and work out how long it will take him to get there, and see if we can't arrange a reception committee. Catch them in the act."

"If we're not too late already."

"Let's make a plan then."

"Hold on a sec. If Windaw's stopping off at Blue Lizard to top up, I'll bet Donnelly's going to be there as well." He let her think about that for a moment. "The Pan Maru must have empty tanks when it arrives, so where did it discharge its oil? What was its last port of call?"

She returned to her screen, and after a while announced "Port Nolloth in South Africa."

"Never heard of it, but it's possible that's where he discharged."

"Not likely, because there's no oil terminal there." She read from her laptop after checking.

"So he must have had another reason for calling-in there… like collecting his pay-off for the oil. Maybe in gold or diamonds, because the Rand isn't worth much these days."

Chapter 16

As usual, Windaw kept his conversation brief on his satellite phone call to Donnelly, but still explained the reason why the Pan Maru would not be docking at the rig until the morning. "You do know there's nearly three hundred of them nomads on board don't you? Are you sure the boat you've got collecting them is large enough?"

Donnelly had to think about that one for all of a second; his mate's trawler had only ever taken a little over a hundred before, but he'd never bothered to ask about available space. He didn't really care if it was big enough, but if not, he might have to tell him to make a second trip. "Did they all pay?" Was his only question.

"Oh, don't worry about that. There's well over a million in the pot. Just you be there, but I might have to wait a bit if the swell's too great."

* * * *

Patricia didn't need a satellite phone to talk to Commander Gibbons. She only had a mobile, and anyway, she had to go through Tates to reach him. She had more than half prepared what she was going to say to him in advance, and knowing that the Commander appreciated short and accurate reports, kept it as brief as she could. She concluded her report stating that time was of the essence, and that the Pan Maru might already be docked at the rig.

"So what course of action do you propose?"

"I need to get out to the rig again first thing in the morning, and want to arrive soon after daybreak. Can you arrange a helicopter for us?"

"Us?" He queried.

"I want to take Justin Crawford with me in the guise of a mechanical engineer." She didn't waste time explaining why, or that she had divulged to Justin most of what was going on.

"Go on."

"I also want international arrest warrants for Jason Donnelly and Michael Windaw." Silence, so she continued. "I'll also need some form of back-up to take them into custody."

Again, a moment of silence while Gibbons considered her requests. He also briefly measured his own position, should she be wrong. "And what if the Pan Maru isn't there?"

"If it's not there, it'll be nearby."

"From what you're telling me, all the hard evidence will be on that ship. Correct?"

"Yes sir."

"So what we must do first is find it."

"Sir, if we wait, it'll be gone, along with all the evidence."

"I'll get back to you shortly."

"Just one more thing, sir. It would be rather unfortunate if Maurice Hamilton got to hear of this."

"Understood." He terminated the call.

* * * * *

As well as running along the river path, Miles Glen liked to keep fit by working out at gyms not too far away from his flat in Sunbury-on-Thames, and to avoid any discernible pattern he rarely visited the same one twice in succession. He also enjoyed the power of his Subaru Legacy that he drove to and from one or another; depending upon the time of day and the traffic.

Early in the afternoon, on his way back from one such gym, he received a text on his mobile, pulled over at a petrol station, and read it. He was used to receiving basic instructions by text which normally required him to attend on Commodore Waters in Northwood. On this occasion, he was ordered to report directly to Lieutenant Commander Greensmith commanding HMS Cutter, currently docked in Portsmouth, by 18.00 hours. The message advised him that his sealed orders would be handed to him there.

He looked at his watch, and knew he had enough time to return to his flat, collect his equipment and change into his uniform. Before he engaged first gear, he smiled to himself at the prospect of driving down the A3 at high speed in his Legacy without threat of retribution from the traffic police.

* * * * *

Hamilton put his brand new Bentley away in his cleanly-swept garage, helped himself to a good portion of pork pie adorned with English mustard, and sat down at his desk. His mobile alerted him to an incoming text from Donnelly which told him to arrive at the rig no earlier than ten in the morning. 'Two hundred and fifty grand' was all he could think about at the time. What he didn't know was that Donnelly didn't want him seeing the boat load of migrants being offloaded on to the trawler, hence the specific arrival time.

*****

'… A fast-moving warm front crossing the Atlantic… ' was announced by the girl on the radio in the kitchen. Patricia paused while spreading ketchup on their bacon sandwiches, and hoped it wouldn't get in the way with what she had planned for tomorrow. She put the plates down on the table in front of the sofa as Justin continued his pacing round the room with his phone to his ear. He suddenly stopped, and she looked up at him in reaction to his expletive. He turned to look down at her as he finished his call.

"You're never going to believe this, but remember I said I won a grand at Ascot on a horse called 'Lucky Bamboo' at twenty-to-one? Well, I've been investigating a syndicate that seemed to be producing winners out of nowhere and staking large amounts on the odds, screwing the bookies out of serious funds." He looked at her, wondering if she might be able to figure out what was coming next. "You can guess who's involved with that syndicate, can't you?"

She knew the answer before she said it. "Hamilton."

"Yup. Bloody Hamilton yet again. But the best thing

now is that the man I was speaking to just now says he's prepared to make a statement, and with that, we can nail the bastard all the way to the gallows. Furthermore, he's got a colleague who also wants to testify, because they haven't been given their pay off."

"Oh God, I hope this gets us a result.."

"So do I, but I can't meet this character until next weekend, when he's over next. Do you think you'll be available then?" Justin knew that if Patricia was present when the statement was made, then his case would be all the more watertight.

"That ought to dovetail in nicely if we can finish this Blue Lizard job in time." She reached for her phone as it rang. Recognising the number, she put it on loud speaker so that Justin could hear.

"Tates here. The Commander has acceded to your requests, and the arrest warrants you asked for will be waiting for you at Northwood. There will also be a letter of authorisation from the Irish government, even though the rig is in international waters. EEC rules are applicable, but only as far as operations are concerned, otherwise rules of the sea apply. The Commander wanted me to remind you that under international law, you have the power to detain any person you suspect of piracy, kidnapping, bodily injury or murder. Smuggling's not on that list because you'll be on the high seas. To assist you with any detentions, a Royal Navy boat is being dispatched from Portsmouth and ought to be in the vicinity of the rig around mid-morning. Your communication codes including your identification protocols will be made available to you at Northwood.

Also at Northwood, Mr. Crawford's identity badge will be issued to him before you board your helicopter, which is due to take-off at 04.00 tomorrow morning." He paused. "Is that all clear?"

There was much to digest in one go, but Patricia was satisfied that she had all that she had asked for; plus a little more, so she confirmed as much with Tates. "Any questions?" He asked in a tone that suggested there ought not to be any.

"Just one. This is obviously legally sanctioned by the British government, but who has overall operational control? The Royal Navy or myself?"

Tates wasn't expecting that one, and delayed his response. "I'll have to ask The Commander. You'll know before you take off. Anything else?"

"Not at the moment." As an afterthought before he rang off, she added. "Thanks, Tates."

Justin had been silently listening in on the conversation. "Bloody hell, that was fast. Somebody up there seems to want to put an end to Blue Lizard and associated crooks. Talking of crooks, if Hamilton is wrapped up in all of this, he'll be one of the first to be told, and we know what a slippery bastard he is when forewarned."

"Shit, of course. We've got to make sure that Hamilton is incommunicado when we arrest the others, How the hell do we do that?"

"We don't know where he is, but perhaps Tates might be able to find out."

"Good idea. I'll text him."

"One other thought, because this is happening ever so fast." He rubbed his chin as if deciding to raise his query. "Could it be that if everything goes wrong, Gibbons has nominated you as the patsy?"

It wasn't an idea that had crossed her mind, but after thinking about it, she dismissed Justin's notion as unlikely. Certainly, if things went awry, then she'd justifiably be the one to blame. She was determined to make sure that they wouldn't.

Chapter 17

On the Portsmouth quay where HMS Cutter was docked, Lieutenant Miles Glen of the Royal Marines stood crisply to attention as he saluted Lieutenant Commander Greensmith.

"3 Commando eh?"

"Yes sir." Miles dropped his right hand.

Greensmith handed Miles a buff envelope, sealed with a red stripe. "The base captain handed this to me just before you arrived, so I presume this will not be a training exercise."

"I presume so too, sir." He responded in a flat monotone; not wanting to reveal that he too didn't know what was within.

"When we get to know each other a little better, you can call me Tug, but not in front of the crew."

Miles recognised Greensmith's friendly gesture, and immediately knew that they would get along. "Yes sir." He purposefully didn't try to correct his response.

"You'd better come aboard as we're due to sail shortly. Stow your gear starboard forward."

Miles followed him onto the Cutlass Class patrol boat that he estimated as being about eighty feet long, noting that the paintwork smelt new as he went below. He wasn't familiar with this type of vessel, but had read that the fast interceptor had a top speed of about forty knots and could berth more than a dozen crew. Primarily, this class of boat was not so much different from her predecessor, but the three Volvo engines were more reliable, particularly in rough seas. Miles didn't have the luxury of a cabin, but he saw he would be sharing a narrow space in which there were two other berths; he noted that there were three other empty ones on the port side.

After placing his rucksack on the upper most bunk, he opened and digested the contents of the envelope. He smiled at the thought of teaming up with Patricia Eyethorne again, and silently laughed at his remembrance of her cursing Donnelly in a back street in the city of Cork a few days ago. He knew she was good, but only now appreciated how good she actually was. Anyone who could inaugurate an operation such as this deserved respect.

He joined Greensmith topside.

"How old is she?"

"Three years old last week, and yes we did crack a bottle of champagne over her bows to celebrate her birthday. Very sturdy boat and not too shabby when it comes to standing up to an unhealthy westerly. Talking of which, I see there's a bit of a storm that we're supposed to be heading through, but apparently it'll be short-lived."

His comment gave Miles an easy opening. "I assume you've received orders to arrive in The Celtic Sea tomorrow morning."

"We have, and at best possible speed, but not the precise location. Let's wait to go over the details until Second Lieutenant Shaw can join us, as I don't like repeating myself. I've put him in charge of getting us under way, which ought to be in the next few minutes." He looked at his watch, and from the expression on his face, Miles could almost tell that if Lieutenant Shaw was late, he'd be thrown overboard.

That didn't turn out to be the case, as at precisely 18.00, HMS Cutter slipped her moorings and motored down towards The Solent at an easy ten knots. They passed Spinnaker Tower off to port, but before they reached No Man's Fort, Shaw increased their speed, so that all aboard had to angle themselves to take the in the extra rake of the decks. Once past Bembridge on The Isle of Wight, and out of the main shipping lanes, Shaw handed over to The Coxswain and joined the other two officers at the chart table below.

It wasn't overly loud, so they didn't need to raise their voices too much to be heard, and in deference to his appointment as master of the vessel, they waited for Greensmith to finish studying the chart before he spoke. "I know our approximate destination and what time we're due to arrive there, but are you at liberty to tell us why?"

"Only if everyone on board is incommunicado."

Greensmith looked at Shaw, who didn't need to be told what to do. He left the senior pair and went to ensure that it stayed that way; he was back within a minute.

"The short story is that we'll be docking at an oil rig and providing assistance to detain certain criminal elements. The longer story is this." Miles went on to explain what he could without compromising what he already knew from his previous excursion on the rig, and what his orders stated. He thought it wise not to mention that he had previously worked alongside Inspector Eyethorne.

"We'll be hard pushed to make it there before 12.00 hours tomorrow." Remarked Shaw, once Miles had ceased speaking. "The Met Office shows that the storm front is weakening, but moving rather quickly, and from my calculations, we'll be passing through it around 0900 hours. Ought to be a lot calmer once we're through."

"Well, we'd better get a move-on now, while we can, hadn't we?" Greensmith looked at Shaw, who scuttled off to see to it. Almost immediately, the boat surged forward at a faster pace; Greensmith and Miles needed to grab a rail to steady themselves.

"I already knew about the weather front, but like to let Shaw think he's contributing; part of his training. It all depends upon the size of the swell, but we'll get there."

"Have you ever docked at a rig before?" Asked Miles.

"Oh yes. We once had to rescue half-a-dozen eco protesters from a North Sea platform. Silly buggers had tied themselves to one of the stanchions without realising that the tide was rising, and before you ask, yes, we did consider leaving them there for a couple of days. Just to teach them a lesson."

Shaw reappeared, lurching from one handrail to another with water dripping on to the deck. "It's starting to get a bit choppy already, and The Coxswain reports visibility down to under a mile."

*****

A haggard-looking Tates was waiting for Patricia and Justin in the brightly-lit hangar which housed the Sea King helicopter that would ferry them out to the rig; she noticed him glance at his watch, probably just to check if they were on time. Up to now, she had never realised just how large these helicopters were; this was reinforced as they followed Tates up the step ladder and embarked into the cavernous space behind the flight deck.

The three of them sat at the far end of one of the two scalloped benches with Tates at the other end; Justin had to crane his neck round Patricia to watch Tates open his briefcase. On the opposite bench, diagonally away from them, sat two armed men dressed in what looked like Commando equipment. Not part of the crew, thought Patricia, and she designated them as Hefty One and Hefty Two.

Tates glanced at them to make sure they were just out of earshot. "You really don't want to know how much this is costing the British taxpayer, and I can tell you now that The Commander had to twist a few tails to coordinate this operation."

Patricia was quick to pick up that it was probably Tates who had had to do most of the coordination throughout the night on Gibbons' orders, but she made sure that she didn't show it.

Tates opened a half-sized folder with clear plastic sleeves. "In the first one, you'll find your operational orders which includes authority over the Royal Navy vessel which is even now travelling to the Blue Lizard Rig, and ought to arrive around noon. This being a Fleet Air Arm helicopter, it also gives you command over it as well, but I have already briefed the pilots. If you're challenged, you can refer them to Commodore Janet Waters. Her direct line is at the bottom of the page. The second sleeve contains a letter from Patrick McEnilee who is the Irish minister in charge of the Department of Agriculture, Food and Marine. It was his department that granted Blue Lizard the licence in the first place, and it authorises you to operate inside Irish territory. I might add that he was happy enough to grant permission after those four men disappeared last week."

A head popped itself round the wide side entrance door that they had boarded through, and eyed up the occupants. "Ready when you are."

"Give us two minutes." Replied Tates.

The head disappeared, so Tates continued.

"In your the third sleeve are the international arrest warrants. Each warrant specifically names Jason Donnelly and Michael Windaw, but there are two more warrants which have yet to have their names filled in, as The Commander thought you would be likely to need them." He looked at Patricia to see if she had figured that one out, but when it was clear that she hadn't, he explained further. "They might have false passports, in which case the named warrants would be useless. You can fill in their names, but don't produce them unless you have to."

"That must have taken some doing." Commented Patricia.

"Don't ask. We've also detailed two sterling fellows from, well, I won't say where, but they're here to make sure you come back in one piece. I'll let them introduce themselves." The three of them looked at the pair of grim-looking fellows in the opposite corner. "Now, in the fourth sleeve are your communication details. Call signs and so forth so that you can liaise directly with

HMS Cutter." He paused, and added as an aside "I think you will find you have a friendly face on board in the form of Lieutenant Glen, who we've also lent you."

Patricia was indeed relieved to hear that, and this time she showed it.

"Thought you might like that snippet of information." He opened his briefcase, retrieved a small wallet and neck dangler ID badge holder. "Here's Mr. Crawford's warrant card confirming his appointment as an electrical hydro-engineer; backdated of course. That gives him a reason for being on this flight and latitude to go more or less where he wants to, once you land on the rig."

He shut and passed the entire folder to Patricia. "Do give me situation reports as often as you can, and I'll pass them on to The Commander. Finally, I have some useful tools for you." He looked over at one of the men sitting opposite, who grasped a large flight case and bought it over to them. "Apart from the communications equipment that you're both going to need, there are emergency location beacons and a selection of weapons. These men here will be able to help you with that."

He snapped the briefcase latches shut, rose, and went to exit down the step ladder, but turned at the last second. "Oh, and by the way, you might come across another familiar face soon after you arrive." He let the last piece of news hang; relishing the moment. "It seems the illustrious Maurice Hamilton will be joining you on the rig."

Patricia and Justin showed their incredulity, but Tates drew out the moment to its maximum before letting on. "He's ordered a government helicopter to take him out to the rig later this morning. Probably after he's had his breakfast."

He took the three steps down the ladder backwards. "Good hunting." No sooner had he gone, the steps were removed, the door shut, and the tug gently pulled the helicopter forwards, out of the hangar.

"That was stunning." Remarked Justin. "All that since yesterday afternoon. You really do have friends in high places."

Patricia had started to look through the folder, but ceased to look Justin in the eye. "Listen. Donnelly is a criminal of the first order and will stop at nothing to get what he wants. Three people have already been killed, probably more, so make no mistake, that unless we're careful, we might also be added to that list. I've no idea how many of his henchmen he has aboard the rig, so this is what I want you to do once we get there."

Justin was trying to pay attention to what he was being told, but this was a side of Patricia that he hadn't seen before, and at first, he admired her air of authority. Then he realised that he also was under her command, and had to ask her to go over her lengthy instructions again.

One of the two personnel sitting opposite got up, reached into a locker, handed them a Peltor headset each, then indicated that the jack socket was above their heads. He raised his voice above the engine whine as the pilots had commenced the start sequence. "You might want to buckle-up once you're connected. It's going to be a bit of a rough ride out there, due to a small storm. Just so that you know, we'll be refuelling at RAF St. Mawgan on the way out." It was obvious to him that neither of them had heard of St. Mawgan, so he enlightened them. "It's not too far from Newquay."

"What time do you reckon we'll reach the rig?" She asked.

"Depending upon the headwind, between 09.00 and 10.00."

Chapter 18

"Thank Christ that's over." Commented Windaw as the wind finally ceded her ferocity to a calmer and clearer sky. All though the night, they had endured a battering from the storm. The winds had generated forty foot troughs and had caused the Pan Maru into vicious corkscrew motions. They both stood close to the binnacle on the bridge, and watched the barometer needle visibly rotate clockwise, ever so slowly, as high pressure took command of the weather.

"You really don't want to go below." Commented Tenmil. "I've never seen so much puke. It's sloshing around all over the deck. And there's an incredibly horrible stench that goes with it. I think even one of the goats threw up."

Windaw wasn't concerned. "Get Efty to hose it down once we get rid of the buggers." He referred to his human cargo, most of whom had never been to sea before; and probably would never do so again after such a night. "What's our position now?"

It was a fair question as the night had yet to give up its darkness.

"About thirty miles south south-west of the rig."

"Right then. We'll circle round and approach from the north, but slowly. That'll give this storm front time to move on, and it'll just about be daylight by then.

Make sure the tanks are empty 'cos we got to fill' em up at the rig. Take over."

Despite the tanker still pitching and rolling a little, his sturdy sea legs took him easily through the connecting door at the back of the bridge, and along a short passageway to his cabin. 'Bloody storm' he said to himself as he sat down in front of his desk, and begrudgingly admitted that it had indeed been a bit on the rough side. He surveyed the copious number of badly-sorted papers that littered of his desktop and chuckled. "Won't have no need for this crap anymore." He leaned forward and cast a particularly annoying sheaf of forms off to one side, looked at the wall-mounted clock, then reached for his satellite phone.

Donnelly would be expecting his call at quarter past the hour. "Change of plan." Announced Windaw.

"Why?"

"There's too much of a swell left over from this bloody storm, and it'll probably take a day or so to calm down."

"That could be awkward." Donnelly was considering the quickest way of altering what he had already set in motion.

"Not half as awkward if some of them nomads tumble into the middle of the Atlantic Ocean. I tell you, this lot are bloody uppity, and there'll be trouble if just one goes overboard. And there's more."

"Go on."

"We can't get there until daybreak, at least."

There was a lull in their conversation, and Windaw almost sensed Donnelly's reaction over the airwaves, so he added. "The sooner we get rid of them, the better."

"Can't you wait until it's dark?" Donnelly was thinking about a few of the rig's crew who wouldn't fail to see the offload of migrants. If they were to continue with their migrant ferrying business, he would have paid them off, but as he and Windaw both planned to disappear soon afterwards, he didn't see the need.

"Not a chance, and like I said, the sea's going to be too rough for a while yet."

"Ok. Ok. I'll make a call."

"'till the morning then."

"Go dtí an mhaidin."

*****

Eamon liked to think that one day he would be able to afford a proper cruiser, like a flashy Sunseeker. In the meantime, he kept his aging thirty-two foot Princess going by overcharging tourists, often Americans, who wanted to see southern Ireland's coastline from the sea. Occasionally, private parties of fishermen would charter his yacht, and as often as not, he'd end up hosing-down the decks to get rid of the regurgitated alcohol, but he didn't mind too much as he overcharged them as much as he could get away with. And then there was Donnelly.

It was almost inevitable that sooner or later, their paths would cross. It wasn't a case of advertising in the local rag 'smuggler seeks man with fast boat', but not far off. All Donnelly did was wander between the quayside bars, ask around, and with the incentive of a few drinks, found his man.

Eamon liked Donnelly. Three or four times a year, he'd receive a call, and knew he'd be onto another cash earner. They'd meet up in the casino after a trip, and he'd receive a nice bundle of notes. If anyone ever asked, having a wad of cash would be easy to explain.

"Change of plan." Donnelly used Windaw's expression.

"Ok. What?"

"I want to be at Blue Lizard earlier than planned."

"No problem. When?"

"Early tomorrow morning."

Eamon didn't have to think about that for long. Experience had taught him to keep one eye on the weather at all times, and he was prepared. "Should be alright, but there's a wee bit of a blow out there at the moment, and it's coming our way. Might be alright once it's passed."

"How long do you reckon this time?"

"Better leave just after sunset."

*****

Jorge Arlesson swore as he replaced his satellite phone back on its keep, and turned to Matt. "Why now of all times?" he commented rhetorically. "Donnelly's coming over just when there's a bloody force ten gale outside. Says he wants to meet up with the skipper of the Pan Maru that's going to be docking tomorrow morning. And then he tells me that Maurice bloody Hamilton's has decided to drop in as well."

Having been around rigs longer that Jorge, Matt

Hewdy was a little more sanguine. "So what?"

"So it means he'll probably want to inspect this, inspect that, check up on us. That's what."

"I wouldn't worry about it. We all know what they're up to, so he's hardly likely to be checking-up to see if we've been skimming-off more oil than we should; which we haven't. Anyway, I expect Donnelly's got some envelopes for us and the crew. They're overdue."

"I know, I know. But why Hamilton's going to be here beats me."

"Probably wants to see how his investment's coming along. No, more like it is that he's the one who'll be handing out the envelopes."

"I hope he's got a lot of them."

* * * * *

Before Hamilton departed in his chauffeur-driven Daimler, he'd spent several minutes padding round and looking over his golden child in the garage. He stood to one side and admired how it gleamed under the luminescent garage lights. All thoughts of his upcoming trip out to the rig evaporated, and even the aspiration of another quarter-of-a-million in his pocket didn't deflect from the scrutiny of his Bentley. He cuffed his shirt sleeve and brushed away a speck of dust that had the temerity to have landed on the bonnet.

He was reminded by one of his security detail that he had a helicopter to catch from Brize Norton, and that due to the inclement weather he ought to take a coat.

Reluctantly, he turned off the light, closed the

door, went to fetch his coat, and came across his two gardeners; one of them was pushing a wheelbarrow.

"Right, you chaps. By the time I'm back this evening, I want my new Bentley washed and polished. Gleaming. Clear." It was a statement, not a question.

Chapter 19

The wind had dropped significantly, but it was still rather breezy. Even the sun was threatening to make an appearance through the clouds, low on the horizon. With the help of winches, the Pan Maru's ropes snaked their way on to the docking platform, but it was clear to all concerned that the gangway's bogey wheels would earn their keep this day. Much as Windaw had predicted, the swell was considerable. The significant rise and fall of the Pan Maru would have made a decent fairground attraction.

Alone, Donnelly had watched the vessel take its time on its approach from his viewpoint on one of the upper platforms for a few minutes, and decided it was quicker watching paint dry, so he went back inside to join Jorge in the office. Anyway, he couldn't see the platform from up there.

"Where's Matt?" He asked, as five minutes earlier Matt had been there.

"He's overseeing the crew tying up the Pan Maru and the hooking-up." He referred to the great flexible pipes that would fill up the Pan Maru's tanks with crude oil. "It takes nearly five minutes to get all the way down there. Why is Mr. Hamilton coming?"

That wasn't a question he was expecting, and to give himself time to think of an acceptable answer, he sauntered over to Matt's chair and sat down. "Oh, it's probably just one of his publicity stunts to say that he's been keeping up with developments. Something he can hold his hand on his heart and say that all's well." Donnelly knew he hadn't any heart, and he inwardly smiled to himself with his own thought that that was why they were in business together.

"The lads could do with receiving their bonus, especially as some of them will be ending their shift next week, and going back home."

In the past, Donnelly had arrived by boat when it had been dark with enough cash to buy the crew's silence. On this occasion, in the knowledge that he would be disappearing for good, he planned to put off those cash payments and keep the money for himself. Besides which, he had no cash to hand out this time; it was all with Windaw. He knew he had to allay Jorge's uneasiness, and once again come up with a credible answer. "The lads' bonus is on the ship, so once that docked, we can sort that one out. Oh, and by the way, I've a trawler that'll be docking next to the Pan Maru, and she'll be taking on some special cargo."

"What, another ship? Oil?"

"No, not oil. Just some odds and sods that Michael picked up along the way, and don't worry about that, because it won't be here long enough for you to log it." After a moment's thought he added "I'll make sure you're both looked after."

Jorge didn't like being asked to turn a blind eye, but he and Matt had done so up to now as Donnelly had always paid handsomely in cash; and there was no reason why he wouldn't do so again. "When's it getting here?"

"It won't be too long."

They both heard a clatter on the metallic outside stair, and a few seconds later, in strode Windaw. He was breathless.

"God, that's a long way up. Why isn't there a lift like in every other civilised building? It's enough to force a man to drink."

They waited for his breathing to return to something approaching normal, and watched him as he hung his heavy coat on one of the hooks. He looked at Jorge. "I told Matt that the manifolds have been checked and the tanks have been vented, so he can start filling 'em up straightaway." He lied, but added "He knows in what order."

Donnelly stood up. "Jorge, Michael and I need a few minutes in private please."

"I have to do my rounds anyway. Even in this weather." He collected his coat and radio on the way out.

Two seconds after the door closed, they crossed the small gap between them, shook hands and clasped each other.

"It's grand seeing you again Michael." He took half a pace backwards and eyed him up and down. "But what's with the fungus?" He gently tugged his newly-grown beard. "And have you lost some weight?"

"Probably. You know I've never worried about my weight, but you look like you've put some on. Must be all them fine restaurants you've been frequenting."

"Palm Island's not bad, but bloody expensive. Even if it's free. If you know what I mean."

"Hey come on now. It'll be my turn next."

"It would be if you could sit at a desk all day and I knew how to sail a ship."

"Tell me about the women another time. Right now, I've got a load of them nomads waiting to throw-up on somebody else's boat. When's it getting here?"

Donnelly pondered for a moment. "This chap has been around quite a bit, and I've known him to smuggle migrants all the way from The Canaries. I spoke to him yesterday and he reckoned he might be here later this morning. Said much the same as you said to me about the weather."

"Yeah, that was a bit rougher than I'd bargained for, but it's clearing away now. All except for the swell."

"So, it's all gone smoothly, and we're nearly in the money." Donnelly was jubilant.

"Yeah. There's a few gold bars, a couple of bags of Krugerrands and over a million in cash in my chest. All we've got to do now is meet our man in Reykjavik who'll swap the gold for Dollars. Er… I take it you've arranged some muscle to meet us in Reykjavik?"

"Yes. Two lads from Ballyandrean will be meeting us there. I told them they could have a two week's free camping holiday, flights included, if they could help us move some lead fishing weights, and make sure we don't get mugged." Donnelly glibly lied.

They both laughed.

"Ok then. We're nearly home and dry. I don't suppose you want to know where the Maru's going after Reykjavik, do you?"

That part of the equation had been left entirely up

to Windaw to find a scrapyard that would take the boat for cash. Having visited a good many ports around the world over the years meant that he had been ideally placed to find such a yard.

Donnelly really didn't care what happened to it, as he planned to vanish with everything in Windaw's chest, but he had to feign interest. As far as he was concerned, cash was king, and not some rusty old tub that might, or might not, fetch a few hundred thousand. "Have you already agreed a price?"

"They've agreed half-a-million US dollars, but I don't know them that well, so I can't guarantee it. The trouble is that once the boat's docked in their yard they could turn round and just tell us to bugger off, but I don't think they will. You see, Jose's brother wants to get involved in what we're doing, and the Maru's the prefect boat for doing just that." He cocked his head knowingly to one side. "Of course, I might have mentioned that there were two other boats in the fleet, and he might have got hold of the idea that they're up to the same tricks as we are as well."

"Michael. You're a canny bastard."

They faced each other in laughter. "We're both canny bastards."

Once they had calmed down, Windaw continued. "I almost wish they would try and shaft us, because I've got some C4 locked away, and I'd like to see what kind of a mess that would make of their yard."

"So would I, Michael, so would I, but let's hope it doesn't come to that." Donnelly still feigned interest.

"Right then. We'll be getting well over five million

for the gold, plus whatever you've agreed with the brokers in Reykjavik for the oil, plus over half a million in scrap, and then there's another million plus in cash from all those migrants." He paused in thought. "I don't suppose you managed to sort out anything on the insurance side of things, did you?"

"Not a chance. It would have made us too visible, and you know how annoying insurance companies can be. Just remember The Salem."

"Oh, The Salem. They were real amateurs, and I'd have been ashamed to have been amongst them. Even if I'd had the chance."

"Didn't you say you once came across one of them; somewhere in the Far East?"

"Oh yes. Drinking his way into an early grave in a Singapore bar after being released from prison. Glad I didn't take him on though, as he might have given the rest of the crew the wrong idea."

Donnelly wanted to change the subject. "That was then and this is now."

"Not bad for a few years work, eh?"

"It's what we always dreamed about, Michael."

Windaw reached into his jacket pocket hanging on the hook, and produced a stainless-steel hip flask. "Let's drink to that."

"Gartha."

"Now, tell me more about Palm Island and those other exotic places you've been to. I might go and visit some of them when this is all over."

"I might ask you the same thing, but I'm not sure if commercial docks can be described as exotic."

"Ha. You'd be surprised then. The best one for nightlife… "

They carried on swapping stories, but Windaw's in-built sense of timing, bought them back to the here and now. "Hey, I'd better go and make sure Tenmil's got it all under control. Don't want any last minute slip-ups. Can't you get your trawler man to hurry up?"

"I'll call him." Donnelly extracted his satellite phone from his pocket. Peering out of the window, which surprisingly didn't give much of a view due to the salty grime on the outside, Windaw overheard one half the short conversation. "Say's he'll be here within the hour."

"Must be in sight, if I could see out of these ruddy windows." Windaw knew what a waste of time it was watching boats dock. Watching paint dry came to mind. "Come and feast your eyes on what's in my chest."

"I thought you'd never ask."

They made their way down a myriad of noisy stairs, along gangways and across metal grids towards where the Pan Maru was docked, and at one point stopped to watch the trawler as she neared.

Windaw turned to Donnelly. "If them nomads were a bit sick on my boat, they're positively going to die when they board yon trawler. Look at the way she's pitching, and not just up and down either."

"Serves 'em right."

"I suppose they want to come to Ireland for the rain, 'cos where they come from, it doesn't rain that much. Well, not as much as in Ireland."

"Nowhere's as wet as Ireland."

"You haven't seen the Monsoon they get out in

India. That's bloody wet. Come on, I'd better get down there before somebody hooks up the wrong cable." Windaw led the way. He needn't have worried because Matt seemed to have it all under control.

"I see you've kept the same name on the boat." Donnelly spotted the painted name om the bows.

"Didn't have a chance to change it, 'cos of that bloody storm. But I don't think it'll matter anyhow. That name will soon be gone forever."

They joined Jorge who had positioned himself on the lowest platform to oversee the trawler's docking. He was constantly on his radio, listening to and giving instructions to those who were tying it up. They were just about to head for the gangway on to the Pan Maru when he took a few paces towards them.

"There's a helicopter on its way in. About ten minutes out."

"Shit. That's bloody Hamilton coming in earlier than I told him to. He must have got up at sparrow fart to be here by now." Swore Donnelly. He turned away so that Jorge couldn't hear him speak to Windaw. "Let's get on board before he gets in the way."

Windaw led the way, but Donnelly suddenly stopped, and sniffed. "What's that smell?"

"I told you. Them bloody nomads threw-up all over the place. Probably the goats as well."

"What goats?"

"Don't ask."

Windaw closed the cabin door behind them, and as they were removing their windproof coats, Donnelly spotted a couple of guns on the floor in the corner. "I didn't think you used them?"

Following his gaze, he replied "I don't. I confiscated them from that lot." He walked over to a hidden drawer under his desk, retrieved a key, bent down and slid a small curtain to one side at the end of his bed, inserted the key into the brass padlock, and opened his oversized chest. He didn't need to say anything, but stood to one side so that Donnelly could look down on their fruits.

A full twenty seconds passed in silence as the pair of them looked upon the ingots of gleaming gold, cross-stacked on top of each other.

"Now that's a grand sight." Remarked Donnelly. He was in awe and hardly dared himself to do it, but eventually he bent down, and with both hands hefted one from the top. He examined the lustre from different angles, first at arms-length, then close up, then rubbed his thumbs and index fingers along its side. He gingerly replaced it as though it might break or disappear.

Looking Windaw directly in his eye, he said "I suppose you've been doing that all these months."

"Not quite. At first I did it almost every day, but it took me quite a while to get used to it being there. It's got an aura about it. A kind of magnetism. Something you can't stop thinking about, and I had to force myself to stop looking at it. How much are we going to get for it?"

Donnelly was still staring at their gold mine. "I've done a deal with our man in Reykjavik and if he's true to his word, and I believe he is, we ought to rake in well over five million."

"What handover arrangements have you made once we get there?"

"In a dockside warehouse, this side of the Icelandic customs. Those two hitch-hikers'll be doing all the carrying, so we don't have to; just in case they get stopped. Our man'll have US Dollars in a briefcase." Donnelly averted his look back to the gold. "Perfect. Bloody perfect. What's that?" He pointed to half-a-dozen brick-shaped items in the left-hand side of the box.

"That's the C4I was telling you about. Safest place for it. We're still meeting up in The British Virgin Islands, right?"

"Yeah." Donnelly grimaced at his next comment. "Our only problem now is Maurice Bloody Hamilton."

"I don't know what dealings you been having with this Hamilton chap, but whatever they are, make sure you don't cross him, 'cos I hear he can be a nasty piece of work. What's he doing here anyway?" Windaw knew his friend had acted in an executive capacity, and knew he had had to make deals over the past ten years, but he didn't know with whom. Now he knew at least a small part of the story.

Donnelly knew this question was coming his way sooner or later. He kept his reply short. "He thinks he's collecting two hundred and fifty grand."

After a moment, Windaw half-cocked his head to one side while he worked out what Donnelly was saying. "I take it he's not getting it then?"

"Too bloody right he's not. That's our money."

"Well what makes him think he deserves some of it?"

"Because that was the price he agreed with Mr. Huseyn in Baku. Part of the deal in setting up this operation. As far as we're concerned, once that gold's converted into cash, and the boat sold, we can vanish, so Hamilton, Huseyn, and the others can fuck off. They won't find us." Donnelly was careful to use the words 'we' and 'us', because he intended to disappear with as much as he could. Windaw could keep the boat. What he had in mind now was a far cry from what they originally planned.

"Hadn't we better and go and meet him then, 'cos we don't want him anywhere near this lot?" He cocked his head towards his chest.

"He doesn't know you or what you look like, only that you exist as the captain of the Pan Maru, so let's keep it that way. Probably best if I meet him alone."

"I'll go along with that. What are you going to tell him about his two hundred and fifty grand?"

"I'll think of something." Donnelly lied, knowing that he was going to tell Hamilton that he would have to wait until they got paid for the oil that Windaw would be delivering to Iceland. Even then, he wouldn't see a penny of it.

"Here, I've just had a thought." Windaw had a glint in his eye. "As I'll be taking the Pan Maru to the BVI anyway, do you reckon they might welcome some fresh water down there... ?"

"Forget it. We agreed this was to be the last run, and if we don't stop now, then we never will."

"I suppose you're right." Windaw's tone of voice betrayed his reluctant disappointment.

"Ok then. I'd better head off Hamilton before he comes looking for us. I'll take him to Jorge's office, and while I'm doing that, you get those migrants onto the trawler."

* * * * *

The trek to Jorge's office from sea level would have tested a fit man, and by the time Donnelly arrived, he was nearly as breathless as Windaw had been earlier. Disembarking from the Pan Maru, he looked up in time to see the helicopter's blades coming to a halt on one of the two landing decks; the highest points of the rig. He couldn't actually see the main body of it, just the tip of one of the blades.

He thought it unlikely that Hamilton would be able to see the trail of humans migrating from one boat to another, and he cursed his early interference as a matter of course. He paused to catch his breath one level below Jorge's office, and mentally prepared himself for meeting Hamilton for only the second time in his life. He chuckled to himself in the knowledge that it would also be the final time they would meet each other.

Two steps into Jorge's office bought him to a complete standstill; he hadn't even reached for the zipper on his coat to remove it. The shock of seeing Inspector Eyethorne sitting in Matt's chair, seemingly holding a relaxed conversation with Jorge, caught him completely off guard, and for the first time in years, he didn't know what to say or do.

"I'm so glad you could join us. Take your coat off and take a seat." There was a worryingly confident tone to her voice, which confused him even further. She indicated to one of the chairs resting against the far wall.

He decided to keep his coat on, and as smoothly as he could he paced over to one of the chairs and wheeled it to a position; nearer Eyethorne than the door, but making sure that Matt's desk separated them. They heard radio chatter in the background through Jorge's radio even though he had turned the volume down.

She waited until he was settled. "I think you have some explaining to do."

He was still grappling with her presence, rather than Hamilton's, and instinctively knew that any comments he made would need to be guarded. Ignoring Jorge, he decided to try and make light of the situation, and gave a little laugh. "I don't think I need to explain anything. I'm here doing my job. One of my many visits. Making sure the rig's running smoothly. Discussing the future with our rig managers. Looking after the safety of our crews. Talking of which, I take it you're here in connection with those missing personnel."

"In a way, yes." On the way over in the helicopter, she'd made her mind up to play-him, like Justin had tried to teach her how to fish. Reel him in gently, perhaps even get him to accidentally incriminate himself. She knew well the traits of criminals, and Donnelly's attempt at laughing-off, was a typical initial reaction. She also knew that she'd have to play him at his own game of blatant lying. "You see, one of those missing men came forward and is being ever so cooperative." She wasn't going to let on that Miles was the cooperative one.

Donnelly was stunned at the news, especially as he had received confirmation from his mate in the employment bureau that the four selected names had been forwarded to the inquisitive authorities. His mate had told him that those four had all emigrated, and that there was little chance of the authorities tracking them down to ask questions.

At the time, it had been a small loose end in the

overall scheme of things, and not one that he had given a second thought about; until now. He decided to go along with Eyethorne's suggestion. "That's good news then. Perhaps he can tell us where they all went that night." He looked over at Jorge, who nodded his head in agreement.

"He has." She bluffed. "But before we get on to that, can you tell me a little more about the Pan Maru." Before Donnelly had a chance to deny all knowledge of the ship, she added "That's the tanker that's tied up below."

This sudden change of subject wrong-footed him. "Oh, you'd better ask the captain about that, because I know nothing about tankers. We tell them to pick up oil in one place and deposit it in another."

"So you wouldn't know anything about where she's been lately?" She asked.

This was tricky ground for him. If he denied knowing where she'd been, it would imply that he didn't have control, whereas if he revealed her latest itinerary, however spurious, it would provide her with another line of enquiry. "I believe she was in The Gulf of Arabia where it was chartered to take some oil to one of the South African countries, and then on to here. You can see that she's taking on oil as we speak. Why do you ask?" He enquired as blandly as possible. He knew full well that the Gulf of Arabia was commonly called the Persian Gulf, and he had said it in the hope of creating some doubt in her mind.

"Is that why you're really here then? To meet with the captain?"

"I don't get to see him often, as he's usually

halfway round the world, but this is a lot nearer than Saudi Arabia or South Africa, so I thought I'd take the opportunity."

"So you've just come from seeing him on his ship?"

"Er, yes."

"And how is Captain Michael Windaw? No side effects from the storm?"

The mention of his name, and more particularly the fact that she knew both of his names, caught him off-guard. He started to feel uneasy, but continued in a nonchalant manner. "I didn't actually ask him how he was, but he looked the same."

"You've known him for a long time then." She led him on.

He realised she'd manoeuvred him into a small trap. "I wouldn't say a long time." He lied. "Just the same as the last time I met him."

"Here. On this rig?"

"I can't remember exactly when, but probably, yes. What's this got to do with those missing men?" He wanted to change the subject, even if it was back to something sensitive.

She judged it was time to get away from the relative small talk, and turn the screw a little. "It transpires that two of those men were looking at the possibility of sabotaging this rig and possibly the Pan Maru as well." Another bluff. She looked across at Jorge, then back to Donnelly; letting her statement hang for a moment. "Neither of you would know anything about that, would you?"

There was negative shaking of heads as their eyes briefly contacted each other; Jorge remained silent, leaving such a question to Donnelly, who wondered where the hell she had picked up that bit of hearsay.

"Now, why would anyone want to sabotage us?" He enquired as genuinely as possible.

"Well, let's see now. It wouldn't be the Greens because they're not into violence, neither would it be the Just Stop Oil protesters for the same reason. And anyway, they don't have any boats, so let's consider other parties who might want to disrupt your operation. How about one of your competitors, for example?" She wanted to keep him guessing.

Donnelly thought he knew how to maintain a straight face, and without much difficulty, he managed to portray a look of being nonplussed. Apart from the constant combination of the air-conditioning and a deep hum that emanated from somewhere beneath them, Jorge's radio was the only item that made any significant noise.

Patricia continued. "Ok then. Maybe it might be one of your suppliers who you owe money to, in which case it would probably be you who they're after, and not this rig. Or the boat. By the way, who actually owns this rig and the other Maru vessels in the fleet?"

"I'd have to check with the parent company to give you a proper answer."

"I suppose you'd have to ask Mr. Huseyn in Baku then."

"Er, yes. He'd know." He cast his mind back to when they had first met, and remembered that she had pressed him then for Mr. Huseyn's name. He wondered if she had managed to track down and ask that gentleman, and if so, she'd already know the answer to that question; along with others. He didn't have time to dwell on the possibilities that went with it, because she was speaking again.

"Of course, there's always the possibility of an insurance scam, and those saboteurs were in the employ of the owners. This rig's worth what? ...several hundred million dollars, and when you include the Pan Maru, it would be most unfortunate if there was an accident while she was being loaded." There was a touch of sarcasm in her voice. "If that were the case, it might explain why those four men went missing. Have they been replaced yet?"

He liked her thinking, but her theory was getting a bit too close for comfort, because he had discarded similar thoughts quite a while ago. "I think that's highly unlikely." His response was tinged with a small laugh, as though to discard the notion as ridiculous. "And we've managed to replace two of them so far."

Patricia surmised that the two thugs that Miles had despatched had been replaced with another pair, and they would no doubt be lurking somewhere on the rig. Now that she had her answer to that, as well as other questions, she felt the time was right to put direct scenarios to him. "Ok then. If they weren't on this rig to sabotage, what were they doing? Guarding something perhaps? Secrets? You see, we know that the oil output figures have been tampered with on the rig's computer, and we know that there's a certain amount of oil from this rig that is not accounted for. What oil that is being produced is of very poor quality and being palmed off as Grade A. We also know that the Pan Maru illicitly visits embargoed countries with that oil, and that most of the money goes directly to Baku. You receive your pay offs when you visit Dubai and squirrel your share of the profits into a bank account in The British Virgin Islands; all tax-free. The crew aboard this rig are paid well above the going wage, as are the men abord the Pan Maru. And then there's the extra cash you have to hand out to them; presumably to buy their silence. All in all, a very profitable operation, no doubt shared with Captain Windaw. Do Jorge and Matt know what you've been up to?" She hoped that by revealing Donnelly's skullduggery it might create a chasm between them. "You do know exactly what's going on here, so don't try telling me otherwise."

Donnelly squirmed in his seat as she reeled off the list. He was too busy taking in what she had just said to come up with a plausible denial, and he didn't even have the time for that, because she was rattling off more incriminating accusations.

"We've been tracking the route of the Pan Maru, and guess what? Every time she's approached this rig, her transponder's off. It magically turns on again when she approaches shipping lanes. It doesn't take a genius to work out why that might be. Her transponder's turned off right now and has been ever since she passed the South African coast, so where has she been that you don't want anybody to know about?"

"Captain Windaw's the man to ask… "

"No. I'm asking you, because just a few minutes ago, you said she goes where she's told. The Gulf to

South Africa to here. Correct?"

He couldn't deny his own words, and was becoming angry with her aggressive nature. One thing was certain; he'd have to get out from under her clutches as soon as he could. "I'll say again, Captain Windaw's responsible for the running of his ship, and I can't answer for his actions. And as far as your accusations concerning the illegal sale of oil to certain countries, I haven't the faintest idea where you're getting this from. You'll have to ask him. Now, if you'll excuse me, I have duties to attend to."

Frustrated, he shoved the chair to one side with his foot as he got up.

"Tell me what Hamilton's got to do with this."

He was gobsmacked that she knew of Hamilton's participation. *By Christ, but this one's a bitch.* He thought to himself. *How the hell did she find out about bloody Hamilton?* He had no qualms about leaving Hamilton in the lurch, and for a brief moment, wondered if he could pass the blame on to him; but there wasn't time to invent a credible story. He couldn't now deny knowing of Hamilton, as he quickly worked out that she probably knew more than she was revealing. "All I can tell you is that I believe he's one of the Blue Lizard investors."

"You know he's on his way here now, don't you?"

"That's news to me." He was beginning to wonder how many more lies he could get away with.

"Now, why do you suppose a high-level government minister would want to come out and visit a rig in international waters today of all days? I'll tell you why. It's no coincidence that both you and Captain

Windaw are here. That's why. Obviously for some sort of pay off."

Jorge's radio crackled in the background, and he turned the volume up a little.

"That's a crazy idea. How am I supposed to know what a government minister's schedule is?" It was all he could come up with.

"Because we found his number on your mobile phone."

Before he had a chance to respond to her bombshell, Jorge interrupted. "There's another helicopter coming in, and from its call sign I'd say it is a government one. I've got to go and oversee its landing." He grabbed his coat off the hook and went to leave. He hadn't liked the way things looked like they were turningout anyway.

Staring Donnelly in the face, she commented in a deadpan manor. "That'll be Hamilton."

Donnelly took his chance, elbowed Jorge out of the way, and ran out of the door ahead of him.

Patricia sat for a moment, gloating at her own performance, then reached into her pocket for her radio. "He's coming your way. Whatever you do, don't let Donnelly get on that motor cruiser."

"Roger." Came the response from one of the two commando types.

So far, her plans were working out better than expected. She knew she had time, so went and poured herself a weak cup of coffee from the machine. She wanted to give Hamilton a head start so that when she did catch up with him, he'd be with both Donnelly and Windaw. All the rotten eggs would be in one basket. She

Zipped up her coat, and with the cardboard coffee in hand, she left Jorge's office and stood outside so that she could at least see in the general direction of the Pan Maru.

After a few minutes of looking around, she was about to make her way down to the tanker when she spotted Hamilton below her, following Jorge, and waited until they were well out of sight before taking a similar route down the maze of walkways and staircases.

Chapter 20

Hamilton cursed Donnelly because there was no one else around to swear at. Every time the helicopter he was in took a sudden dip, up or down due to the storm front that they were traversing, he was violently jerked in the opposite direction. It hadn't helped loosening his seat belt. The seat itself would have been comfortable enough for most people, but one edge dug into his buttocks every time there was an unexpected up or down surge. He had insisted that there was no need for his close protection officer to accompany him, which was probably just as well, as otherwise he would have been at the sharp end of his curses.

His Peltor headset squawked in his ears. "Coming up on the rig now, Minister."

Up until about an hour ago, it had been dark outside, and he hadn't noticed that it was daylight; such was his misery at being thrown around. He looked out of the window as the helicopter gently banked to circle the grey metal structure. To him, it looked like it was growing out of the rolling waves and would turn turtle at any moment, but it grew larger, and more solid as they descended. The pilot, judging the strength of the wind, hovered a short distance away for what seemed an eternity, giving Hamilton the opportunity of surveying the Pan Maru.

At first, he didn't take in the snake-like trail of people

disembarking, but his curiosity got him wondering who they were; there were certainly an awful lot of them. He craned his neck a little further and saw them milling around on the platform next to what looked like some sort of fishing boat that heaved up and down with the swell. Just as he wanted to see more, the pilot steadied the helicopter and gently landed it next to the other one on the large platform. His view of the Pan Maru was blocked, but he'd be sure to ask about those people.

Still looking out of the window, he watched yellow-jacketed men running around outside as they tied the helicopter down. Not long after, the side door next to him was opened, and the steps were unfolded by a burly man who waited to one side for him to disembark. Upon standing up, it took him a few seconds to steady his legs that had been immobile for several hours, and he had to cling to the side rail to prevent himself from tripping over.

Having been in many helicopters over the years, he instinctively ducked to a half-crouch as he walked towards a man who beckoned him from outside of the peripheral circumference of the slowing blades. Once down a set of metal steps that took them to the level beneath the landing deck, the man waited for Hamilton to catch up. Here, with a raised voice, it was quiet enough to hold a conversation.

"I'm Jorge Arlesson. General Manager of the rig. We weren't expecting your arrival until much later."

Hamilton didn't feel he had to enlighten the man, but said "Last minute change of plans. I here to see Jason Donnelly."

"He's gone down to the Pan Maru. That's the

tanker that's docked up against our lower platform, but you can't quite see it from here. I'll take you to him."

"Do you have a toilet nearby?"

Hamilton hadn't traversed the full length an oil rig before, and certainly not from the very top to the lowest docking platform. Jorge led him down and along the myriad stages and walkways, which for most of their trek were accompanied by various sizes of pipes and conduits; often randomly appearing and reappearing at ninety degree angles.

The legacy of the leftover storm in the form of a respectable swell produced a fair-sized spray through the blow-holes, and despite them threading their way across to the Pan Maru, there was little option other than to endure the occasional Atlantic showering. As a consequence of the salty sea spray that caused him to half-close his eyes, he initially didn't notice that there were two other vessels tied to the docking platform. He only tried to focus on the vastness of the Pan Maru. What he couldn't help noticing was the stream of odd-looking people coming down the gangway against his direction of travel. Shielding his eyes, he looked along the queue which meandered its way over to one of the other boats.

"I expect you'll find Mr. Donnelly up there with the captain. That chap there'll show you the way." Jorge pointed across at the side of the tanker, having to raise his voice over the sound of the waves as they surfed their way across the underside of the platform.

There was an orange-jacketed man standing inside of a hatch at the top of the gangway, who seemed to be staring into the middle of nowhere. Hamilton elbowed his way against the tide of humans who reluctantly parted to let him through, just about noticing a particularly unpleasant odour as he passed them. The further along the gangway he went, the more he felt it rise and fall, and he had to hang on to the side rail to steady himself until he finally set foot inside the steel hatchway. Even there he could feel the tanker riding the swell.

"Donnelly." He had to raise his voice above the chattering of the crowd that separated him from the man in the orange jacket. "Jason Donnelly." He repeated without any recognition from him. He forced his way through the human caterpillar that was shuffling towards the hatchway, and stood next to the man. "Where's Jason Donnelly?"

The man had a blank look on his face, but eventually replied. "I not know a Jason Donn....." Hamilton reckoned he had a thick Eastern European accent, and then realised that this chap probably wouldn't know Donnelly's name. He certainly couldn't pronounce it.

"The captain. Where's the captain?"

He understood the word captain and gestured towards a corridor.

"Bloody foreigners." Muttered Hamilton as he walked through another hatchway and into a semi-grated corridor. There were a pair of big metal shutter-type doors on one side, but the other had what looked like a lift, and he dutifully pressed the call button. He was relieved that it did turn out to be a lift, but as the steel door opened, out came a dreadful stink. He paused before getting into it, wondering what he might be stepping into, took a deep breath and trod carefully on a clean part of the lift's floor.

It was large enough to accommodate more than a dozen people, and obviously doubled-up for utility purposes, but the brownish mass off to one side on the floor looked anything but utility, and was obviously the source of the acrid smell. It looked like shit, and indeed it was. He faced the control panel which was fortunately marked, and pressed 'bridge'. It started with a jolt, causing him to steady himself. On the way up, he couldn't prevent himself looking down at the mass of liquid faeces, and wondered what kind of ship this captain kept.

The lift jolted to a halt, and with an annoying screech the door opened on to an enclosed corridor. He turned the wrong way and found himself looking at the deserted bridge of the tanker, so he turned around and tried one of the only two other doors.

Despite it being a considerable time since they had last met, he and Donnelly instantly recognised each other, but it was clear to him that he had interrupted something, because of the look on the face of the third man.

Windaw broke the silence first. "So you're 'Bloody Hamilton'. People on board my ship usually knock before entering someone's cabin."

Donnelly spoke quickly, without giving a chance of a retort. "I believe 'Bloody' is your official nick name, so don't take offence. This is Michael Windaw, captain of the Pan Maru." He stepped forward and held out his hand; hoping that this would prevent the two of them coming to blows. Now was not the time, especially as there were important items to discuss.

Hamilton and Donnelly's last meeting had been some three years ago in Blue Lizard's offices in Baku. Hamilton had been appointed to represent the UK at an OPEC-organised oil conference, and at the suggestion of a Mr. Huseyn, had stayed on an extra couple for of days to discuss certain future possibilities. With the aid of some local women, and copious amounts of five-star food and alcohol, it hadn't taken much for Hamilton to see that there were significant benefits to investing in a profitable scheme. While he recognised that it was probably illegal, with a little bending of the rules, the principle and simplicity of the operation was foolproof; only requiring him to approve certain protocols at the UK end of things.

They had parted as business partners with a handshake, and right now Donnelly wanted nothing more than to maintain the illusion of that same business relationship.

Hamilton stepped forward and they shook hands, but neither he nor Windaw went to do the same. Probably due to Windaw's first words, there was now an intangible aversion between the two of them.

Donnelly took the lead. "I was just explaining to Michael here that we don't have much time because of that bloody police inspector. She knows too much."

"Pity you didn't tell me about her before, otherwise I'd not have stopped here now. I'd have anchored-up sooner in The Gambia, or even Dakar, and waited for the all-clear."

"That still doesn't alter the fact that she knows about the rig's operation and that the oil is being sold to blacklisted countries." He turned to Hamilton. "It means that I can't give you your next bonus, if I can put it that way, because that was coming from the next off load in Reykjavik. That's where the Pan Maru is heading once she'd filled up here."

Windaw recognised that he was choosing his words carefully by avoiding any reference to the gold, and in fact diverting Hamilton's attention away from it.

"She's not going there now?" Queried Hamilton. He was primarily concerned that he might not receive his next payment.

"She can't go there now. Not now that the word's out, and that inspector probably already alerted the Icelandic authorities."

"Why would she do that? Who else knows where this tanker is headed?" Hamilton was displaying his ignorance of how the oil-broking business operated.

"Because trading is done weeks, or often months in advance, and once they've been notified, they'll not want to do any further business with us." Donnelly explained.

"And I wouldn't want to be impounded along with this boat. It's as simple as that."

It took Hamilton a couple of seconds to realise what had been decided. "So what you're saying is that this is the end of our venture."

"Right."

Another couple of seconds passed. "Where is this inspector now and who is she anyway? I might be able to make a call and have her taken off the case."

"Not this one you can't. I left her up in Jorge's office." Donnelly didn't add that he had legged it. "She's also bought a couple of armed monkeys along with her, and they're guarding the other two boats." He turned to Windaw. "I say we sail this boat out of here. Now. Disconnect those pipes and forget Iceland."

Windaw rubbed his chin in thought. "If we wait a few hours, the tanks'll be full and we can sell it elsewhere."

"We don't have a few hours. Only a few minutes before that inspector tracks us down and calls on her monkeys to arrest us."

"That serious eh?"

"Damn right it's that serious."

"I didn't think she could arrest us in international waters." Windaw was aware of maritime law, and in any case, he was reluctant to concede defeat.

"She can't, but with her armed helpers, she could detain us until the authorities arrive, and claim that we were people smuggling."

"Hang on a minute." Interrupted Hamilton as he put two and two together. "They're migrants, aren't they - That lot out there… and you're transporting them in this ship… and then offloading them onto that smaller one, aren't you." They were statements rather than questions. "That's what that bloody awful stench was." His nose wrinkled at the recent memory." You're smuggling people… and that's why there are two armed guards there. You've got me mixed up in a migrant scam haven't you, and that's probably why you've got an inspector on your back. You're bloody fools, and I want nothing to do with transporting migrants. If word of this gets out, I'll be finished."

"You're finished anyway." Patricia Eyethorne announced in a firm voice.

Nobody had seen or heard the cabin door open..

Chapter 21

She stepped confidently into plain view and closed the door behind her.

Windaw gawked at her, partly because he hadn't seen such a pretty face for a long time.

Donnelly briefly closed his eyes and inwardly groaned.

Hamilton was astounded and imitated Bob the fish with his open mouth. He was, however, the first to recover. "Not you again."

She turned on him with a vicious tongue. "If you weren't such a misogynous shit head, I wouldn't need to be here, and this time, you won't be able to wriggle out of it. Your mere presence here confirms that you're an accessory to all sorts of the criminal activities that your fellow shit heads have been up to."

"I'm here on official…"

"Oh shut up, you outdated turd. That old story is wearing a bit too thin for you to hide behind. You're here for your pay off, aren't you? What have they promised you? Cash? Diamonds? Gold?" She stretched-out her comments in the hope of seeing some sort of reaction from the other two, and was rewarded. Windaw couldn't help himself flick his eyes towards his strong box which he hadn't yet covered up. "It's gold, isn't it?" She tried not to sound too triumphant.

"Don't be absurd. How am I going to carry around a bag full of gold… "

She didn't let Hamilton finish. She took three paces forward and confronted Windaw. "Why did you stop at Port Nolloth?"

"I don't have to answer to you." He replied morosely.

"The question still stands, because there's no oil terminal at Port Nolloth, so it must have been for some other reason. Like collecting your pay off in gold."

"There's no gold in Port Nolloth." He said just a little too quickly. He wasn't used to being questioned by someone as adept as Patricia. He was more used to dealing with dozy port functionaries, who, as often as not, preferred a bribe.

"You'd know that because you've been there."

His response was delayed as he sought an answer. "Everyone knows there's nothing at Port Nolloth."

"Especially an oil tanker, so why did you turn off your transponder just before you got there?"

He glanced towards Donnelly for a bit of help, but his face was impassive.

She continued before he had a chance to reply, and from memory said "It was off for three days, and the only port of any significance that was within reach during that time was Port Nolloth. It came back on again soon after you left, and two weeks later, the track stops again just before you reach the waters off Liberia. It comes on again after another three days, and lo and behold, the track disappears again two days ago. Yet here you are now." She let the obvious conclusion hang in the air.

He glared at her without responding.

"You turn your transponder on and off so that there's no record of which ports you've been to, and you've been doing that for years. But all one has to do is fill in the gaps, and then it's easy to see where you've been calling at. You hadn't thought of that, one had you?"

She saw the guilt reveal itself all over his face, and knew she was right.

"What was worth stopping for in Liberia?"

When he didn't respond, she shifted herself half a pace towards him. Even though she was slightly shorter than him, she found that this sort of physical strategy often pressured her accused into an admission. It didn't work with Windaw, but she carried on anyway.

"Let me guess. Port Nolloth is South Africa's northernmost port on The Atlantic coast, and because it's quiet and well out of the way for large amounts of commerce, it suits you perfectly. South Africa is famed for producing a good portion of the world's gold, so that's where you picked up your latest pay-off."

She kept looking directly into his eyes.

"Liberia is still strife-ridden by local warlords, so that's where you collected your passengers. You take advantage of those poor souls by taking the last of their money, when, in desperation, all they want to do is escape from a feudal system. But what you're really doing is swapping one regime for another, because they haven't got enough money, and have sold their souls and their families into slavery in another country. That must make you a very tidy profit, and I don't suppose you care one iota that it's morally wrong."

She paused her tirade. Her intuitive Anglo-Saxon

decency hoped that her moral point would somehow strike a note, but she immediately realised that it hadn't. "Where exactly are they off to now?"

Windaw kept his mouth clamped shut.

"We can ask them that later, but if they don't know, we can always find out from the trawler captain."

Hamilton was also putting two and two together. He'd just about noticed the line of foreigners queuing up, but up to now had thought nothing of it. Her comments directed at Windaw had him realising that his two fellow accomplices had been hiding this part of the oil operation from him. He knew that there were organised criminal gangs supplying inflatables to migrants to cross the English Channel almost on a daily basis. As Northern Ireland Secretary of State, he'd been briefed on the growing problem of migrants using Southern Ireland as a springboard to cross the soft boarder into Britain. Now he knew how, and this posed a dilemma for him.

On the one hand, he should be pleased that Inspector Eyethorne had managed to uncover an illegal people smuggling operation, but on the other hand, he hadn't been asked to 'turn a blind eye', and so he hadn't been profiting from it. What was of more concern to him was that Donnelly had concealed this side of their venture and was cashing in on it with Windaw. He wondered how long this had been going on and how much money was involved. More to the point, where was that cash now, and in what denominations?

"Let's get back to that gold." Patricia announced as she backed away from Windaw.

The previous mention of gold had peaked Hamilton's

interest. While Patricia had been putting Windaw on the spot, he had been speculating about it. If there was any chance that it might exist, Eyethorne would be the person to find out. He hazarded a comment. "Yes. I'd like to know about that gold as well."

All of a sudden, Patricia knew she had an ally in the form of Hamilton; but only as far as the gold was concerned. "I'll bet you it's somewhere on this ship." Her eyes briefly met with Hamilton's. "And it'll be close, because it's not the sort of thing you entrust to anyone else. What's in that strong box over there?"

Windaw hadn't redrawn the curtain that had previously concealed his sea chest. Rectangular in shape, and much bigger than a generous picnic hamper, its black painted steel gave it a look of solidarity. Hinged handles at each end made lifting it a little easier. For security, a sturdy hasp and staple connected the lid to the front face when closed, and completing the look was a brass and steel padlock; the old-fashioned type.

"What's in there is mine and you've no right to look in my private box." He said ferociously and shifted sideways a little to stand between them and his chest.

"No gold then?" She proffered. When he didn't respond immediately, she took the chance to keep him on the back foot. "Then why don't you prove it?"

"I don't have to prove a damn thing to you." He retorted angrily.

"But you do to me." Hamilton stepped a pace forward. "If there's no gold in there, then there's no problem."

Unsure what to do, he stood there looking from one inquisitor to another.

"Open the box, Windaw." Hamilton demanded.

He was still uncertain when Patricia tried a well-used ploy. "Don't tell me you've lost the key."

Once again, he couldn't help himself; his eyes briefly darted towards his desk.

"Will you open it or shall I?" She took a step nearer him, and noted that Hamilton did likewise.

He knew that he had lost, but remained rooted to the spot.

The three of them were so engrossed that they didn't notice Donnelly as he silently crept behind them. They also didn't notice him bend down and pick up the pistol that had been placed on the floor in the corner. "I think that's enough of that."

The clear menace in his voice had them turning to look at him. Gun in hand, it was clear who was going to have the last word. "You'd better think twice unless you think I'm not capable of using this." He was pointing it midway between Hamilton and Patricia, but when Windaw stepped out from behind them to join him, he found Donnelly aiming the weapon at his midriff. "Stay where you are."

Windaw stopped mid-stride alongside the other two. He clearly struggled to understand why he was being told to stay still.

Donnelly edged back against the wall to give himself more space between him and the trio, reached into pocket, brought out his phone and dialled. "Come in lads." Was all he said, and a moment later, two men entered the cabin and stood next to him; one produced a revolver and pointed it in the same direction, while the other just stood there blocking the door. Neither of them said a word. "I don't need to tell you, but I'm going to anyway. Don't do anything foolish, otherwise Seamus here will shoot you in the stomach, and Paddy will kick the shit out of you just to make sure you suffer a slow and painful death that will surely follow." He narrowed his eyes as he said it. "Darlin'." He looked at Patricia. "I believe you're carrying. Take it out and toss it on the floor over there." His head indicated in which direction. "Throw your radio over there as well."

Once she had complied, he addressed her again. "You've been a real fucking bitch and deserve all that's coming to you. I'm going to make sure you're going to regret even knowing my name." He let that sink in. "You're lucky I don't believe in hitting women, but I will if you give me any trouble." He bent down and put her gun in his pocket.

Hamilton rued not bringing along at least one of his security detail, but he was still confident that he would be able to come out of this alive. After all, he and Donnelly were partners. Weren't they?

"And you." He motioned at Hamilton with his pistol. "What d'you want to come here early for eh? I thought I'd told you not to get here before ten o'clock, and if you'd done as I'd told you, you wouldn't be here now. You're an interfering arsehole of a busybody and believe you can solve every problem by talking about it, but you're not going to be able to talk your way out of this one."

"But I thought… "

"You thought wrong." Donnelly was starting to enjoy himself. "I'll tell you what you thought you were coming here for today, shall I? You thought you were going to collect quarter of a million, didn't you? Well, you're not getting it because I'm keeping it. And I'm also taking the gold... all of it." He looked Windaw directly in the eye. "Sorry Michael, but it was always going to end this way. You doing all the hard work going back and forth across the globe, while I had to play the businessman with the likes of him there."

Windaw was fuming. "What about our pact? You remember. The one we made to each other when were guttersnipes without so much as a penny between us. I covered your arse when O'Brien came after you, and again when Father Arnott threatened you with the police. Does that not mean anything to you?"

"It did then, but not now."

"For the love of Christ. I watch your back and you watch mine. Isn't that what we agreed?"

"It is, but things have changed."

"What's changed?

"I'll tell you what's changed. Our world's got a whole lot more complicated ever since the invention of the internet, and now you can find out anything about anyone at anytime. Disappearing has become next to impossible, and it's going to take a lot of money to stay hidden. There's not enough in there for both of us to stay away from prying eyes, and now that everybody seems to know who and where we are, it's time to cut and run." He motioned towards Patricia and Hamilton with the pistol.

"Fer fok's sake, I'm not just anybody. I'm your lifelong partner, and I've kept up my end of our bargain. Don't you feel you owe me something? Loyalty even?" Windaw pleaded.

"Honour among thieves. Is that that it? I think you'll find that that idea died a long time ago."

For all his faults, Windaw was beginning to see where this was heading, and he didn't like it one little bit. "We agreed to go our separate ways after this last deal, and I haven't the faintest as to where you'll be disappearing off to. You don't know where I'm off to either, so that hasn't changed."

"But I do know where you're going, don't I? And I'm pretty sure you can make some educated guesses as to where I'd be. It wouldn't matter how much money I had if you were still around. Would it?"

"You're a right bastard."

"We're both right bastards. But I'm a bastard who's going to live to enjoy being one."

"And what about them?" Windaw already knew the answer, but wanted to hear it from Donnelly's lips.

"I can't buy their silence and you're a loose end." He raised the pistol and shot Windaw in the centre of his forehead.

Chapter 22

Such was the suddenness that neither Hamilton or Patricia managed to move as Windaw crumpled to the floor. Both of them had experienced death at close quarters by gunshot, Hamilton more so from his days in the army, but it still came as a shock to them.

Once again, it was Hamilton who reacted first, but he gulped before he spoke. "I suppose we're next."

Donnelly now pointed his pistol back in their direction. "You're next alright, but not here. He was about to become indiscreet." He said in a flat tone of voice as he briefly looked down at the body. "Can't be having that now, can we."

"If there's no one left, how can he have been indiscreet? Asked Patricia.

"You're not the only ones. Seamus and Paddy here don't know me like he did, and as things stand right now, as far as they're concerned, they never set eyes on this chap. He knew far too much about me, and sooner or later, he would have found me."

"And what about the bullet you've left in his skull? Don't you think it'll be found and questions asked about who pulled the trigger, and then there'll be a world-wide man-hunt out for you."

"What... the bullet from an unknown gun that'll be at the bottom of the sea?" Donnelly sniggered.

"Anyway, it'll be difficult to find that bullet once this place is destroyed." He had to wait a few seconds for her reaction, and when none came, he added "Fire is a great cleanser."

She saw him smiling, and a chill ran through her. "So if you're not going to shoot us, what are you going to do?"

"I'm sure we can come to some sort of arrangement." Hamilton thought it well past time to try and add his own solution to what was looking like his own demise.

"I'm not going to talk to you about the rubbish you're going to offer me." Donnelly retorted angrily. "Words and more bloody words is all you're good for. And they're not worth listening to, so shut the fuck up."

Donnelly was starting to become agitated. "Paddy, you have a look for that C4 and the detonators. He'll have kept them apart, but they'll be somewhere in this cabin. Then use the trolley outside to get that chest over to the boat. Let's get this pair over to the chamber." He said to Seamus.

"Why not just shoot 'em here?"

"Because I want them to suffer a slow and painful death. Especially her. You first." He looked at Patricia and indicated that she should leave the cabin ahead of him, and as she did so, he added. "Just one wrong twitch from you… " He jabbed his pistol into her kidney.

Seamus made sure Hamilton stayed close behind the pair as they exited the corridor and headed for the gangway. All the migrants had moved away towards the trawler and were still queuing up to embark. As they made their way across the docking platform, Patricia mournfully looked for her pair of commando types, but they were too far away and engrossed in their duty of searching those getting on the trawler.

As they were escorted across the breezy platform towards one of the massive stanchions, both Hamilton and Patricia were lost in their own personal worlds trying to imagine what the chamber was.

"Open it." Ordered Donnelly as they approached a vast wall of steel, interrupted only by an obvious hinged door; very much wider than an average doorway.

She leaned forward to unlatch the two iron levers that held the door firmly closed against the elements, and depressed the long bar that released the opening mechanism towards them. All the while, she kept an eye on Donnelly in the hope of being able to snatch the weapon out of his hand, but he was too wary, and kept a suitable distance away. Once opened, he flicked his pistol to one side, indicating that they should go in.

Patricia hoped that there would be an opportunity to evade Donnelly once she stepped-over the raised threshold, but it immediately became apparent that one didn't exist. As soon as she entered the drier internal environment, she saw that it was enclosed; in a manner of speaking.

"Over there." Donnelly motioned to one side while taking a few steps backwards in the opposite direction. Hamilton joined Patricia and the pair of them stood mournfully together while Seamus firmly closed the heavy outer door, which resonated with a loud clang.

The room wasn't really a room at all, but was the inside of one of the massive support columns of the rig. It was lit with evenly spaced lights, but it was difficult to estimate how far either up or down the ends were. Trapdoors in the thick-grated floors would allow a person to ascend or descend via welded rungs, protected by tubular ribbed cages. Permanently, there was the distinctive sound of the sea as it edged its way around these vast columns and reverberated in a soothing manner, but one couldn't tell from which direction if it was either coming or going. Coupled with a background odour of oil which left a sickly, sticky sensation in the back of one's throat, the unfamiliar hallucinogenic surroundings could affect those suffering from either agoraphobia or claustrophobia.

Hamilton and Patricia were struggling to take in the extraordinary environment, and instead were looking at an enclosed elevator that looked like it could hold about ten people. It was directly beside them, just where the grating stopped, and was attached to the inner wall of the column by a pair of sturdy railway-track type runners that descended somewhere beyond sight.

Donnelly walked up and surveyed the control panel, paused, then pressed a couple of buttons, and at the sound of a mechanical pump and a slight hiss, the part-glazed door of the elevator opened evenly. "Welcome to the diving chamber."

Once the thick oval-shaped door was fully open, they could see that inside there were two benches opposite each other, several valved pipes with a pair of analogue gauges and a communications telephone; nothing much else apart from a pair of recessed tubular lights.

"It's used by the divers to decompress after extended dives on underwater repair jobs. Every rig has a decompression chamber but this one, being in waters this deep, lessens their recovery time considerably by being able to come up from the bottom at the same time. It also has the added bonus of being able to prepare them in advance. It travels on these rails either up or down, and I can control it all from here." Unusually for him, he went theatrical, and bent forward, pretending to inspect the panel closer. "Oh, look. It says here that its maximum pressure is 30Bar. Let me see now... that must be over a thousand feet if I'm not mistaken."

He returned his gaze to look at them. "But don't worry. The seabed here is only about seven hundred." He smiled at them as he made the last facetious remark. "Let's see now." He attended to the panel. "Let's set the descent speed at... something nice and slow so that you get to appreciate it... ten feet a minute... no, that's too fast. Let's make it five... and increase the pressure at the same rate." He dialled-in the parameters. "After about thirty minutes, I reckon your eardrums will burst, then you'll start bleeding through your nose... maybe other orifices as well. I don't know what'll happen next, but it won't be pleasant." He didn't know, but he wanted it to sound nasty. "And just to make sure, we'll program it to flood at say... five hundred feet?" he looked at them. "But by that time your lungs won't be able to scream, because they'll have collapsed."

He finished with the panel and took a few paces towards them, making sure he was not blocking Seamus's firing line. "Unfortunately, I won't be here to see your bodies implode or you gasping for air in your final moments, but I'll at least have the satisfaction of knowing that I've fucked you up, like you've fucked me up."

"You don't have to do this, you know." pleaded Hamilton. "I've got access to millions."

"Oh, I think we're well past that stage." Donnelly dismissed his offer out of hand. "You're more likely to use your millions to try and track me down. You see, I know what kind of a person you are, so don't tell me I'm wrong."

Hamilton didn't have an answer for that, but Patricia was thinking more clearly and had her own questions.

"Why the double-cross on Windaw?"

"He was just a means to an end. Always was, but sooner or later, he would have worked that out. He was a loose end and it was quicker to put him out of his misery now rather than later. You see, I can be compassionate."

His oxymoronic statement stalled Patricia, but she recovered quickly. "And what about Mr. Huseyn. Is he a loose end too?"

"He'll not be a problem, once I've rearranged things with my gold broker."

"Who is your gold broker?"

"Why the fuck should I tell you?" Donnelly shouted at her; his mental stability was toppling.

"Because it won't matter if I'm dead, will it?"

He grinned at her acceptance of her fate. "No, I don't suppose it will." He walked to the side of her, but still kept well out of arm's length. "Henri." He blurted out. "And that's all you'll ever know. Now get in the fucking chamber."

Seamus edged closer so that he and Donnelly, with

guns levelled, appeared to be herding their prey. Patricia went first. Hamilton's complexion had turned to an ashen grey, and he turned just as he went to lift his leg over the door's lip. "Look, can't we do a deal? I can… " He received a hefty blow on the side of his head from Donnelly's pistol, and would have tumbled to the floor inside had Particia not put her arm out to steady him. By the time he had seated himself opposite Patricia, all the pair of them could see through the door was Seamus pointing his gun.

Chapter 23

The door closed ominously, and they heard the hydraulic locking bolts firmly seal it, creating a dead hush.

Hamilton recovered, stood up, and banged his fists on the glass door panel in desperation. "Let me out, let me out. Please let me out. I can make you rich beyond your dreams." He started to sob. "I've got gold you can have. Please… " He sunk to his knees. "You can have everything I've got."

"Oh, be quiet you quivering heap of jelly. He's not going to let us out of here." Patricia didn't have to raise her voice very much to get through to him, as there was no sound or even the faintest echo in the stillness of the air chamber.

"You heard him. We're going to die. He's going to suffocate us… and then drown us. I can't put up with this. We've got to talk to him." More desperate, he thumped the glass with his fists again, but stopped as the chamber started its downward descent with a gentle jerk. "Arrgh… nooooo!" He cried; his first real tears since his childhood. He dropped to all fours on the floor and sobbed.

For nearly a minute, Patricia watched him make an exhibition of himself and listened to his plaintiff cries. She watched out of the window as the floor steadily seemed to rise. "Listen, as these are our last moments, why don't you tell me about your life, and I'll tell you about mine?"

His sobbing eased, and he turned his head to look up at her. "What's the point?" He hung his head back down.

"Well, I don't want to waste my last precious moments, do you?" There was no response from him. "Tell me about your love life." Still no response other than a snivel. "I thought you had wonderful life entertaining all those women. Were there really that many?"

The mention of women finally distracted his misery away from his impending doom. He lifted himself up off the floor and sat directly opposite her; face to face a foot apart. "You're not really interested in my life. You just want to distract me."

"Now that's a thought." She sat back as far as the side of the chamber allowed. "But seriously, you must have real stamina the way you get through them. I'd love to know what your secret is."

He took one last forlorn look through the window, then turned back to her. "No secret really, just a natural urge that I had to satisfy." He paused reflectively. "From the moment I got out of bed in the morning, I felt I had to... well... relieve myself, and what better way than to do so in the company of a woman."

"From what I've heard, it was women, and not just one at a time."

Hamilton was emerging from his state of depression. "And why not? If one can enjoy one, why not more, and before you ask - yes, it was wonderful."

"How about young girls? Teenagers? Boys even?"

"No boys. I'm not like that, but on occasion, young girls." He reflectively paused. "But I found that those approaching middle age were the best. They knew how to control themselves at the right time. It was the Far Eastern women who knew how to pleasure me the best."

Patricia congratulated herself that she had managed to distract him enough, and felt it was like being in an open confessional box, so she egged him on. She saw his tears had begun to dry up. "There must have been those with whom you swapped sex for secrets."

"Oh yes. They were the easy ones, but not usually as pleasing and they were merely a means to an end. I could usually tell that they were after some sort of information and willing to trade their bodies for it. So at the appropriate moment, I'd give them some low-level, out of date rubbish and send them away happy. All except Gertha. She was one of the EEC's commissioners."

"And what about your wife?"

"Oh, she was different; at first. But before long, I found her love-making boring, so we came up with an arrangement that kept us both happy. She allowed me to play away just so long as I was discrete about it, but I think jealousy got the better of her in the end. Shortly before I left, I found a note saying that she's divorcing me, and that's one of the reasons why I came out here to see if Donnelly could help."

"In what way?" She frowned trying to work out what he meant.

"I was going to ask him… " Hamilton paused.

"Go on. You might as well tell me, because it soon won't make a difference."

"I was going to ask him to get rid of her. I couldn't have her ruining my life with all the scandal and other whatevers coming out into the open, I really couldn't. Not with being in the running to be the next Prime Minister. If all that came out, I couldn't have lived with myself."

Patricia hid her instinctive reaction of horror, knowing that he might clam up, so she altered tact, and led him on as gently as she could. "I suppose you were concerned that some of those women might have come forward, which would have put an end to your way of life. Have you always had a great sexual appetite?"

"Ever since my school days. You see, once I started, I just had to carry on, and it became an obsession with me. I enjoy being around women;especially when it comes to their final surrender."

"Even if it means raping them, including me?"

"Er, yes. Sorry about that." She concluded that his unexpected apology was only forthcoming because of their inevitable death. She could still visualise the moment when he had tried to rape her in his apartment, and it sent a slight shiver down her spine. "But in my experience, I find that women actually enjoy being raped at the moment of orgasm."

"Well, I'm sorry that I disappointed you."

"You nearly gelded me for life. You know that, don't you?"

She couldn't hold back the hint of a smile as she recalled how hard she had kicked him where it hurt most. She felt a slight but gentle increase of pressure in her ears, and knew she had to extract more out of him before he descended into reticence. Even though she wanted to continue learning more about his outrageous sexual exploits, it was time to move on to other subjects. "And what about that mole hunt you had me working on? That nearly ended my career."

He blinked at the change of subject. "Yes, that was also unfortunate. You were a lot smarter than I gave your credit for; you and that partner of yours."

"Did you find your mole?" She didn't reveal that she already knew the answer.

"Oh yes. We found a whole nest of them in the end, but I suspect there's more of them hiding somewhere."

"So why did you try to frame me in that drugs bust?"

"I have to admit that you were a thorn in my side at the time, and it seemed the easiest way of having you removed from the investigation."

"Where did you get hold of those bags of cocaine? That couldn't have been easy?"

"Umph. That was easy. As a senior cabinet member, I had access to almost anywhere, and the depository in Belfast was no exception. You managed to wriggle out of that one as well. I say, did you feel that?" He poked an index finger in his right ear and wiggled it. "How are you going to get us out of this one?"

Patricia too experienced the pressure increase. "Try yawning, like you'd do on an aircraft to equalise. Hold your nose and blow your ears out. Like this."

He did. "How much longer do you reckon we've got?"

"He said about half an hour." She lied, not wanting him to focus on what was ahead of them; at least, not just yet. "What about that platinum mine scam in

Bulgaria? How did you get on to that bandwagon?"

"That too was easy. These third-world country leaders look to the UK as a source of wealth, and quite naturally, want some of it for themselves. The idea that slush funds don't exist is a myth, and when international trade agreements are signed, it's naturally assumed that there's a bribe that goes with it." He leaned forwards a little. "Why shouldn't I help myself when all those around me are doing the same? If I don't get any of it, then somebody else will get a cut, and before you ask; yes, I did make over a million." Having made his point, he sat back.

"And I suppose the same goes for this little enterprise?"

"Of course. There's more money floating about in the oil industry than they know what to do with. We're talking about billions. Corruption is a way of life, especially when it comes to the west African nations, not quite so much in the Middle East, and nobody's going to notice the odd million here and there going missing."

"In gold?"

"No. I didn't know about that, and still don't. Did you see any?"

"Nah."

"That must have been from something else on the side that they'd been running. Maybe human trafficking. Ouch." He pressed his hands to his ears and massaged the side of his face, while Patricia opened and closed her jaws a few times. "Tell me how you managed to track Donnelly down." He asked and blinked a few times.

"That wasn't easy, because he's a slippery sod." She wondered how much to tell him, but needed to keep the conversation going. At least it would distract her as well. "It was a simple treasury request that started it all off. They were wondering why Blue Lizard wasn't making enough money to generate taxes, and when one of their operatives went missing, it raised red flags. I was called in but when I went to interview Donnelly, he sent me away with a flea in my ear, so then I knew I was on the right track."

"But you didn't know I was involved."

"Not initially, but almost insignificant snippets of information came to light."

"Such as?"

She didn't want to get drawn in to a blow-by-blow account, but gave an example. "You were seen at Ascot rubbing shoulders with people from OPEC."

"Ah, them." He said ruefully. "I never gave it a second thought, as it was just the sort of thing one does as minister."

"It wouldn't have mattered under normal circumstances, but it just happened to coincide with my investigation at the right time. Is that where you receive your pay offs? Somewhere in the middle east?"

"No. I wouldn't trust them with my money. That's in the BVI."

"BVI?"

"British Virgin Islands. It's in The Caribbean and a previous British overseas territory, but more importantly, outside of British financial scrutiny. It's a safe place to put one's money if you don't want it to be found. I believe it was you who managed to put a stop to my Isle of Man account."

She nodded. "How much have you got in the BVI?"

He was trying to remember how much he had amassed over the years, but the effect of increased air pressure didn't help. "Over ten million." He said at last.

"All tax free."

"All tax free." He conceded. "For what it's worth, you can have it all if you can get us out of this bloody contraption." He winced and scrunched his head to one side as the pressure began to take a more serious toll. "Are you finding it difficult to breathe?"

"Just a bit." She looked at her watch and saw that nearly fifteen minutes had passed. "Talking of money, how did you manage to cash in on the platinum?"

He wheezed a little as he gathered his breath to respond. "They told me when they were going to dump it on the metal market, so I just bought or sold at the right time." He keeled over to lie down on the bench. "I can't take much more of this."

Patricia was becoming concerned, and edged herself along the bench to prop herself up in the corner. She reached over and pressed the green button on the telephone receiver, waited and pressed it again; and again. She felt the edges of unconsciousness creep nearer as her vision began to narrow, and felt a warmth creep over her entire body. She shook her head to delay passing out, and saw that Hamilton's eyes were now closed. This was the moment she had been waiting for. With great effort, she reached over to Hamilton's pocket and extracted his mobile phone; it took two attempts to place it in her own pocket.

Just about able to see, she was horrified when the chamber took a sudden lurch downwards; or at least she thought it did. Immediately the pressure climbed, forcing her to lie down on the bench, and all the while, she kept pressing the green button, which kept going in and out of focus.

Chapter 24

Time is meaningless when one is unconscious, and Patricia had no idea how long she had been cataleptic. Opening her eyes and immediately shielding them from the relatively bright white light, she discerned someone standing over her. At the same time, she was aware that people were speaking, so she risked opening her eyes a little further. Focussing was hard, but both sight and sound were gradually returning.

"Welcome back, beautiful."

She tilted her head to see Justin crouching down level with her, and she let out a moan as she tried to sit upright, but felt a hand on her chest holding her down. "God but I ache. What's this?"

"It's an oxygen mask, and the doctor says you've got to keep it on for a while."

She relaxed and tested her limb movement. "It feels like I've been through a meat grinder."

"At least your senses are working properly. He tells me that that's normal. Fortunately, you weren't down there very long, so there ought not to be any permanent damage."

She closed her eyes for a moment and recalled her last conscious moments. Still with her eyes shut, she asked. "How about Hamilton?"

"He's been stretchered over to the rig's hospital,

but the doc's not sure if he'll make it." Justin waited a few seconds before nervously asking his next question. "What was it like?"

She slowly opened her eyes; this time without any focussing problems. "Not very nice. You ought to try it sometime." She watched a smile grow over Justin's face. "Can I get this bloody mask off me now?"

He helped her with the elastic round the back of her head and took care of the tube that came from an oxygen bottle on the floor. She sat up. "How do you feel?" He watched her carefully in case there were any signs of her passing out, but was relieved when she stretched her arms out wide.

"I've got a headache, but nothing a hot bath couldn't help with." She rotated her head a couple of times as if testing to see if it all worked properly. "Go on then. Tell me what happened to you."

"You first. Before you pass out again."

She took a deep breath and started from where they had parted company on the helicopter landing pad. She was about halfway through when she remembered. "Is his lackey still on board the ship?"

"Yes he's there, or at least he ought to be there. I laid him out cold and left him tied him up in Windaw's cabin. He left soon after you did with a big black chest, but I got him when he returned. Why do you ask?"

"Just as we were leaving his cabin, I heard him say to get the C4 and detonators. Did you find any?"

"Don't worry. Yes, I did find the C4 and I've hidden it."

"Thank God for that." Real relief showed on her face.

"What happened next?"

She continued, but when it came to the part when she persuaded Hamilton to pull himself together, she reached into her pocket and brought out her phone. "I hope this is still working."

He watched her as she attended to the screen, and listened with increasing incredulity as the voice recording progressed. It was rather muffled and the occasional word needed to be guessed at, but in the main, it was all there.

"Bloody hell. You had the forethought to start recording." He shook his head. "I wouldn't have thought of that, knowing I had only moments to live."

She leaned forward and pecked him on the cheek. "That's what makes me special, and I've got another present as well. He'll miss it, but he won't know where it went." She produced Hamilton's mobile. "Lots of lovely information. Now it's your turn. How did you manage with Donnelly and Seamus?"

"When I followed you down to the docking platform, I noticed two fellows just hanging about down there. They didn't seem to be rig types, and when they followed you onto the Pan Maru, I knew then that there'd be trouble. You were clearly outnumbered, even with me, so I just hid next door until they went into to Windaw's cabin, then listened in. I almost came in to break it up, but I'm glad that I didn't, otherwise we would never have got Hamilton's confession."

"I don't suppose it crossed your mind that there was a decompression chamber in here did it?"

"You're right there, but I couldn't sneak up on them

after they closed that big door, so I waited on the other side of this upright until they came out."

"You took your time rescuing us."

"I had to wait until they were well out of sight. With both of them armed, it would have been suicide if they'd turned around and seen me on the open platform. Nowhere to hide and I didn't fancy having to dive into The Atlantic if they'd spotted me. I nearly did come in, but those two big door levers put me off. They wouldn't have failed to see me if I'd opened it and presented them with a perfect target."

"Do you know where they are now?"

"The last I saw of them they were getting on that motor cruiser."

"Weren't the two commandos there to stop them?"

"They were too busy checking everybody trying to board the trawler. I understood that that was their instructions... and they obviously did as well."

"Oh, bugger. That means Donnelly can take off any time he chooses. Let's go and check."

"Hang on a mo. The doctor said you were to rest here for a while."

"Bollocks to the doctor. I'll thank him later, but right now, we've got to stop Donnelly." She stood up a bit too hastily, because she had to steady herself as she exited the chamber.

Heading for the big iron door ahead of him, she stopped and looked at the control console. "You didn't have any trouble operating that, then?" She queried.

"Erm. No, not too much, but I got the hang of it in the end. Why?"

She gave him a look. "I'll tell you later."

Chapter 25

They emerged on to an empty platform. Immediately Patricia felt the Atlantic breeze bite through her clothing, and attributed the chill she felt to her recent experience.

"They've gone." Commented Justin as he looked over to where both the trawler and motor cruiser had been when he had entered the support column. "But the Pan Maru's still moored-up."

"Shit." She looked around. "Can we get out of this wind?" They went across to what looked like a large electrical cupboard and stood in its lee. "I hope our commandos have returned to the helicopter? Have you still got your radio? I lost mine."

"I told them to guard Hamilton, so they're probably in the sick bay." He handed his radio over and watched her raise it to speak; but then she stalled. "I can't remember my call sign."

"You're Dolphin." He said in a matter-of-fact tone of voice, realising that she still hadn't fully recovered.

She received confirmation of her suspicions thirty seconds later, and relayed as much to Justin. "He says both vessels left about the same time less than half an hour ago."

"I know. I heard." He pointedly looked at the radio that was on loud speaker.

"Oh, sorry. I'm still not quite with it. Bloody hell, I'm cold."

Justin did the gentlemanly thing by removing his own coat and putting it round her shoulders. "Better?"

"Much. I'm just wondering where our support vessel is. HMS... "

"Cutter. Why don't you call them up on the radio and ask them? They might be in range." He looked at his watch. "It's due here anytime soon. Channel eight." He reminded her.

She dutifully followed his instructions, and was rewarded with more voice than crackle. After ascertaining who was who, she gave them docking instructions; right where the trawler had been.

"Half an hour away, so can we find somewhere warm in the meantime?" She asked.

They sought shelter on the empty bridge of the Pan Maru, and Justin helped himself to a spare jacket that was hanging on a hook. "Better view from up here and we should be able to see them coming."

Patricia opted to sit in one of the tall seats that was anchored to the deck, rested her forearms on the console in front of her, and stared out of the windows at the ocean. She reflected upon her near-death experience and wondered if she could have avoided it, if only she had had one of the commandos with her. She knew Donnelly was a bastard, but knew now that he was a dangerous and sadistic one as well. She remembered an acronym from one of the manuals. He was an AWEC which stood for 'Approach With Extreme Caution'.

Thoughts of what she'd do to him, if ever she came

across him again, were put to one side as she really wasn't feeling like doing anything to anybody right now. "Justin?" She needed him by her side, but there was no reply. She didn't feel as though she had the energy to turn round and see where he was. Instead, she looked down at her hands and saw that they were shaking. She called his name again and was rewarded when he appeared at her side bearing a cup of coffee. "Oh Christ, thank you." She cupped it in both hands and sipped it.

"It's out of a machine, so it probably won't make your shakes any worse. Look what I found in Windaw's cabin." He placed a block marked C4 in front of her.

"Is that what I think it is?"

He didn't need to answer.

"And he was going to explode this, wasn't he?"

"Had it wired up to Windaw's bedside alarm clock. It's ok now. I removed the detonator."

She reached out and fingered it. "Bit like putty."

"Donnelly's got a lot to answer for."

She stared into middle space. "Justin. You're thinking clearer than I am. What are we going to do now?"

"Now we wait for the cavalry in the form of HMS Cutter."

"No, I mean, once it gets here."

"Ummm. I see what you mean." He walked up to the glass for an extended view while thinking. "Well, all our enemies have fled, so there's no point in staying here. One thing we've got to do is get you back on terra firma and a comfortable bed for you to recover in." He turned to see her reaction to his suggestion.

She finished her sip. "We've got two targets. I don't want Donnelly getting away, and we've got to intercept that trawler, so which one do we go after? Trawler or cruiser?"

It took him little time to come up with an answer. "The trawler's a slow boat, and that can be intercepted at any time before it reaches landfall, but the motor cruiser's much faster. From what our commando friends said, and if I were in his shoes, I'd bet that Donnelly's on that faster boat. And I saw one of his chaps loading a big box on to it, presumably with the gold inside, so he'll be on that one."

She mulled over his logic after another sip. "I agree. So we go after the motor cruiser."

He took a couple of steps towards her and leaned on the opposite side of the console so that he could look into her eyes. "Do you think you're really up to chasing boats across the Atlantic to god knows where?"

It must have been the coffee, because she was beginning to feel more lifelike. "I'll be fine, and anyway, I reckon I know where he's going."

He stood upright. "Where?"

"Ireland." She saw him thinking it over, but continued. "It's the closest landmass, and he'll want to be on land as soon as he can, so that he can disappear again. He can't do that while he's on a boat this far out. He's got his office in Cork, and I'll bet you a pound to a penny that's where he's headed because he's got money stashed away there. He'll feel safer on home turf." She paused in thought. "He'll also have evidence he wants to destroy, maybe in his office or house. Fire usually does the trick."

"Makes sense to me, but he might figure out what

we just have, and head in another direction."

"I doubt it. He won't want to land on British soil as that comes under our direct jurisdiction, and France is that bit further away, so it has to be Ireland."

"I hope HMS Cutter is fast, because he's got a fair lead on us. Do you know what kind of ship it is?" Justin asked as he turned and looked out of the windows.

"Not the faintest, nor how fast it'll be."

"There it is. Over there."

Patricia joined him, and through the salt-stained glass discerned a boat coming towards them at high speed. "The rate they're going, they'll be here in five minutes. Come on. Let's meet them."

The morning's previous swell was beginning to subside to a more manageable level, and as the patrol boat drew alongside, it was evident that the crew knew their business well. Even before it kissed the rubber fenders, two crew members jumped the short distance across to the docking platform and tied off the mooring ropes. Two others produced a short gangway, along which Lieutenant Shaw confidently strode. Patricia was surprised when he stood directly in front of her, introduced himself and saluted. She made a pathetic effort returning it.

"The captain asked me to convey that he understands that we're under you orders ma'am, and requests that you come aboard."

She didn't know how to address someone who was technically her junior, so didn't attempt anything naval, but felt that she needed to project an air of authority. "This is Mister Crawford and he'll be joining us. We'll follow you." She quickly glanced at Justin to see his reaction; straight after Shaw turned around. He led them onto the stern of the boat and along the starboard side to a door that opened outwards, and held it open for them.

To her, Lieutenant Commander Greensmith looked like he would be more suited to being a school headmaster, but his naval uniform told a different story. "Welcome aboard, Inspector." He looked over her shoulder, and she introduced Justin as Mr. Crawford. "I understand from Mr. Glen here that you two have worked together before."

It was a small enclosed bridge, but somehow Miles had managed to make himself inconspicuous on the far side, right up to the point of Greensmith's comment. "Hello again. When they told me you would be here, I knew you'd managed to get your man, but I'm surprised it was out here, halfway across The Atlantic." He smiled wryly.

"Yeah. I cornered him alright, and he cornered me as well. I'll tell you about it later, but he's not here."

The smile evaporated from his face. "That's a shame."

"It might not be if we can catch him in time." She turned to Greensmith. "We believe he's heading for Cork and he's got an hour's head start on us. "Can I bring you up to speed once we get going?" A thought flashed into her head, and she tactfully added "That's if you can agree to it?"

"We're supposed to be under your orders, and I'll have to clear it with the Irish authorities if we're going to enter their waters. They might be our allies, but protocol demands that we observe certain niceties." He glanced over her shoulder again. "Shaw."

"Right away sir." Shaw closed the door behind him and they heard him shout casting-off orders.

They were under way in less than a minute. Greensmith gathered them round an elevated screen at the back of the bridge, and after a moment, a coloured chart appeared. "Cork's the best part of three hundred miles from where we are now. At an average of thirty knots, it's ten hours. What kind of vessel are we after, and how fast is she?"

They all steadied themselves as the rake of the boat tilted under power. "Do you mind if I sit down?" Patricia looked at one of three tall swivel chairs, and once more comfortable, she outlined who they were after and why.

"If you know the name of the boat were chasing, we can find out what her performance is, and from that, we'll know if there's any chance of catching her before we run out of international waters." Stated Greensmith.

She looked at Justin, but he was no help.

Greensmith got them to describe the length of the motor cruiser, but neither of them had paid enough attention at the time, and their estimates varied between forty to sixty feet. "Assume she can cruise at twenty knots. That'll take her some fifteen hours, which means we can catch her in time, but if she can manage any faster, then it's going to be nip 'n' tuck. "Let's have a look at the radar then. If we can see a boat heading in that direction it'll show up if it's within about thirty miles."

He turned to face forwards. "Jessop. Anything on the radar?"

"No sir. Not a dicky bird other than the rig." Came the response from the rating that was manning a console on the other side of the bridge.

"It's probably a waste of time checking Marine Traffic." Volunteered Patricia. "This lot are famous for keeping their transponders turned off, but it's worth a shot."

"Jessop."

"On it sir." He'd overheard Patricia's comment.

"What's our speed Ahmad?"

"Thirty knots sir."

Greensmith made his way forwards to look out at the sea conditions, then leaned over and pressed an intercom button. "Shaw."

"Yes sir." came the metallic voice from the open bridge above.

"Do you think the swell will allow us to go a little faster?"

There was a five second delay. "Not much, but I'll give it a go."

They all felt the increase in speed.

Greensmith turned to them. "I'm concerned that we might catch up with that damn weather front that delayed us on the way out here, and that'll slow us down again."

"The same will apply to Donnelly's boat, won't it? And he'd reach it before we do." Justin offered.

"I'm aware of that, which is why I want to make as much speed as we can now. A storm front like that has a habit of interfering with our radar." He looked at Patricia pensively. "If we do manage to catch up with them, what are your intentions?"

*****

With a smile on his face, Donnelly relished the moment as he watched the top of the chamber disappear downwards at a sedate pace; but not for long. He had other things on his mind such as keeping an eye on Paddy, and hoped he had done what he had been told. By now, the chest ought to be aboard the motor cruiser, but he wanted to start a fire in Windaw's cabin first. That would distract everyone while he made his getaway.

He and Seamus made their way over towards the cruiser, and he looked over at the trawler. As far he could tell, there was hardly any space left on the open deck as the migrants shuffled their way between themselves to get comfortable for the final part of their journey. The skipper had obviously given departure orders, and he watched the final rope snake its way back on board.

"I'm glad those commandos have fucked off." Commented Eamon as they jumped aboard. "Once they'd finished checking them migrants out as they got on the trawler, they started sniffing around here, especially when Paddy turned up with a bloody great trunk. Christ, but that was heavy. What you got in there? Lead bars?"

"Guinness."

"What?"

"It's full of Guinness."

It took a moment for Eamon to cotton on to the fact he was being told to mind his own business.

"I hope it's safe."

"In the cabin there."

Donnelly disappeared but only to confirm that it was indeed where it should have been. "And Paddy?"

"Last I saw of him, he was heading back to the tanker."

"Right. Get ready to get underway while I go and fetch him."

Donnelly gave a soft curse under his breath as he walked across the platform to the tanker; he'd told Paddy to stay with the chest. It was a bit eerie getting on to an almost deserted tanker, and he presumed most of its crew had opted to get on the trawler. He wondered what Windaw had said to them before his demise.

He let out an indecipherable Gaelic curse when he opened Windaw's cabin and saw Paddy tied up on the floor. Blood had coagulated down one side of his face, but his moans attested to his conscious state.

Once he had removed his gag and freed his hands, he asked "Who the fuck did this to you?"

"If I knew, I'd have his bloody balls." He rubbed some of the sticky blood away from near his eye, and explored the lump at the back of his head.

"I'll hold him down while you cut 'em off. Where's that C4?"

Paddy motioned over to Windaw's desk.

"Right. You get yourself back to Eamon. I'll finish off here." He waited until Paddy left the cabin. A thought crossed his mind that he could have left him trussed up, but he had to consider what the others would say to him. He looked around and attended to the C4.

Twenty minutes later, he felt a euphoric wave of relief as the heel of the motor cruiser dug into the ocean. They were all in the cockpit. "Well done lads. Another few hours and we'll be celebrating in O'Malley's."

"With what you're paying us, I won't have to share with the two Bettys anymore." Seamus gave a wide grin.
"But you told me you liked to share." Responded Paddy.
"That was before her sister joined in."
They all knew about Betty and her twin sister.

Chapter 26

"That storm front should be clearing the Dingle Peninsula within the next hour, so it looks like we'll have a clear run, but the swell's increasing the nearer we get." Informed Greensmith after consulting the weather repeater.

Patricia had just emerged from the bowels of the boat, where she had spent the past four hours asleep in one of the cramped bunks. She'd paid no attention to the two other crewmen who were sleeping in the bunks above her, and wasn't aware that Justin had occupied one of the remaining bunks soon after she had put her head down. She still had a slight headache, and her sense of balance was a little out of kilter, but overall, she felt more human and capable of coherent thought.

"Any sign of them on radar yet?"

"No, but if you're right, they should appear very soon." He went and sat on one of the seats while she chose to stand; stabilising herself by hanging on to a deck-mounted rail. "Are you able to tell me who we're after and why?"

It was a question she hadn't considered before, and while there was no state secret involved thought it best not to divulge more than necessary. "We're after an Irish national called Jason Donnelly who's up to his eyeballs in smuggling, human trafficking and murder, amongst other things." She went on to tell him a few more details. "You'd better know that Maurice Hamilton is also involved as well."

He blinked. "The MP, Maurice Bloody Hamilton?"

"The very same. Donnelly tried to kill him as well as me, at the same time, and he's currently in the rig's hospital."

"Well, that's upped the game rather."

"I think you've got hold of the wrong end of the stick. Hamilton was in on Donnelly's scam."

"Ahhhh." Greensmith said pensively. "Sounds like they fell out with each other then."

"There's obviously no honour among thieves."

"Are they armed?"

"Yes." She described what guns she had seen, and went on to tell him about the C4 explosive Justin had found.

"Do you reckon he's got any more with him?"

She had to think about that one. "He might have. I didn't see how much there was in the first place."

"We're going to have to treat these characters with extreme caution then. Now that you've told me that, I'll have to warn the Irish coastguard."

She braced herself a little more as the boat rebounded off the waves a bit more severely.

Greensmith reached over to the intercom. "Shaw... How's the swell looking?"

"A bit dicey sir. We were just talking about that. Looks like we're catching up with the tail end of that storm. Can we trim some speed off?"

"Go ahead. Who's with you?"

"The Coxswain sir."

"You might as well both come down to the cockpit."

"Aye sir."

Greensmith took a good look out of the window. "Shaw's a good sailing man, and I know exactly what he means by a bit dicey. We may be in for a rougher ride than I'd hoped for."

The engine note muted a little and the boat instantly felt more stable. A minute later Shaw and the Coxswain entered through the side door.

"Contact on the repeater sir. Twenty-eight miles dead ahead. Course zero four zero. Same as ours." Jessop announced.

Patricia felt a satisfying buzz run through her, and her eyes briefly locked with Greensmith's.

He glanced at the clock. "More or less halfway."

"More contacts sir."

"We're entering the shipping lanes." He explained to Patricia, then addressed Jessop. "Don't lose them in the traffic."

"Aye sir."

"Shaw. Work out where we'll intercept."

A thought occurred to Patricia. "Will he be able to see us on his radar set?"

"Probably, but only if he's keeping a keen eye glued to it. The other vessels are a bit of a blessing and will show up as much larger than us, so he'll probably miss us; at first. Let me show you."

He guided her towards the portside where Jessop dutifully stepped to one side of his console. He pointed with his finger on the black and green screen. "We're in the centre, and this is our chap near the top, here. These two much larger contacts here and here look like they're containers, and a fair bit larger than the Pan Maru. I expect we'll come across one or two others shortly, and possibly the Santander ferry."

She watched the mesmerising sweep of the solid radar line as it picked out the vessels he had described. "Is he still headed for Cork?"

"At the moment, yes. Shaw?"

"About three-and-a-half hours at our present speed sir."

"In or out of the twelve-mile limit?"

"Just about on it sir."

"I take it that's Ireland's limit?" Queried Patricia.

"Yes. The waters are international outside of that twelve-mile limit, and maritime law applies. Inside, it's Irish. We'll wait a little longer and see how close we're going to get before I contact the coastguard."

"And what difference is there between the two? Maritime and Irish I mean?"

"It means we have to go through official channels and obtain permission to enter Irish waters, and that's likely to take time. I can't cross into Irish waters until we receive that." The tone of Greensmith's reply suggested that he'd encountered this irksome issue before.

"And what if I told you that we already have that permission?"

He tilted his head slightly, then watched her reach inside her jacket and produce a folded plastic envelope. "Here's authorisation from Patrick McEnilee. He's a minister in the Irish government." She handed him the letter to inspect, which he handed back to her after a few seconds

"You'd better keep that safe, because that's our 'Get Out of Jail Free' card." She returned it to the envelope, and saw him staring at her. "There's more to this than just catching crooks isn't, there?"

Their eyes locked on to each other, and it took a moment for her to respond. "You're right. Donnelly's the man we started out being after, but when we discovered that Hamilton was involved, it changed. Hamilton's been around long enough to make some powerful enemies, and that's how I came to be in possession of McEnilee's letter of authority. So you see, we already have the Irish government's blessing to pursue Donnelly." She could see that Greensmith still had doubts. "I've even got international arrest warrants with me."

"Really." His eyebrows lifted in genuine surprise.

"Like I said, Hamilton's got enemies who would like to see him sidelined. Permanently. I'm as much an instrument in this as you are. I've been sent to detain Donnelly, and you've been sent to help me catch him. If Donnelly manages to reach dry land, we'll never find him again, so if it helps, you can always blame me and say you were following orders."

Greensmith's eyes narrowed as he made his mind up. "Now that you put it that way, I think we can satisfy both the British and Irish governments' desire to see justice done." He looked out of the window. "I don't suppose you'd be one of Hamilton's enemies would you?"

"He and I go back a little way, so yes, there is a personal element to this as well." She smiled at his preceptive comment.

"Then let's hope we catch them up before it gets too dark."

* * * * *

As good as Shaw's word, a little over three hours later, the lights of the motor cruiser could just be seen in the deepening dusk. "We'll be approaching the twelve-mile limit shortly sir." He reminded.

Twenty minutes earlier, Greensmith had been conversing with the coastguard station at Crosshaven, just south of the city of Cork. He had been told that their rescue boat was in dry dock for hull repairs, and would not be available to assist, but permission to enter Irish waters had been given. He wondered if they might have refused, had he told them that the men that they were chasing were more than just smugglers.

"Post look-outs and darken ship. Reduce speed by half Coxswain." Justin and Patricia heard him order from their corner of the cockpit. The interior lights changed from white to red, and Greensmith explained to them. "No point in advertising our presence, so I've ordered our external running lamps extinguished, but in the same token, I don't want to be running down an innocent fisherman. They clearly haven't spotted us yet. Looks like you're right as they're heading directly for Cork, but they might bypass Crosshaven and head for one of the smaller marinas further up river. That's when tracking them on radar becomes tricky, because they could well lose themselves amongst all the other pleasure cruisers. We'll know in a few minutes. If he turns to port, it's Crosshaven, otherwise… "

Miles entered the cockpit and joined them in the corner. "I presume we're nearing our destination."

"I was beginning to wonder when you'd put in an appearance." Remarked Patricia.

"There's only so much sleep a man can have, so instead, I've been studying a manual."

"Studying what?"

"It was titled 'How to survive a shipwreck in The Atlantic.'"

It took a second before they reacted predictably to his humorous statement.

"Well, as you can see, we're nearly close enough to swim." She looked out of the windows at the twinkling lights on the mainland.

"Where's our man?"

She peered harder out of the windows. "Can't see him right now, what with all the other lights in the background, but the radar shows him heading for Cork. That's it there, dead ahead."

"So he's heading home. At least we're both familiar with that part of Cork."

"Might not be the same part as we're not sure which marina he's heading for yet. That chap on the radar will be able to tell us in a minute… I hope."

"What's my role in all of this?"

She had to think about his question. "I think that the powers that be thought I could do with some additional help, seeing that they've already lost one man. Someone to watch my back, if you like, so, depending upon how things turn out, do just that. Only you and I know what Donnelly looks like, oh, and Justin as well. We think there's three or four of them, probably all armed, and I reckon they'll want to vanish once they reach the mainland." She gently nibbled her lower lip while considering what might transpire. "His got to move that heavy chest, so he'll have arranged for some form of transport. A big car, or a van, which means there could be at least one other person. I don't know. But what I do know is that he'll shoot anyone who gets in his way."

"We know he's already murdered his partner, and he's got two pistols that we know of. One of them being Patricia's." Offered Justin as emphasis.

Miles summed up what they were now all thinking. "So we'll have to catch them before they transfer the gold into their van."

Realising how true his words were, Patricia approached Greensmith who was standing next to Jessop at the radar repeater; both of them were looking intensely at it. "There he goes now, sir."

Greensmith waited a moment before addressing Patricia. "Looks like he's heading for Crosshaven. That makes sense, as it's well away from Rushbrooke naval yard, and easier to slip in and out of. No islands to have to navigate your way around either."

"Can we get there alright?"

"Good question, but as it's a relatively new man-made marina in a natural valley, there's plenty of depth.

Far more than one would normally expect, so there's no problem."

"We've got to catch up with him as soon as he lands."

Greensmith looked out of each side window, then down at the scope again. "Now that we know where he's heading, there's no need to potter around anymore, plus he can't escape to the open sea now that we're in the estuary. He can't get past us. Shaw."

"Sir?"

"Turn the navigation lights back on and catch up with them. Smartly."

"Aye sir." Shaw gave orders and the boat surged forwards again.

"Captain."

He turned to her.

"Have you got any armament I could borrow?"

He looked at her sceptically at first. "What have you got in mind?"

"Nothing too large. A pistol perhaps?"

"Wait here." Two minutes later he returned. "This ought to do you."

She took the leather holster from him, which housed a 9mm Glock. He watched as she checked that the chamber was empty then expertly worked the action. "Perfect. And thank you."

"I'll detail a boarding party, but please try not to get into a firefight."

"Target's slowing sir." Jessop called out.

Greensmith took three quick steps to share the repeater. "He's heading for the yacht club moorings.

Watch your heading, Coxswain. There's plenty of boats anchored at their moorings." He returned to the trio. "When he moors up, I suggest we draw alongside, then you can board directly."

"How far ahead of us is he?" Asked Patricia.

"Not too far. He'll have less than five minutes before we're on him. Get yourselves ready. Probably better to go from the aft deck."

He waited until they disappeared, then turned to Shaw. "I want you to have the deck gun manned, but unloaded. Remember, we're in friendly waters and I don't want to start a war, so let's drift up to them nice and quiet, and see if we can't catch them by surprise. Detail two two-man armed teams, and get them to report to me."

"Aye sir."

They felt the engines more than heard them as they quietly pulsated somewhere beneath their feet. The boat inched forwards towards lines of yachts that were tied up to their respective moorings in a series of jetties on their left, and there was the familiar clank of loose lanyards betraying those whose owners had not tightened them enough. Patricia and Justin were suitably attired in dark navy coats, but Miles, lying flat on the far side of the deck and dressed in camouflage, was virtually invisible but for the whites of his eyes. She had time to comically wonder if he ever needed to apply white face paint, just to break up his silhouette.

"Justin. I know you're not armed, but please stay close to me. I know it sounds silly, but, you know... in case... "

"I wouldn't want to be anywhere else in the

world right now, and besides, I'm getting very good at rescuing you."

Greensmith appeared out of nowhere. "We can't board him directly as he's berthed between two other cruisers, so we're going on to the next jetty but one. You can see it over there." He pointed uselessly in the dark.

What little light there was came from tall shore-mounted lampposts and dim, evenly-spaced hip-high posts down each jetty, and it was barely adequate enough to be able to make out where he intended them to land; it was at least a hundred yards further on. As they passed Donnelly's boat that had squeezed itself between two others, from its own cockpit lights they could see them securing the stern with ropes.

Patricia craned her neck and spotted a Range Rover type vehicle parked more or less opposite where Greensmith intended them to land, and even though one would expect to see a Range Rover parked in a marina, this one had its internal light on. "Miles." She called in a loud whisper.

Once Miles had slithered over to her, she told him what she wanted him to do, and he dutifully disappeared out of sight towards the front of the boat.

She could now see the lip of the concrete dock, and heard the engines briefly roar as they slowed the boat down to nudge the big rubber tyres. She was aware of one sailor removing the safety cable that ran above the forward gunwales, and two more jumping down with ropes to secure the boat to the quayside; safety cable-man then produced a gangway from nowhere. Then, out of the corner of her eye, she thought she saw the spectre of Miles leaping across the narrow gap and vanishing into the darkness beyond.

"Right behind you Ma'am."

She turned to see four armed sailors, and gloomy though it was, they were obviously awaiting her command. She was so glad Greensmith had decided to provide her with additional help. She wasn't sure in the dark, but the one on the left may have been female. She didn't know how much they'd been told, so thought it best to give them a clear idea as to what she expected of them. "On that boat over there are several armed men smugglers, and we're going to stop them reaching that Range Rover. One of those men is wanted for murder, and he'll shoot anyone who gets in his way, so mind yourselves." She wanted to add so much more, but time was now turning against her. "You block off the end of their jetty, then follow me up while I confront them."

Four blank faces stared back at her, so she added. "Clear?"

"Yes Ma'am."

"Let's go, then."

Chapter 27

She walked purposefully, even though her mind wanted her to run at a half-crouch, and as she reached the start of the jetty she looked round and saw that they had paired-up; two over her left shoulder and two over her right. Justin was behind them all, in the shadows.

She spent the last half-minute wondering how she would present herself to the criminals on the boat, and worked out that she would be the last person on earth that Donnelly would be expecting. She'd use those valuable few seconds of confusion, and could picture Donnelly's face when he saw her. Withdrawing the Glock from her pocket, she winced at the tell-tale sound that it made as a round slid into the chamber, but she needn't have worried as those on the boat were far too engrossed in what they were doing to notice anything else.

It is a well-known fact that when standing in a lit area, or a building, one cannot see anything beyond the influence of the lighting; more than a foot or so past the pool of light, and one is oblivious to what is going on. It is completely dark out there. Quite the opposite applies when looking into an illuminated site; one could be one yard away or a hundred yards away; it would make no difference, as those within are clearly exposed.

Now only a few feet away from the lit boat, but

still in the shadows, she could clearly see two of them struggling to get Windaw's chest over the rear transom and onto the planks of the jetty, and she presumed that the man waiting there was the driver of the Range Rover. Donnelly stood wordlessly next to Eamon by the wheel in the lower cockpit without lifting a finger to help him, and waited until the chest was safely on the side. He eventually went over to it, unlocked and opened it, and handed out what looked like several bundles of cash to those who had gathered round. This was the pay off they had all been waiting for.

Just at the point where another step would have revealed herself to them, she stopped dead. No more than thirty feet away was the person who had so far outsmarted, belittled and tried to murder her, and memories of her previous entanglements with this obnoxious man threatened to overwhelm her into inaction. With a serious bite on her lower lip, and a glance over one shoulder to make sure her armed escort were where they should be, she took a deep breath and shouted in as firm a voice as she could manage. "You're a murdering bastard, Jason Donnelly."

The shock to him was exactly as she had envisaged. In reaction, his body stiffened, and his eyes widened as they looked around for the source of the accusation that seemed to echo in the night. Seamus and Paddy had similar reactions to what must surely be a ghost, but Eamon and the driver weren't quite so afflicted.

She stepped slowly out of the shadows and into the illuminated arena that could have been out of a stage scene when the director shouts 'freeze'. Her intent was very threatening as she levelled her Glock at the middle of the circle, but the driver had other ideas. His hands were already in his pockets, and it didn't take much for him to curl his fingers round the grip of his stubby revolver, and fire it at her through his coat. The report of the gunshot acted as a signal to the others who all reacted in different ways. It was as though someone had thrown a Thunderflash into the fire.

Predictably, Seamus and Paddy each produced their guns as they dived in opposite directions; Seamus back into the boat, while Paddy unwisely hid behind one of the flimsy jetty lights. Eamon ducked down into his boat with thoughts of retrieving his gun from one of the cockpit lockers.

Donnelly disappeared behind Windaw's chest as it offered the most immediate and solid cover, and fought to free his gun from his pocket, but instead of firing at the apparition of Inspector Eyethorne, he took the time to think about his predicament.

All of them were now aiming at where Patricia had been, but she had dropped onto her side clutching her leg. In his haste to shoot her, the driver's haphazard aim had been hampered by the shape of his pocket, and unable to elevate his gun far enough, the bullet had ricocheted off the jetty's planking and grazed Patricia's thigh. His second shot went hopelessly wide. He was the first to be put out of action by a well-aimed shot to his shoulder.

The second person to be incapacitated was Paddy. Trying to hide behind a light, which actually lit up his face, made him an easy target, and with a scream he dropped his gun as a bullet ripped into his forearm.

The four sailors from the boat, acting in tandem, now eased themselves carefully forward into the lit area, and pointed their rifles at the remaining threats, or where they had been a second ago; both of those threats were in the boat, but not visible.

Justin hadn't seen where the driver's bullet had hit Patricia. Fearing the worst, he rushed forwards to help, and breathed a sigh of relief when he saw most of her body move. "Where are you hit?"

"In my left leg."

Ignoring the others, he positioned himself to have a better look and saw that there was a decent bloody patch on the outside of her thigh, just where her trouser had a tear in it. His initial reaction was to drag her to safety, just a few feet away outside of the pool of light, but felt resistance from her, so stopped pulling. "Come on. Let's get you away from here."

"No." She winced at the pain. "I can handle it." She moved herself into a more comfortable upright position, taking the weight off her injured leg. While she did so, Justin looked around at the situation and was reassured by the presence of the four sailors; a pair each side of them no more than ten feet away. One of them looked at them and mimed what they should do next. She held her hand palm down indicating that they should remain exactly where they were.

"Where's Donnelly?" She asked Justin in a low husky voice.

He looked at the scene again. "Can't see him."

She groaned at the prospect of Donnelly escaping,

but turned her attention to the chaps who had disappeared into the boat. "Come out with your hands up." She shouted, even though it hurt a little to do so.

Nothing happened for a moment, then one arm appeared, slowly followed by another; then Eamon's head appeared. He stood up in surrender. "Seamus?" They heard him say. "There's six of them against us." He looked down to where Seamus still hid below the level of the boat's lip.

When Seamus suddenly stood, it was clear that he had no intention of giving up, as he aimed his gun in their direction. It may have been the light, or it could have been the realisation that there were five weapons pointing at him, but whatever it was, it caused him to hesitate, and before he had decided which person to aim at, a bullet took him in the shoulder. He collapsed out of sight back into the cockpit.

"God bless you Miles." She said loud enough for only Justin to hear. "Help me stand." As he did so, she swore. "Fuck, but this hurts."

Justin looked down again and saw that the bloody stain had spread. "Rather you than me."

She gave him a withering look. "It might be you if we don't find Donnelly." She turned to the pair on her left and told them to cover those in the boat and those lying prone on the jetty. Then to the pair on her right, she said. "Stay put but keep a sharp eye out. There's one more of them somewhere. Don't kill him. I want him alive."

She and Justin looked around, trying to figure out where Donnelly had gone, and there was only one place left. With Justin's help, she took a few steps, then pushed his arm away from her as she got used to the pain in her leg. Pointing her borrowed pistol ahead of her, she hobbled towards Windaw's open chest; but he wasn't hiding behind it. "Shit. He was here a few minutes ago, but where's the bugger gone now?"

They looked left and right at the rows of moored yachts, both wondering if he'd managed to hide himself on one of them. "You take the left. I'll take this side."

To most, it would have been an obvious choice, but from what little she knew of Donnelly she reckoned that he'd have avoided that option. She closed her eyes and listened, while applying her detective's mind to the problem. She ignored what she expected to hear; the slapping of the waves, the clacking of the lanyards, the occasional gurgle from eddies, and even a sharp cry of pain from the boat where they had been a moment ago.

An unexpected muffled chink of something metallic, like a chain, made her open her eyes and look in the direction of the end of the pontoon, but it was too dark to see anything. Slowly, and with her gun pointed down, she made her way to the end of the jetty; her eyes slowly adjusting to the darkness the further she went.

She stopped when she reached the end and strained her eyes to see if there was anything out of the ordinary, but nothing jumped out at her until she looked down and could just about make out the outline of her own Browning pointed directly at her. It was less than two feet away. She knew how powerful it was and instinctively feared what would happen to her if he decided to pull the trigger.

"I don't know how you managed to escape the chamber, but it doesn't matter now. You're a fucking pain in the arse, like a terrier that won't let go. A…" She heard some form of Gaelic interspersed with vague English swearing, which was obviously as uncomplimentary as it could be. It gave her time to think, and look at what he was standing on. From the way he moved, she surmised that he was in a very small boat; from its outline, probably an RIB that he had managed to find.

She still held her pistol in her right hand, but knew that if she dared to point it anywhere near him, she'd be dead in an instant.

She saw the barrel of her Browning flick to one side and back again. "Drop it. I don't fancy being shot by a poxy woman; especially you."

She realised that she had no choice in the matter. She could hardly see him since he melded into the blackness of the sea, but with light behind her, she knew she'd be a very easy target. Rather than toss it into the water, she let it drop, and it landed on the wooden decking with a dull thud by her foot.

"I'm going to drill you, but before I do, I want to know how you got out of that chamber."

"Why the fuck should I tell you anything?"

"Because I can make it painless for you with one shot to your head or take you apart piece by piece, and I'll start with your other leg. I'm told the kneecap is extremely painful." He altered his aim so that the muzzle of her Browning, only a foot away, pointed at her right knee.

"If you pull that trigger, they'll hear you and know where you are."

"And then I'll just vanish into the night. Now tell me." He insisted.

If only she could keep him talking a while longer; Justin would come to her rescue.

"And if I do, you'll just sail away without your gold."

"I'll have to make do with the two bars in me pockets. Now how did you....."

They both heard the unmistakable hiss of escaping air at the same time, and a moment later, a louder, more urgent hiss. Donnelly was the first to react by whipping his head round in the direction of escaping air, and quite rightly realised that the RIB he was standing on was losing buoyancy. They heard the sound of a third, and much louder air source. Patricia took advantage of the distraction by falling to the deck, a fraction before Donnelly pulled the trigger; the bullet whistled away into the night, missing her knee by millimetres. She cursed as her elbow painfully encountered her Glock, which was now under her.

At the first sound of escaping air, both of them automatically went into self-preservation mode, but it was Donnelly's whose predicament was becoming desperate very quickly. The RIB started to cant over to one side, and he hardly believed what was actually happening. His logic told him that it was sinking, but it also told him that that couldn't be true because he hadn't moved, and therefore there was nothing that could have caused an air leak.

Steadying himself, he looked up at where Patricia had been a moment ago, but all he saw was an empty space, and hoped his shot had smashed her kneecap to bits. He quickly returned to his own problems as seawater began to swirl around his feet, and this time he had to lean heavily on one of the side ribs, but as he applied pressure with his outstretched hand, it gave way beneath him, and allowed more water to flood into the boat.

In an attempt to stay upright, he fell backwards, his head glancing off the cowling of the Mercury outboard, and instead, ended up sprawled across the width of the narrow boat. His now thoroughly-soaked clothing clung to him and restricted his movements as he wallowed around in several inches of cold water, and somewhere along the line, he let go of Patricia's gun. Desperate to escape from the bottom of the boat, he tried to pull himself up by grabbing hold of the outboard's handle, but with little to hold it in place it slipped from his grasp, causing him to fall sideways off the stern, and into the sea.

As he submerged, he instinctively reached out and grabbed part of the rubber side which compressed as he closed his fist around it, but it was no longer inflated enough to support him, but still he hung on. He spluttered out a mouthful of cold seawater, and coughed-up whatever was left.

Patricia gingerly lifted her head beyond the end of the jetty and watched Donnelly flailing around. When she had collapsed onto the decking, not only had she encountered her Glock, but also a loose coil of rope.

She bent down, picked it up, pulled it through her hands and traced its origin to the RIB.

The sudden appearance of torchlight from the far side of the RIB took Patricia by surprise, until it illuminated Miles' face as he trod water, and she thought she saw the glint of a knife in his hand. It all became clear to her that it was he who had slit wide openings along the flanks of the RIB, but she didn't dwell on that thought for long. She heard and felt thumping footfalls running towards her from behind, and glanced back to see that Justin had found a torch from somewhere.

He drew alongside her and shone it down at Donnelly, who was making all sorts of peculiar noises at the rear of the quickly sinking RIB. Miles' torch lit him up from the waterline and revealed his stretched neck as he struggled to keep his head above water.

He pleaded with them in between gasps. "Help me... I can't... gold's too hea... rope... aargh." The last thing he saw was Patricia, only a few feet away, standing stock still at the end of the jetty, holding up the rope that he so desperately needed. With a final gurgle, he disappeared beneath the waves.

Nobody said anything; they didn't have to.

Chapter 28

The sky gradually turned from dark to light grey as the dawn reluctantly began to break, and its wan light revealed further greyness in the form of a dockyard. Leaving Shaw in charge of refuelling at the Rushbrooke naval yard, Greensmith joined them in the warm bowels of his boat, and as he entered the mess they ceased talking. He didn't say a word until after he had seated himself, conveniently at the head of the table, and one by one, he surveyed the trio. He then purposefully cast his eye to one side to scrutinise the large chest that took up far too much space. It reminded him of the adage that there was an elephant in the room.

His voice was even. "You can probably guess what I'm about to say, but I'll say it anyway. I need to make two reports, one to The Admiralty and the other to the Irish authorities. The first can wait until they've finished their breakfast, but the Irish need an explanation a bit sooner as to what went on last night. No doubt you have your own reporting to do, and I'd rather present a coordinated version that doesn't conflict, so therefore welcome any comments you might like to make." He theatrically looked down at his watch. "I have less than an hour before their base commander comes aboard, and I expect he'll have the local Guarda with him."

Justin and Miles sat across the table from each

other, while Patricia was sandwiched between them with her leg propped-up on an adjacent chair. She had accepted the boat's medic's offer of a painkiller as he had bound her flesh wound.

"Tell them the truth." She proposed.

Her comment had them all wondering why she had suggested what seemed to be a rash statement.

"Oh, I intend to." Replied Greensmith. "But there's some explaining to do when it comes to those three Irish Nationals now lying in hospital with gunshot wounds, not to mention a fourth missing one, and I expect the captain of the motor cruiser might have something to add."

Patricia had had time to think about events while her leg had been attended to, and her analytical mind had concentrated on the problem. "Well, start at the beginning and break it down step by step. You advised the coastguard, and had permission to pursue smugglers into Irish waters, and that pursuit terminated here in Cork. Correct?"

"Correct." Said Greensmith.

"They were seen by four members of your crew, dividing their booty on the pontoon. Correct?"

"Correct."

"Did any of your crew fire a shot?"

"No. I gave them specific orders that they were not to fire unless in self-defence, and only then if it was life-threatening."

"And they obeyed that order. Correct?"

"Correct."

"And you can prove that by accounting for any

ammunition that was handed out and returned. Correct?"

Greensmith nodded this time.

"Then it's obvious that the villains had a serious falling-out and shot at each other."

"Now, wait a minute. They'll tell a different story that they were shot by an unseen marksman."

"Is it normal practice for a patrol boat to have a marksman on board, and do you have one among your crew?"

"No." His eyes flickered to Miles.

"Then it's the smugglers' word against yours. Their versions of what happened will differ from each other anyway, to such an extent that nobody's going to believe what they say."

"And what about Donnelly, because he'll be found sooner or later?"

"Like I said, tell them the truth, because that will certainly be in my own report. He was trying to escape with the gold, and we can show them exactly where he went down. The Irish will be most grateful for our help in pointing out his location, especially when they find two gold bars worth over a million quid in his pockets. The fact that they were all armed, and that shots were fired, reinforces the fact that there was a fire-fight on the jetty."

"Then who was he supposed to be running away from?"

"That's obvious. He was trying to get away from the others with the gold."

Greensmith still had scepticism, but it seemed she had an answer to everything. "Ah, but what about that chest?"

"What about it?" She let him mull on that one for a moment. "The Irish don't need to know about the chest, do they? Nobody saw your crew lifting it on board in the middle of the night. Anyway, they'll be distracted enough sifting through evidence and inaccurate statements. They'll be overjoyed with finding Donnelly and his two gold bars at the bottom of the riverbed. Even if his cronies do say that there was a chest full of gold, there's no proof that it ever existed, and it might become one of those myths, like Drake's treasure, and X marks the spot."

"Um." Was all Greensmith managed.

"Annother thought has just occurred to me." Announced Patricia.

They all looked expectantly at her while she strung the moment out and considered what she was about to say.

"I haven't seen inside the chest, but I'll bet you Windaw had what gold he'd collected over the years, melted down so that it's now unmarked."

Nobody said anything while they pondered what she had just said.

"Hadn't someone better look inside and see what is actually in there?"

It was such an obvious question that at first, nobody reacted while they individually thought it over. It was akin to opening Pandora's Box, and the worrying notion simultaneously crossed all of their minds; that there might not be anything of value in it at all. To Miles, it was logical. Justin wondered why he hadn't thought of it before, and Greensmith cursed himself for not having done so when it had first been carried on board.

In an unspoken agreement, and after looking at each other across the table, they left it up to Greensmith. He stood up, walked over to it, lifted the lid on its hinges, and silently gazed down. His lack of movement prompted both Miles and Justin to follow suit, but Patricia remained seated.

When the chest had been in his cabin, Windaw had proudly arranged its contents so that he could look down and croon over the fruits of his labours. Gold bars were stacked crosscross style on top of one another on the far right, two open blue canvas bags of Krugerrands on the far left, permits, passports and other such documents clipped together in the middle. Sheaves of cash, elastic-banded together and separated by their denomination, were in the front.

Now, however, with the chest having been manhandled and trolleyed from one vessel to another on two occasions, tilted to one side or another, and generally treated for what it actually was, its contents had been thrown around and were no longer in the neat and tidy state that Windaw had left it in. The heavy gold bars had been flung from one side to another, crushing whatever had been in their path, and were now haphazardly heaped towards the back. Most of the Krugerrands, having spilled out of their bags, and were lying loose on the bottom.

Three stunned men looked down in silence on what was a considerable horde of treasure; the sort of treasure one imagines pirates duelling over.

Miles was the first to react. "Now that's what I call a treasure chest. All that glitters isn't gold, but it is here."

Justin reached down and scooped-up a handful of Krugerrands, which he palmed from one hand to the other, then handed half of them over to Miles to feel, and while he did so, Greensmith bent over and lifted one of the gold bars out.

None of them could take their eyes off the booty until Patricia interrupted their cerebral thoughts. Still sitting with her leg propped-up, she surveyed the three transfixed men as they greedily ogled their catch. "Those Krugerrands are about three grand each and a gold bar over half-a-million."

It took a bit more than a moment for each to react to her comments; once again, it was Miles. "Three grand each?" He queried, trying to work out how much he was holding in one hand, and once he had repeated her rough valuation, Justin did his own calculations before looking down into the chest at the splayed bags. He gave up. "There's an awful lot of them in there."

Greensmith now registered what the others had been talking about and did his own, easier, calculations, and had to drag himself away from concluding how much, when Patricia repeated her question aimed at him. "I asked, any markings on it?"

Miles and Justin watched him examine it closely by rotating it in the light. "None that I can see." He replied.

"We'll that proves my theory correct that he's had it melted down, but we'll have to wait and see how fine it is."

"You mean how pure it is." offered Greensmith, still looking closely at it.

"Something like that." It was time to bring them

back down to earth. "Unless it's just gold paint over lead, and those Krugerrands are ninety-nine percent copper."

That shocked them out of their daydreams. Greensmith first, followed by the other two, returned their prizes back to the chest.

"I don't suppose… "

"No." Patricia said firmly with an authoritative voice in response to Justin's expected question. "And before you ask your next question, the answer to that is no also."

Once Greensmith gently closed the lid; the brief enchantment they had experienced ended abruptly.

"What happens now?" Asked Miles.

Patricia was prepared, and looked at Greensmith. "Now, it's down to our captain here to decide what he's going to tell the Irish authorities."

All eyes turned to Greensmith as he pondered the conundrum, and they could tell he was in two minds. "I need to have a word with you in private." He said to Patricia.

Miles and Justin filed out and they headed for the lee side of the foredeck to watch the refuelling.

He sat down opposite Patricia. "You really know how to put someone on the spot, don't you?"

"I thought I was saving you from having to be put on the spot. By the Irish."

"How do you work that one out?"

Despite her recent experiences on the rig and her throbbing leg, Patricia's mind was working perfectly. "If you tell the Irish about that chest, all sorts of questions will be raised. Like, where did it come from, who melted it down, where's it going, is there a fence involved, who sanctioned that number of Krugerrands and why. That will then lead to questions about oil, embargos, government ministers, the rig we've just come from, the Pan Maru. For every ten questions answered, there'll be ten more, and leading to why you and I were pursuing them. That'll mean someone in Whitehall having to answer awkward questions, and therefore scrutiny of what happened last night will surely focus on our actions. Whatever answers we give will be contorted to whatever political response is desired at the time, and probably won't accurately reflect on what really happened. You and I will be looked upon as mere pawns that will be played on a level far above our pay grades, and if necessary, sacrificed in order to satisfy the diplomatic status quo."

Greensmith had not come across someone like Patricia before; someone with executive contacts who looked beyond the horizon to foresee what was over it. As a career man in The Royal Navy, he had aspirations of promotion and up to now, it had all been plain sailing, but a whiff of an unsavoury diplomatic incident might well dampen his prospects.

Patricia didn't know what he envisaged for his future, but did appreciate the quandary he was now faced with, and added. "Use the KISS principle."

"I'm aware of the Keep It Simple Stupid term, but withholding information from the Irish might turn out to be not so simple if extraneous factors came to light afterwards. For example, I'm sure there are things you have not told me because they might compromise your own position, and you expect me to do likewise. Yet here we are discussing the pros and cons of suppression, to suit our own ends."

"I know what you mean, but in this instance, there is very little chance of the whole truth ever coming out. There were no onlookers, none of the public were involved, there was no damage to any third party other than an RIB, and we apprehend ed those carryingout illegal activities as ordered to do so. And don't forget, we've got that 'get out of jail free' card. So, why not prepare a brief written statement, all of which can be corroborated, and hand that over to the base commander for him to forward as a matter of course?"

"You make a convincing argument." He conceded pensively. "Do you really believe that's what I ought to do?"

"Most certainly. Just give him the salient points, and make it as brief as you can. I'm not going to give you the 'I was never here' story, thus leaving you with all the awkward explaining to do, because I've just given you a perfectly credible version that won't raise any eyebrows." A thought crossed her mind. "Have you met the base commander before?"

"No."

"Then treat him like an equal, and report this episode as just another smuggling operation. Run-of-the-mill, but with a golden ending in the form of Donnelly."

Greensmith looked at his watch. "I'd better go and start that report."

"Just one more item to consider, and that's the trawler full of migrants. It might be wise not to mention that until we're well under way and in international waters. If you can locate it again, then that would be the time to report it via radio, and leave it to the Irish to deal with. That'll be another feather in your cap."

Greensmith left, leaving her alone to muse; if he got it wrong, it wouldn't be just his own future that was in jeopardy. Without the pressures of having to concentrate on recent events, she felt a wave of weariness come over her. She closed her eyes and tried not to think about her leg that seemed to throb the more she thought about it, and she gingerly probed her bandaged wound with her fingers, but quickly decided not to go any further.

Justin, followed by Miles, came back in. "I take it you managed to talk Greensmith round to your point of view?"

"I hope so too. He did seem a bit happier."

"They're just about finished refuelling, and I take it we're taking the slow boat back to England."

What with all the goings-on, she hadn't considered the helicopter and the two commandos waiting for her back on the rig; and then there was Hamilton. "Shit, of course. Greensmith'll be busy, so can you ask Lieutenant Shaw if he can spare a minute?"

Justin went in search of the lieutenant leaving her and Miles alone.

"You look a little weary, but I suppose you've a right to be." He commented.

She gave a pip of a laugh. "Do you know what I'm looking forward to most right now? A hot bath. But I suppose that'll have to wait until I get home." She repositioned herself. "And then the bloody medics'll tell me not to get my leg wet." Their eyes met. "I haven't thanked you for what you did last night."

"All in the course of a day's work, and there's no need to thank me. It's not every day I get to use my rifle for real."

"You must have been well-positioned to have hit them where you did without killing them."

"It was pretty much as you said it would be. What you said to me on the boat before we landed, but I couldn't have done it in daylight, because I'd have been too visible."

"Where were you?"

"On the deck in the shadow of a telecoms box at the end of the jetty; just over eighty yards, so not too difficultwith the night sight... except when you got in the way."

"Then I'm glad I didn't stay still. But what prompted you to knife Donnelly's RIB and how did you get there so quickly without being seen?"

"While you were rolling about clutching your leg, I watched Donnelly slip those gold bars into his pockets and slink away down the far end. He'd figured out that I was the hidden sniper, and that he'd never be able to get past me and reach the mainland, so there was really only one place he could go. He cut the rope attaching the RIB to the yacht on your right, and it was obvious that that was how he intended to escape. The others were taken care of, so I simply slipped into the water and swam to the end under the jetty."

"I thought RIBs were difficult to sink."

"So they are, but we know where the flotation cells are, and which ones to pierce. It's something we've been trained to do, and I've actually practiced that before."

"Thank God for practice, and thank you anyway."

He looked at her thoughtfully. "You know, most people suffer from PTSD, but you don't even have the shakes. Have you been trained?"

"I can't claim to have had any training in that department, and I suppose it's just the way I am. Mind you, living with Justin produces its fair share of surprises. Talk of the devil... "

Justin and Shaw filed into the mess; the latter addressed Patricia. "You certainly know how to excite the crew." He sat down next to her and pointed to the chest. "They're making bets as to how much treasure there is in there, and if they'll get a share of it. Prize money, like they used to hand out in the old days if you like. Diamonds, rubies, pearls, gold and silver platters, you name it, and they've already thought of it. We're going to have to tell them something. Perris, he was one of the four that was backing you up, reckoned he saw bars of gold."

"I'm sure we can come up with some plausible explanation once the captain is free." Patricia didn't want to think about that right now as she had other things on her mind; namely Hamilton and the waiting helicopter. "I presume you're able to contact the helicopter on the rig still?"

"Oh yes. Assuming they're manning their radio."

"Well, I'd like to talk to them if possible, then once the captain's finished with the base commander, I'd like to talk to him too."

"I'll see what I can do." He got up and left.

Chapter 29

"You'll get fat, and then you'll waddle down the aisle instead of gracefully arriving at the altar like an angelic bride should."

Attired in a short loose-fitting dressing gown, Patricia held the spoonful of raspberry trifle in mind air, and looked up at Justin from her comfortable position in one corner of the sofa. With the television placed directly opposite, and her leg rested on cushions over the other seats, well within reach on the table beside her was a cup of warm cocoa. "Well, you'd better hope I don't get so heavy that you won't be able to carry me."

"No chance, not the way I've been waiting on you hand and foot the past two days. What did your last slave die of?"

"Ecstasy. Unbridled ecstasy." With a seductive look and with a wide grin, she shovelled the spoonful of trifle into her mouth, then enticingly licked her lips.

"I thought the doctor told you to eat plenty of protein? What you've got there hardly fits the bill!"

"Then you can cook me a nice juicy steak with all the trimmings for supper."

"And I suppose you'll want another pot of trifle for pudding afters."

"That's a good idea."

"Serves you right if you're sick afterwards."

"Anyway, I need to get my strength back up again quickly. Gibbons wants to see me at New Scotland Yard the day after tomorrow, at nine o'clock sharp."

"Was that him on the phone half an hour ago?"

"No. That was Tates."

"What's he told you about Hamilton?"

"Apparently, he's made a good recovery, but being older than me, suffered more from nitrogen poisoning. He regained consciousness sometime around the time we cornered Donnelly, and started swearing at anybody within earshot, so much so that he had to be locked in the recovery room. Those two commandos were ordered to accompany him back in one of the helicopters."

"Where is he now?"

"Tates didn't say, but he did say that he had trouble walking."

"Serves the bugger right."

"No doubt I'll learn more from Gibbons. Oh, by the way, can you give me a lift, 'cos I don't fancy battling my way across London with this leg?"

"I'll tell you what I will do."

She looked at him quizzically. He bent down and gently lifted her up with both arms, being very careful to avoid hurting her leg, and carried her into the bedroom.

"Just because you've got a gammy leg doesn't mean you can't enjoy my company to the full." He said as he laid her flat on the bed and undid her dressing gown, revealing her nakedness.

Under her watchful gaze, he undressed himself, knelt at the side of the bed, caressed his fingers ever so gently up and down, each side of her bandaged leg; and kissed it. "That's to help it get better, because I don't fancy being married to a peg-leg."

"Justin... !"

* * * * *

Justin dropped her off in Victoria Embankment and watched her hobble the several yards across the stone pavement and in through the glass-fronted entrance of New Scotland Yard. She was early, for two reasons; She did not want to be caught-up in London's infamous congestion traffic, thus causing her to incur Gibbons' displeasure, and while waiting to be summoned, it gave her time to prepare herself. She'd already presented her report electronically, but knew he would want to look into her eyes when answering pertinent questions; questions that could only be answered face to face.

Tates held the door open for her, and she sat directly opposite Gibbons as comfortably as she could. She knew he would notice her limp, and guessed that he would not be commenting upon it.

"When you sat there for the first time some months ago, I told you that my first rule was that you should not draw attention to yourself. You were to remain invisible, and as far as the general public were concerned, you did not exist."

She didn't quail at his opening remark since she had expected something similar.

Gibbons continued. "It's just by the grace of God that your incursion onto Irish soil happened at night, and that nobody was there to witness what actually happened." His tone of voice inferred that if it had happened during daylight hours, that there would have been dire consequences. "But as things stand at the moment, the Irish have only raised one low-level enquiry as to the type of wounds that three of their Nationals received. You see, upon examination in the naval hospital, where they're more used to seeing gunshot wounds, their doctor quite rightly raised an eyebrow when she discovered that their injuries seem to have come from the same high-powered rifle, and not the weapons that were retrieved. We've already advised them that they should be looking for an unknown assassin, who obviously fled the scene, possibly from a rival organisation. It's small details such as this that can lead to conjecture as to what really occurred, and in my experience, minor particulars can lead to rumours which impinges on the operation of Special Branch, and that's why I insist that you are as circumspect as possible."

"Sorry sir, but it was the only way I could think of at the time to resolve this whole issue."

"I know. I've read your report, and I think you acted correctly." He conceded, much to Patricia's relief. "Tell me more in detail, starting from when you landed on the rig."

She was aware that Tates was taking notes, but as far as she was concerned, that didn't change anything, and she started on what turned out to be a monologue lasting nearly twenty minutes; except for an occasional interruption from one or other of them. She couldn't help but shudder when it came to the part where she had passed out in the chamber, as that was as close to death as she had ever come.

She finished by extolling Miles's actions, and for some unknown reason added that should the opportunity ever arise, she would feel comfortable working with him again. She wasn't a Catholic, but she now realised what it must be like leaving a confessional box.. Relieved that it was all over, all that remained was for Gibbons to absolve her of all her sins. She realised that Gibbons and Tates were talking to each other, but such was her state of mind that she didn't take any of it in. Her leg started to throb again.

She waited for an opportune moment. "I have a few questions of my own, sir."

They both looked expectantly at her.

"What happened to the chest and its contents?"

Tates replied first. "That's a question that you ought not to ask."

Gibbons followed that comment after some thought. "I think we can allow a little latitude seeing that you were responsible for its recovery. It's not been confirmed by The Treasury yet, but it seems that there was over ten million in gold, cash, and diamonds, and we are still sifting through several documents which will probably reveal Captain Windaw's worldwide contacts. Once we have ascertained who and where these people are, we'll have to decide what action should be taken; if any."

"Some of the crew on board HMS Cutter might have seen the gold. What about them?"

"I think that's a matter for The Royal Navy to deal with, but I expect they'll be bound by The Official Secrets Act." Gibbons said flatly.

"I know I shouldn't ask, but do you think there'll be any recovery money coming my way?" Before Gibbons could rebut her suggestion, she continued. "If we hadn't prevented the Pan Maru from being blown up, which would have undoubtedly damaged the rig, the insurers would have had a particularly large claim on their hands. Additionally, there would have been an environmental claim for oil pollutionalong with probable loss of life claims. All of that taken together would have amounted to tens, if not hundreds of millions of pounds. All the time, insurance companies reward those who assist them, so why not us? You see what I'm getting at, don't you? I'd like to think that our actions deserve a little more than a pat on the back."

She let him chew over that for only a moment. "I presume the Irish were happy at discovering those two gold bars in Donnelly's pockets, and that will have reflected well in somebody's books."

As she recited her half-rehearsed piece, she saw Gibbons' face betray a look of concern; but she hadn't finished. "And if we hadn't caught up with Donnelly and recovered a gold mine… "

Gibbons held up his hand. "Ok, Ok, I see your point." He turned to Tates. "Is that TOPOLOV scheme still running?"

Tates scratched his head. "If it's what I think you're referring to, then yes." He addressed Patricia. "TOPOLOV stands for 'Tanker Owners Voluntary agreement concerning Liability for Oil Pollution', and it's something that's been in place ever since The Torrey Canyon oil spill back in the Sixties. It's not something that those outside of the industry know about, but basically all tanker operators contribute into a global fund to cover oil spills. You probably haven't heard of he Torrey Canyon, but it was a large tanker that ran aground of the Cornish coast, but you will have heard of The Deepwater Horizon disaster in the Mexican Gulf. That was partly covered by TOPOLOV."

"Thank you for that brief history lesson." Remarked Gibbons. "Under the circumstances, I think we can provide a sum for reimbursement. Arrange that, will you." He said to Tates.

"Thank you sir. Just one more question."

Gibbons raised his eyebrow a smidgeon; it was the first time she had seen him do so.

"What's happening with Hamilton?"

Tates answered; "Nothing much at the moment, as he seems to be recovering from his strenuous trip in his London apartment just across the river there." He indicated with his eyes out of the window which overlooked The Thames. "No. 10 has issued a statement to the effect that he contracted pneumonia while visiting an oil rig off the Irish coast, and that he will remain under medical supervision for a few days. All standard stuff, and so far, nobody has queried it."

Gibbons continued; "However much The Press suspect that there's something else afoot in response to a typical diplomatic stock answer, there's little they can do until he emerges from his hideaway. Anything they might come up with is pure conjecture, and potentially libellous, so they tend to stay schtum unless something new comes to light, but he can't stay in there forever."

He tapped the tablet on his desk. "Your report is pretty damming, but you've got no proof."

While resting on her sofa over the past couple of days, Patricia had had plenty of time to consider how, or even if, she was going to prove Hamilton's guilt. In her report, she purposefully hadn't mentioned that she had recorded Hamilton's confession while they had been descending in the chamber. Her concern was that if she had, her superior in the form of Gibbons, or even those in government, might apply pressure into suppressing such damning evidence. It would be pretty useless to her if her evidence was filed away for use by those who would seek to release it at their own convenience. She knew she wasn't adept enough in the art of political manoeuvring to be able to utilise the recording herself, so had to sound out what Gibbons' views on it might be.

"And what if I told you that I had proof? Is it the sort of thing you would feel obliged to present to the Prime Minister, or make it public?"

Gibbons' eyes narrowed before he replied. "You present me with diametric choices, but it's not that simple. It never is. One has to be prepared to temper one's own position when it comes to dealing with cabinet ministers, because there's always a quid pro quo, and issuing charges can often rebound. Hamilton's got some very powerful friends, and enemies, and one would need to weigh-up the pros and cons before issuing such accusations. What form of proof do you have?"

"Irrefutable." She was aware that Gibbons was considering the repercussions; even his own position.

"Not good enough."

"Before I tell you, I need to know if you'll back me or sack me. That's my ultimatum."

"Young lady, I'm not going to be blackmailed by you. My position is clear, and my first duty is to the security of this Nation, and not to some lowly employee. If what you say is true, then I need to consider whether or not it is in the country's best interest."

"But you already know that Hamilton's a crook."

"All politicians are crooks at heart; they have to be in order to do their jobs. The issue here is not whether Hamilton's a crook, but if he's endangering the security of the nation by his actions. Does your proof meet that criterion?"

She thought about that one for a moment. "In a roundabout way, yes. It's certainly something The Treasury would be interested in, and I recall you saying at the outset of this operation that it was a Treasury enquiry that started it all off."

"Well, we'd better hand this back to the Treasury then. Take your evidence to them."

It was a rebuff that Patricia wasn't expecting, but she now knew where she stood with him.

* * * * *

Dismissed by Gibbons, she phoned Justin as she made her way out of New Scotland Yard, and learned that he had managed to find an expensive parking meter not far away; he picked her up from the same spot.

"I've some good news, some bad news, and the glimmer of an idea. Just drive around in circles while I think this through." she announced after settling gently into the passenger seat.

London traffic was its usual self, and Justin stayed well below the twenty mile per-hour speed limit without difficulty as he drove them along Victoria Embankment, over Waterloo Bridge, onto The South Bank and headed for Elephant and Castle.

Patricia eventually spoke. "I'll tell you the good news later, but basically Gibbons dismissed my claim that I had solid evidence, and told me to take it directly to The Treasury."

"What, even after listening to Hamilton's confession?"

"No. I didn't tell him about that. Only that I had irrefutable proof."

"I'm not surprised he turned you down. I think I would have as well."

"I had to make sure he was on my side, otherwise it's just the sort of thing that would get buried among the diplomatic bullshit that permeates in those high-level circles. More than likely, Hamilton will have got to hear about it, and do his usual trick of squirming out of it. If Gibbons won't take the necessary action, then we will. This time we do it ourselves."

"What have you got in mind?"

"Hamilton's supposedly recovering in his London apartment, in the Marriott just round the corner, so let's go and see him, because I'm going to blackmail him." She said gleefully, looking across at Justin, who instinctively glanced back at her as they passed The Oval cricket ground.

"You're mad… or brilliant."

"Reserve ye judgement until after you've tasted it."

"Is that a quote?"

"Not from Gordon Ramsay it isn't, but I'm going to enjoy this."

Chapter 30

They pulled up in the familiar parking area behind the Marriott and were immediately accosted by an attendant, who directed them to a space after Patricia showed him her badge. They took the lift up to the top floor and walked down the wide corridor towards Hamilton's apartment. It was easy to recognise which one was his, as outside it were two men from The Diplomatic Protection Squad; one sitting in a chair in a recess further along, while the other casually walked up and down. From his previous employment as one such officer in the DPS, Justin recognised the walker, but couldn't immediately put a name to him; it was fortunate that the man had a better memory than Justin did.

"I'd heard you'd moved on from this job, or have you just been reassigned?"

"It was a reassignment of sorts. A different kind of protection." Fibbed Justin with a straight face, thinking that protecting Patricia could be construed as a form of protection. "You now permanently on Hamilton's detail, or just a one-off?"

"Mainly on Hamilton's, but you know what it's like. Are you here to take over from us?" He looked sideways at Patricia.

"No, we're here to speak to Hamilton."

"You know the rules. I can let you in, but not her."

Particia stepped forward and showed him her badge. "Ah. That's different."

Justin, in particular, was relieved that they had managed to circumvent Hamilton's security detail so easily, and wondered what he would have done had the roles been reversed. "How is he today?"

"Um... The lack of female visitors makes it far less exciting than it used to be, and the nurses aren't nearly as pretty."

"Anybody with him now?

"No. A couple of doctors left about twenty minutes ago, and his secretary a while before that, otherwise he's now on his own. Are you going to be long?"

"Not too long." Justin indicated that they were ready to go in, and the walker obliged by swiping the key card against the lock.

The first thing they noticed was a wheelchair folded against one wall in the hallway, and they looked knowingly at each other. They knew the layout of his apartment, and slowly made their way through another reception area, past one bedroom, and into the sitting room. Hamilton had a ministerial-looking briefcase open on the table in front of him and was seated in one of the winged arm chairs, which faced towards the Palace of Westminster over the river Thames. He looked round at them as they neared.

"I wondered when you'd turn up. It seems that my security chaps aren't worth their own body weight in salt."

Those few words told them both that he had regained most if not all of his mental faculties.

"We wouldn't want to disappoint you, and anyway, from what I've heard, you need the company." Patricia said as she sat down on the sofa opposite and was joined by Justin. "Your wheelchair?"

"I struggle to walk any kind of distance, and I don't want to been seen in one. Bloody doctors and nurses won't leave me alone for more than half an hour, and do you know what? They even provided a specialist to help me in and out of bed. I send those bloody busybodies away with more than a flea in their ear. Don't need their kind round here."

"I can imagine." Said Justin with a hint of sarcasm.

"I suppose you're here to gloat." He remarked pointedly at Justin.

"Not at all. If it wasn't for me, you'd be six foot under by now."

"So you say." He fiddled with a paperclipped sheaf of papers, and looked at Patricia. "Go on then, tell me, because no other bugger round here has. I suppose you're going to say it was him who rescued us from that bloody chamber." He pointed firmly at Justin.

"It was." She replied flatly. "I half-suspected Donnelly might try something, but didn't know what. I had to draw him out in order to get him to admit to what he was up to, and I told Justin to shadow me once we landed on the rig. Had I known he was going to murder Captain Windaw I'd have done things differently, but as it turns out, he was going to kill him anyway, and keep it all for himself."

"Yes. That was a shocking incident."

"Perhaps his plan was to kill you all along as well."

She hypothesised. "We found a quantity of C4 explosive on the tanker, and it would have been easy enough for him to have had you knocked out and left in Windaw's cabin when it went off."

"I've come across those with sadistic streaks in them before, but what he tried to do to us went beyond sadism."

"I think he was hoping the authorities would find you and I in the chamber, thus diverting their enquiries, and giving him more of a chance of a clean getaway."

"And has he got away?" Hamilton's face portrayed genuine concern.

Patricia stalled; she hadn't prepared an answer for that question, but Justin came to her rescue with a half-lie. "We believe he was seen stealing a boat from one of the Cork marinas, but God knows where he is now."

"That means he's still out there, and could come after me."

"I doubt it." Answered Justin. "Why would he want to do that?"

"Because he's obviously a vindictive bastard."

"And you're not?" Patricia accused.

"Touche. But I know when to stop. He's not the type that does."

"I'm sure you'll be the first to know if he does reappear." She was careful not to divulge what she already knew about Donnelly, as she preferred to let that information come from the Irish side.

"Thank you for those comforting words." Sarcasm oozed from him as he placed the sheaf of papers back into the briefcase. "And now I assume you've come here for your reward, but you must realise that promises made under duress don't have to be honoured."

"I expected nothing less coming from you. In other words; you're backtracking on your word." She knew he'd come up with some excuse or other.

"Everything was going fine until you stuck you oar in, so why should I?"

"Quite simply, because we saved your life."

"By turning up on that ship and confronting Donnelly, you limited his options." Hamilton said vehemently. "It was your fault that we ended up in that damn contraption, not mine, so I don't see why I should give you a bloody thing."

"I'm sorry you see it that way. What do you think what your life is worth?"

"A damn sight more than yours." He retorted indignantly.

"Ten times more?" This was one of the parts she had rehearsed in her own mind while Justin had been driving her across London.

Hamilton frowned, wondering where she was going with this. "More."

She let him ponder her last question for a moment, and watched him as her inference sunk in.

"If you're about to suggest that I give you a tenth of my fortune, forget it." He stuck his jaw out in defiance.

"You offered me ten million in the chamber."

"I can't remember doing that, and anyway, I haven't got ten million."

"You have in the BVI. You told me."

"That was a lie, and what on earth makes you think

I would tell you such a thing?"

"Because you were about to die. I think ten percent of your wealth is a fair payment."

"A million." He exclaimed. "Bugger off. Now if you've finished badgering me… "

"I'm going to appeal to whatever miniscule of goodwill you've got left in your body, and give you one last chance. I'm not a vindictive person, but I'll make an exception in your case. Pay up or face the consequences."

"Get out." He roared. Prominent veins stood out on his neck, and the way his hands gripped the arms on his chair attested to his ire.

Throughout their exchange, Justin had remained silent in the background. In fact, he was fascinated by their aggressive conversation, and admired the way his fiancée goaded Hamilton.

She made to get up, but sat down again. "Just one more item before we go." She produced her phone, set it down on the table, pressed the screen, and sat back to listen to the recording between Hamilton and herself as they had descended in the chamber.

She stopped it after a few minutes. "Now do you remember, or shall I continue?"

"Oh please, let's continue." Suggested Justin, even though Patricia had already made him listen to the full conversation.

Hamilton kept a straight face throughout. "No need. I'm still not giving you anything. None of that is admissible in court, and any newspaper you care to pass it on to won't dare print a word of an uncorroborated story like that. Especially as it's blackmail."

"So you admit everything on there's true?"

"Of course it's true. You don't think I would have told you all of that unless I had to, do you?"

"No, you wouldn't have. Talking about corroboration, do you think those messages on your mobile might be viewed as confirmation?"

She watched him begin to mentally squirm, and knew she almost had him by the balls; but not quite yet. "Let me see now..." She feigned temporary memory loss by looking up to the ceiling behind him. "One particular text from Gertha is a perfect example. She's quite specific when it comes to her demand for inside information as to the government's position on EEC fishing quotas. Then there's another relating to a squeeze on Guinness, to increase the demand for it, and how about the lovely Eileen? She was the delegate from The Northern Ireland Assembly who thanked you for your concessions regarding the Anglo-Irish border. I'm sure this would all be of great interest to Special Branch, The Home and Foreign Offices, MI5 and 6... "

"Ok, ok. You've made your point."

"Oh, there's more. You forgot to delete some of your WhatsApp messages. I must say, from the photographs, you do go for chesty women."

"A hundred thousand." Hamilton blurted out.

"There's several on there from your bank in the BVI, and judging by the sums involved, they obviously value your business."

"Alright. A million then, but no more."

"Are you sure?"

"Yes, yes, I'm sure."

"Good. Here's the bank details where you can transfer it to." She held out her phone so that Hamilton could see.

"I can't do it right now. They're not open yet."

She knew he'd stall. "Oh yes they are. They opened half an hour ago. I checked. And don't go telling me you can't remember your account details, because I have them here. They're used to seeing large amounts being transferred in and out of that account, so this won't be out of the ordinary and won't raise any red flags. Just do it." She demanded.

Hamilton reached for his new mobile phone, not realising that it was Patricia who had lifted his old one when they were deep in the chamber. Justin nudged Patricia so that she glanced at him, and saw him mouth a question, but she brushed it away with a reassuring look.

"It's done, damn you." He announced two minutes later.

She pretended to inspect her phone. "Right, one last thing. You're to resign from the government."

"Like hell I will." He retorted.

She faced Justin. "I just knew he'd say that. We'll just have to present our findings about how he plotted his wife's murder to the police. It's a straightforward case of attempted murder. Then there's the murder of Captain Windaw. Just the spectre of an accusation would be enough; don't you think? I'm still a detective inspector in the Thames Valley Police, so it would be easy to begin an official investigation."

"Don't forget his involvement in migrant smuggling.

Human trafficking is a hot topic at the moment." Justin played his part.

"Now wait a minute. You've no proof of any of that." He said defensively.

"Oh yes we have. Not only did you admit it to me in the chamber, but you've also admitted that everything on that recording is true, in front of an independent witness." She referred to Justin, who produced his own mobile. "Besides which, we also recorded this conversation."

Hamilton raged. "You bitch. You fucking bitch."

"At least I'm not a murderer."

The air turned blue with expletives.

Patricia reckoned it was time for a final twist of the knife. "And you've just bribed me."

"What?" Hamiton was incredulous.

"You've just transferred a million, and I have the proof right here." She tilted the phone in her hand for him to see, but only for a second.

For once in his life, Hamilton was speechless. Never before had he been put in such a position, and he didn't know how to react. Realisation that he had been beaten crashed down on him, and it felt like the end of the world. Never before had he considered defeat in his many enterprises, but now his way of life was about to come to an end, and he realised that there was nothing he could do other than concede.

The three of them sat in silence; Patricia in particular savouring the moment. "Don't even think of offering more money. You're to resign and resign now."

With chagrin written all over him, he eventually nodded.

"Why don't you write it on your House of Commons

headed notepaper in front of you?" She indicated to his ministerial briefcase on the table.

His hands shook as he used his fountain pen, and was halfway through when he looked up to see them both staring at him. "I have to give a reason, and can hardly put 'to spend more time with my family', can I? That's the usual wording."

"Why not cite health? That way you're not lying." Suggested Patricia.

With an odd look at her, and compressed lips, he continued, and once signed, he silently handed it to her for inspection.

"You don't mind if I photograph this, do you? Just in case." Looking back at him, she thought she saw an already changed man. His head hung a little lower, and his shoulders slouched.. "I'll deliver this to Downing Street for you."

"Where will you go now?" Asked Justin.

"I expect I'll go home." He sighed.

Chapter 31

The captain of the trawler kept a metaphonical look over his shoulder as he headed away from the rig, on a diverging course from Eamon's gin palace. From the moment the two commandos put in an appearance, he knew something wasn't right, and changed his plans to stay well away from Donnelly who he assumed was heading for Cork. He initially steered a westerly course to put as much distance as he could between the two boats, then headed for Kinsale on the River Bandon.

His major problem was that due to the trawler's draught, there weren't many quays along southern Ireland's coast, where he could moor his boat. His other headache was that he needed to offload his human cargo away from prying eyes. He knew of one such pier that was just about remote enough on the outskirts of Kinsale; providing that he arrived in the small hours. He would have to impress the importance of keeping quiet upon his passengers when they got off, but wasn't confident that all two hundred a fifty of them could disappear in such a small community, overnight.

He looked to his right where Tenmil Brajan easily swayed with the boat's motion, and asked himself again why he, and most of its crew, had abandoned the Pan Maru. He didn't believe Tenmil's story that all of them were fed up with not being paid because he saw a group of them playing cards on the aft deck with what looked like gold coins. He also knew Donnelly, and what he was like when it came to nefarious expeditions, and had come to the conclusion that he'd best keep well away from him.

He'd already ascertained from Tenmil that they were only transporting migrants, and that there were no consignments of drugs on board, but again, he wasn't certain if he was being told the whole truth. Certainly, he had been paid handsomely for transporting the poor wretches, so couldn't complain on that front, but his sixth sense told him that something was seriously wrong.

He governed his speed so that they would arrive at Kinsale well past midnight the following day, all the while keeping one eye on his radar, and could hardly wait until they entered the busier shipping lanes where they could hide amongst other marine traffic. He started to feel more relaxed as the sun began to set, but out of nowhere, and heading towards them from dead ahead, his radar showed a fast-moving vessel. He thought it unlikely to be a pleasure craft this late in the day, especially as there was nothing but the open ocean behind him, and correctly concluded that it was one of the Irish coastal patrol boats. He knew he had nowhere to hide or go, so reluctantly, throttled-back his engines, and waited to be boarded.

* * * * *

There'd been a serious accident on the M4 motorway, so Justin drove them through Slough on the A4; neither of them said a word to each other, both of them lost in their own thoughts and both of them waiting until they got home. They were about ten minutes away when Justin broke the silence. "Fancy fish 'n' chips for supper?"

"The last thing I want is anything to do with the sea, but I'll settle for something more earthy; like an Indian."

"I know just the place."

Half an hour later and in front of the television, they settled down on the sofa with plates of rice, bhindi bhaji, lamb pasanda, papadums, and a cold can of Guiness each.

"Wonderful. Absolutely wonderful." Announced Patricia as she spooned in the last mouthful. "I reckon that trip down the rig's shaft improved my taste bids."

"I'd have preferred it hotter myself. Another Guinness?"

"Go on then."

By the time he returned, Patricia had changed channel on the remote. "Look." She exclaimed. "Hamiton's officially resigned." She turned the volume up to listen to the newsflash.

"Well, what a surprise." said Justin as he sat down and handed her a fresh can, but it slipped through her fingers and landed on the carpet. She was so engrossed in the newsreader reporting on Hamilton tendeding his resignation due to ill health that she forgot the golden rule when opening a freshly dropped can. When she pulled the ring, Guinness spumed into her face and thoroughly soaked her.

"You git! You did that on purpose!"

"I can't help it if you can't hold a beer can properly. Would you like a ladies' glass instead?" He jested.

"Bluddyferrigwatsamaffing." She got up and went to change out of her sodden clothes, and returned in her diminutive dressing gown a short while later.

"They're laying Hamilton's epitaph on a bit thick." Commented Justin as she sat down next to him. "Talk of him no longer being in the running to be the next Prime Minister and making him out to be almost a national hero. Ex-public school, ex-army, devoted his life to serving the public and all that kind of bullshit. If only they knew the truth."

"I haven't told Gibbons yet, and it'll come as a bloody great surprise to him. I expect Tates will be on the phone to me, demanding that I send in a report by midnight; if not by yesterday."

"Well, now that our nemesis is behind us, we can concentrate on the future. Talking of which... " He leaned over, parted her dressing gown, and positioned himself directly in front of her. "Time to clean you up."

"Eh?" She was bemused.

His tongue started licking sensuously between her breasts; and stopped. "Can't waste good Guinness."

* * * * *

They lay side by side; each contemplating on their latest, and most satisfying, sexual feats that had started on the sofa and ended up in the bedroom.

"You want to try that again?" Asked Patricia.

"Give me five minutes and I'll tell you."

"It's just that I've remembered something that happened in Ireland."

"What's that?"

She'd almost forgotten about the dishevelled woman who had accosted her in the Cork hotel and had to jiggle her memory, as the incident had paled into insignificance when compared to the last few days. "Oh, she was just a gipsy-type going from pub to pub, reading palms, but it felt like she really did have insight."

"And what revelations did she come up with after you had crossed her palm with silver. That's the traditional payment, isn't it?"

"Um, most of what she said came true, but she was quite emphatic on one thing."

"Go on."

"She predicted that I would conceive."

"I think most people could have predicted that. No surprises there."

"Yes, but it's the way she said it. No ifs or buts."

"Well, it's up to you now, because I've done my part."

She gave him a playful whack on the arm.

Justin took his punishment. "Talking of surprises, I have one for you too"

"That's not a surprise." She gave a smug laugh.

"Shut your eyes."

She sensed him shift out of bed, and after a moment, gave a slight flinch as a piece of cold metal made contact with her flat stomach.

"Guess what that is."

She fingered the metallic disc, lifted it up and opened her eyes to see a gold Krugerrand. She wasn't sure what to say as she looked into his eyes.

"For the baby." Was all he said.

* * * * *

As sure as day follows night, Patricia was summoned to Gibbons' office the following morning to explain what she knew of Hamilton's unexpected resignation; unusually, Tates wasn't present. She kept it short, admitting that she and Justin had visited his apartment. "He's was in a dreadful state, suffering from what was effectively decompression sickness to such an extent, so that he was no longer capable of making coherent decisions. I'm not surprised he decided to resign, so I offered to hand deliver his resignation letter myself. I think he wanted to avoid being seen in a wheelchair." She added the last part to pre-empt Gibbons' next question, and before he could ask her anything else she moved on to the matter of monies. "I have to admit that I bullied him into making a small donation into this department's bank account."

For the second time in her life, she saw Gibbons raise an eyebrow. "Bullied?"

"I think he was trying to buy his way out of being connected to Donnelly, so I suggested he ought to at least make a small compensation donation for the cost of a helicopter and a patrol boat."

"How small a donation?"

"Just a million."

Gibbons blinked in disbelief, but only for a second, as she continued. "If you follow the money, I think you will find that it originated from a bank in The British Virgin Islands, and that looks like being the end of one of the paper trails you originally asked me to find."

She thought it better not to mention how she had coerced Hamilton into resigning.

*****

Upon tendering their resignation, ministers were expected to visit No.10, and personally present their letter to the Prime Minister, but on this occasion, and despite a summons from No.10, it was the other way round. Partially due to his incapacity to walk upright, Hamilton refused to come out from his sheltered apartment to be badgered by an army of reporters and their photographers. He was dammed if he was going to be seen hobbling from a wheelchair into a car.

Without prior notice, Andrew Barrows and his obligatory entourage arrived at the Marriott, but the short drive from No.10 Downing Street across Westminster Bridge had automatically attracted a crowd of onlookers. They mingled with the throng of reporters and generally got in the way.

Upon being shown into Hamilton's apartment, and accompanied by a member of the DPS who tactfully stood in line of sight as far away as he could, Barrows was taken aback when he set eyes on his old friend. "I see now that reports of your ill health haven't been underestimated. You look awful." He sat down on the sofa opposite.

"You don't know the half of it."

"So it's not pneumonia then."

"I've never had pneumonia, so wouldn't know it even if I did. No, this is from being forced into some sort of diving chamber at gun point by a lunatic on that bloody rig. They tell me it's roughly to do with nitrous something or other that got into my bloodstream and joints, and before you ask, yes it bloody hurts. Permanently."

"Where was your close protection officer?"

"Didn't think I needed one all the way out there." He lied, convincingly. He briefly thought about trying to blame Eyethorne, but didn't have the energy to concoct a plausible story. In fact, just talking with his friend made him feel weary.

Barrows looked around the room, noticing a well-stocked drinks trolley in one corner, and noting that Hamilton had not even offered him a drink. To him, that summed up how his friend was feeling.

"Well, even if you were to change your mind, and reconsider your position, it would be extremely difficult for you to return to top flight politics now; not now the whole country has been told. Most of the party whips are naturally disappointed, and they're looking around for someone else to put forward to take over from me as PM. Not all of them are that keen on my replacement frontrunner, so is there anyone in particular you might like to endorse?"

Hamilton took in only half of what was being said. His mind drifting, he took him time before responding dejectedly. "No. Nobody springs to mind."

Barrows saw his friend as he never had before. No longer was he the bombastic type who thought he could convince anyone, and achieve anything. Someone who he had grown up with and someone he could rely on in a sticky situation. Now, even his frame was beginning to look fragile. He had come with the hope that he may be able to change his mind, but now, seeing him in person, knew that that was not a realistic option. "I presume the wheelchair I saw on my way in isn't a prop."

"I despise the ghastly things, and I'm told I'll need it to go any sort of distance. My legs aren't working properly yet."

"I can see now why you didn't want to be seen." He let out a reluctant sigh and glanced at his watch. "Well, as much as I'm sorry to learn of your afflictions, I still have a country to run, and can't stay." He gave a short laugh. "I expect I'll be joining you soon, wherever you're going to be, but I'll make sure you're given some sort of honour in my own retirement list. What are you planning to do next, anyway?

Adjusting his gaze from nothing in particular, Hamilton looked up. "I expect I'll go home."

* * * * *

Two days later, around lunchtime, the interest in Hamilton's resignation had waned to such an extent that there was only one hopeful freelance photographer lurking outside the Marriott. Hamilton was wheeled along the corridors and out to a waiting government Daimler, but this time, there were no DPS officers following him around. Instead, he had to share the back seat with a burly male auxiliary nurse, whose job it was to push him around in the wheelchair.

The chauffeur drove them northwards up the M40 towards Worcester, having received instructions from Downing Street to deliver Hamilton to his country residence, not far from Stratford upon Avon. Even though Hamilton had been gazing out of the window at the passing countryside for most of the journey, he didn't take in the beauty of Shakespeare's County and it was only when the chauffeur announced that they had arrived did he begin to recognise where they were.

Apart from the usual number of cars parked, there were three tall removal lorries directly outside the front doors. Caroline stood by the entrance directing an army of brown-coated men who carried furniture out of the house and loaded it, into one or other. She looked over at his arrival, and marched over; Hamilton obligingly pressed the down button on his window.

"It's no good you being here. I've sold it."

Hamilton struggled to focus on the issue. "What? The furniture?"

"No. The whole house, you idiot. I'm taking the furniture with me."

It took him more than a moment to comprehend what she had just said. "You can't do that, it's… "

"Oh yes I can. If you remember, you signed everything over to me when you were worried about that public affairs probe into your finances a couple of years ago. You said to me that you'd transferred it all into my name so that your estate wouldn't show up on the parliamentary register. I distinctly heard you say that you'd rather the devil take your money than the bloody taxman. Well, I'm not the devil here. You are. You and your hareem of women you've been flaunting about with in London all these years. All I have to do is go down the High Street and people look at me as though I'm one of them. They ask me awkward questions when I go into shops, and the delivery men have started to leer at me. And then there's the children. They're being asked embarrassing questions, and it not right at their age. I don't give a hoot about your reputation. It's mine. You're a rotten, selfish, pig-headed chauvinist who doesn't have any concern for those around you, especially your family, so we're leaving. You've ruined my life, and I'm starting afresh. I've sold the house and the grounds to an American, and I'm not going to tell you where we're going. You might as well go back to whatever hovel you've just come from, and screw the first tart you come across."

Hamilton sat in the back of the Daimler trying to take in all of her tirade, but couldn't; not all at once. It was only when he spotted one of the brown-coats carrying the model of his golden Bentley did he react. "You can't take that. It's mine."

"Not anymore." She spun round and flounced back to directing the removers.

The nurse had overheard Caroline's outburst, but readied the wheelchair anyway, and bought it round adjacent to the back door of the Daimler. With his mind focussed as much as it could be, Hamilton directed the nurse to push him over to the garage; the door began to open and the inside lights came on automatically as they approached. A sense of relief flooded over him as his eyes feasted over his prize possession, but as the door fully opened, he saw that it didn't seem to gleam as it should.

Trepidation coursed through him as he reached forward to stroke his golden baby, but he recoiled as his fingers detected a course surface instead of a smooth mirror-like finish. Under his direction, the nurse wheeled him to one side so that he could see down its length. Whereas before it had been the perfect picture of what a mirror sheen should be, now it was mottled and miscoloured with a mixture of flaky gold and battleship grey.

He remembered telling those two oafs to polish it, then polish it again, and wondered what they had done to it, but he couldn't comprehend what had gone wrong. The nurse pushed him towards the back of the garage so that he could inspect the back, and as they neared the shelves on the back wall, he spotted a neatly folded pile of rags next to a series of large tins. Several were dedicated to car polishing, but at the far end was one branded 'BRAKES FLUIDS'.

Even he knew that brake fluid stripped car paint, and cursed those two oafs for getting it wrong. He never knew why, but he suddenly remembered where he had seen the twins before, and closing his eyes, he pictured scenes from over thirty years ago, when he had been their Company commander in Northern Ireland. Eric and Ernie had had their revenge.

Tears welled up as he whimpered at the realisation that he had lost everything. He dug his fingers into his scalp and let out a scream of agony, then wept uncontrollably.

* * * * *

"Let's take a week's holiday, because we've certainly earned it, and it'll give my leg time to recover fully. Somewhere where I can swim, like Corfu. Where the sun and the sea's nice and warm."

Justin looked up from the newspaper. "I assume we can just about afford it." He said facetiously.

"Ah, I forgot to tell you. You know that million I got out of Hamilton? Well, it didn't go into our account. It went to Special Branch."

He thought about that for a moment. "That's a relief, because I don't think I could have lived with that hanging over our heads. Sooner or later, the Inland Revenue would have found out, and then we'd have been in serious trouble. But my question still stands. Can we afford it?"

"Oh yes, we certainly can." She reached for her mobile and played with the screen. "We've just received a hundred thousand pounds, and it's posted as coming from TOPOLOV."

"Well in that case, we can go fishing, can't we?"

* * * * *